SAFE AT HOME

MEL SHERRATT

PROLOGUE

The force I hit him with doesn't surprise me, yet the damage I cause sends shockwaves through my body. But then I've been holding everything in for years, knowing one day it might erupt again.

Knowing one day it will have consequences.

Repercussions.

Similarities.

After all, it's bred into me.

I stare down at him. 'Now look what you've made me do!'

I've fought against it – oh, how I've fought – but holding back is always in vain. I know how it works. Because in the end, it all boils down to one thing.

I am just like my father.

CHAPTER ONE

There's something about a red door. It's welcoming, jolly even. Regal, like a pillar box. Soothing, like a puddle of fresh blood. As I stand at the top of the driveway in front of the house, to my surprise, it's one I'm familiar with. As a youngster, I've passed it many times on my way to and from school. Often, I imagined living there when I grew up.

Cedric House is on the edge of the Bennett Estate, a mixture of privately owned and social housing. The pre-war detached property is on a busy road, but it overlooks a park and has thick privet hedges surrounding it, making it a little more secluded. It's double-fronted with bay windows. Five steps up to the entrance.

I press the bell for flat number three, glancing around as I wait. The garden is laid to lawn, winter flowers around a neat border and hedges trimmed. There isn't an ounce of rubbish strewn across the path, and considering it's mid-morning, it is quiet out on the road. So far, so good.

'Hello,' a voice calls out, sounding tinny through the system.

'Hi, Mrs Fisher? It's Clara Mansell from Stoke Helps Out.'

A buzzer goes off near to my ear, and I push the entrance door open. I find myself in a spacey hallway, stairs to the left. Original Minton tiles chequer the floor, high skirting boards and ceilings recently painted. A row of post boxes stand in a line attached to the wall at chest height, a round antique pine table below with a large glass vase filled with artificial flowers.

On first impressions, it seems well-kept. I can't see any dust, and there's a smell of summer breeze reaching my nose. Another tick in a box.

The house has been converted into four flats. Number one is on my left, to my right flat two. I always enjoy guessing who lives behind each door. According to my case notes, the woman waiting at the top of the stairs is seventy-two. She's wearing a navy woollen dress underneath a thigh-length cardigan, with flat black boots. Her thin grey hair is tied in a plait and suits her oval face. She smiles at me with ruby-coloured lips and offers her hand the moment I draw level with her.

'Thank you for coming,' she says. 'I'm so pleased to meet you.'

'Always happy to help, Mrs Fisher.'

'Please, call me Roberta.' She holds her arm out to the side. 'Come, this way. I'll apologise now for the mess. I'm sure you can understand.'

I step inside flat three, squeezing down a passage

that has so many boxes piled high along one wall I can't see whether it is plain, painted, or has wallpaper hung on it. The carpet is threadbare under my feet as Roberta shuffles past.

'There's room for you on the settee, while I take the chair.' Roberta goes through a door at the end. 'It was the first space I commandeered.'

I know that Roberta's husband, William, died about eighteen months ago. Before that, for twenty years, he'd been a hoarder. What I hadn't intended to see was so much stuff! There are boxes stacked in every available space. Some are sealed with brown tape; some have items spilling out of them. I can see piles of clothes, and a pair of wellies full of rolled-up newspapers. Books, magazines, toy cars of all things, and a pile of diaries going back to 1994.

'We bought this property as a home for us and a family,' Roberta goes on, 'but sadly, I wasn't able to have children.'

'Oh, I'm sorry.' I don't have to feign sadness. I know how devastating the loss of a child can be.

'It was a long time ago now. We both had good jobs and went on lots of holidays instead. But then we decided to retire early by changing the use of the building. It was a labour of love, but it kept Bill busy. And once it was finished, well, his illness took over. If I hadn't put tenants in, he would have filled all the rooms with junk.' She points ahead. 'The flat across the way should be bringing in rent, but his stuff overflowed into there.'

I nod in sympathy, all the while writing notes.
Empty flat. Rent?

She seems nice, if a little dizzy.

How on earth did they live like this?

'So it got worse?' I ask, trying to resist the urge to grab either a hoover or a duster.

'At first, it was the odd collection, that I didn't mind,' Roberta tells me. 'Then he started going to car boot sales and bringing back so much tat.'

'How did you cope with it all?'

'I didn't really. But I loved him. He was a kind soul, even if a tad eccentric. We spent forty-seven years together and, apart from that, he was like anyone else. It isn't easy to throw it all away, but it has to go.' Roberta's eyes glaze over as she struggles to keep in her tears. 'Bill died of a bleed to the brain. We'd been watching *Countdown* one minute and he was gone the next.'

'I'm sorry to hear that.'

'Thank you, it was a shock at the time.' Roberta sniffs. 'It's so kind of you to help. I've been wanting to clear the property for quite a while, but I really don't know where to start. I'm in a bit of a mess.'

'Nothing that we can't sort,' I quip. 'We could perhaps tackle a room at a time. It won't seem as daunting then. I can start this week, if you like. Visit for six weeks and see where we are after that.'

'Now, that does sound like a plan.'

Yes, it does. Excellent.

I let myself out after another twenty minutes. I really like Roberta and know I can help her, and it will be an interesting, as well as satisfying, job.

I jog down the stairs and open the entrance door. A man and a young girl are walking along the path towards me.

'Hi,' the man says. 'You're not here for flat one, are you?'

'No, I've been to flat three,' I reply.

'My name's Isla,' the young girl says, jumping up the steps and down them again. 'This is my dad, Tom to you.'

I glance at Tom. He reminds me of an Irish actor, with his spiky brown hair, thick groomed eyebrows, and blue eyes surrounded by layers of lines. He's almost clean-shaven above the bright-green scarf wrapped tightly around his neck.

'I'm very pleased to meet you both,' I say. 'I'm Clara, and I expect we might bump into each other over the coming weeks.'

'Oh, you're here to help Roberta clear out the rubbish?' Tom queries.

'I am! There's quite a lot of it. Do you know her well?'

'Yes, I've lived here for fifteen years, five before Isla was born.'

'I'm ten,' Isla clarifies.

'What a lovely age to be.' I smile, lying through my teeth as I recall my tenth year. Some kids get all the luck.

'There's only the two of us now,' Tom goes on. 'My wife died of cancer last year. I – we're still coming to terms with it.'

'Oh, I'm so sorry.' I pull another sympathetic face, while making a mental note of the details. Single male, a widower at that, and a cute kid.

'Thanks.' An awkward silence falls between us.

'Well, I'll let you get inside.' I step down onto the

path. 'Nice meeting you both.'

'You, too. I'm sure we'll see each other around.'

I watch them go indoors, Isla chatting about a maths test. I wave before Tom closes the door, and I have to refrain from skipping to my car. It's a great start, much more than I bargained for.

If everything goes to plan, I'll have friendly neighbours when I move in, too. Because that empty flat is perfect for my needs. As long as I don't screw things up this time.

CHAPTER TWO

I fasten my coat and flip up its fur-edged hood. It's rained for the past few nights, but thankfully, this evening it's dry. However, it's bitterly cold now.

I take my usual route, across the spare ground at the end of the street and then on to the main road. Through the row of shops, where the local kids hang around making nuisances of themselves, and off the estate. Shuddering involuntarily, I march quickly past the gates of my old secondary school. I relished running out of them like an escapee on the last day of term, not that I spent many days there during my final year.

From there, it's wherever my feet take me. Having been back in Stoke-on-Trent for several months, mostly through the darker winter nights, I know the places I can see into. They are full of families who keep their curtains open so I can see straight in. No one knows I watch them, and I only stay a few minutes outside each property.

First up is the Mini family. There are always three

Minis parked, two in the driveway and another on the road. Tonight they are all at the back of the room, sitting together at the table, eating, joking, and laughing. I linger for a few minutes, wishing I could hear what they're saying, join in with their jokes and laughter. Belong to them, even.

I have nicknames for most of the families I watch. There are the tea makers, a family who huddle around a fire on two settees, the youngest lad of about eight on the floor at his father's feet. If I'm lucky, I'll be there to see the row breaking out as to who is going to make a brew. Usually it's one of the boys. Usually it's after *Coronation Street* has finished. They're as regular as clockwork if I'm here at that time.

Then there are the dog lovers, whose three Labradors take over the settee. The game players who mostly sit on the floor with handheld equipment and headphones. The book readers, who barely interact with one another as their heads are in different places. I like to imagine what they are reading; what games have been played; what time the dogs are due a walk.

One day, I'll have a place of my own with children sitting on the floor while I watch TV with them and their dad. Even so, I'd close the curtains as I wouldn't want people gawping in the way I do. Still, it does no harm. They don't know I'm here, and it helps me to stop feeling so lonely back in Wedgwood Street.

I'd started walking during the first lockdown when Coronavirus was travelling fast through the country. Once I was able to go out and exercise for an hour daily, I found the evenings were better suited to me. I liked the feeling of being alone but surrounded by people.

It had been summer then, so I'd scanned gardens for people sitting out, having barbecues in their bubbles, and volunteers helping people to get by. Once autumn had come and the nights were shortened, I'd still kept the same routine. With curtains closed, however, the sense of loneliness became stronger, so I found myself staring through windows I could see into. It made me feel as if I belonged, on the periphery but part of something.

I stop at Mr Old and Mr Young TV. The couple are always wearing casual sports gear and look as if they could be on *Gogglebox*. I'm not sure from where I'm standing if they're father and son, uncle and nephew, friends, or are in a relationship. Either way, they are always glued to the telly. I often smile when I see them laughing together at something on the screen.

But Mr Young TV is asleep. As there isn't much to see, I continue to the last family on my grand tour, glancing in other windows with delight if I see a light on.

This family is my favourite. A young couple with a newborn. I found them when the woman was first showing her pregnancy. By the time the baby arrived, it was a special moment. I watched them cooing over a tiny bundle dressed in blue. I hadn't anticipated how much it would make me cry, but it was a beautiful moment.

Sadly, they're not home this evening, so I head back to Wedgwood Street. There aren't many curtains open along here, no doubt its residents don't want to show off what they have for fear of getting burgled. I've walked this street so many times I know every crack in the pavement. I know, too, about Mr and Mrs Kerrigan at number forty-two who are into cocaine. You'd never have guessed, her with her high-and-mighty attitude, and him up for being a councillor, too.

At number seventeen, you'll find Mandy Adams and her daughter, Imelia. Mandy's husband, Anthony, went missing many years ago after one affair too many. Rumour had it back then that she'd done him in, but he was seen several times in the big Tesco so he must have moved to another estate. It was fun guessing at the time.

Next door to me are the Raynors. They're okay as neighbours go, but I didn't like them much when I was here earlier, and now I'm back, I realise why. Trevor Raynor is a fat idle bastard who's never earned a day's pay in his life. He sits in the armchair in the front window watching the world go by, pretending to be ill with mobility problems. I can't tell you how fast he legs it to the bookies once his wife has gone out to work.

So many secrets behind closed doors. And those are the people I know about. Mind you, not much changes about Wedgwood Street. It's still as scratty as ever.

There's a group of teenagers sitting on a wall, and they mouth at me when I go past. My razor-sharp wit puts one of them down, dissed in front of his mates. There's laughter once I continue on my way, feel the lads' eyes burrowing into the back of me.

I open the front door with a sigh and, within minutes, make my way to bed. Alone again.

Naturally.

CHAPTER THREE

I never thought I'd return to Stoke after what happened to make me leave, so I'd been shocked when Nan rang to tell me she was terminally ill and wanted me to come home.

Home, I laugh inwardly. It had been more like a persecution camp. I hate stepping inside it every evening, but at least there are only ghosts of the memories to harm me now.

Needing a bit of cash while I was there, I'd taken a job as part of the support team at the Stoke Helps Out charity. It's a fixed-term contract for twelve months, twenty hours a week and, more importantly, they are flexible, so I'd been able to work around my nan's care at the time. If I go in for four hours during each weekday, I'm fine. The pay isn't great, but what can I expect in my position? A six-figure salary?

I had thought of handing in my notice after my nan's death but found myself attached to a few of my vulnerable clients. Eventually, I decided to wait until the house is sold and make up my mind whether or not to leave then.

'Did you finish that report I asked you for, Clara?'

I jump out of my thoughts, looking up to see my supervisor, Sam, peering over my shoulder.

'Yes, I sent it to you about half an hour ago.'

'I haven't got it.'

I hold in a sigh, clicking onto my emails. 'Here.' I point to the screen. 'It's gone and been read.'

'Not by me. Send it again.'

'You're the boss,' I mutter to his disappearing back. 'Knobhead.'

He turns sharply. 'Did you say something?'

'No.' I shake my head.

Sam stares at me, daring me to speak. He's a charmer, I'll give him that. He wears his forty years well, distinguished with a full head of blond hair and a floppy fringe, and his dress sense is smart casual but always trendy. When I first met him, he reminded me of an older Jack Lowden, one of my favourite characters in *Slow Horses*.

Now I know him, there are no redeemable features at all. I hold his gaze until he relents and storms off. Rolling my eyes, I mutter more expletives.

Sam has been giving me his big-man ego for the past fortnight. It's a good job I'm going to my anger management meeting soon. Otherwise I might lash out at him, and that won't do me any favours. I sigh. It's all so exhausting.

I often wish I could be normal, because people don't have a clue what goes on inside my head. It's why I never get close to anyone anymore. It seems easier not to form friendships. And of course I'd never socialise with colleagues outside of work. I don't join in much when I'm at my desk either, even though I know it annoys the hell out of them because I'm so secretive.

But I am always watching, waiting, listening to what's going on. I've learned *so* much that way.

Like how my supervisor is screwing Tess the temp after work. I saw them flirting in the corridor, they thought discreetly, and then as they left for the day, I followed close behind. They got into his car, wrapping their arms around each other almost immediately.

It's pathetic really, quite risky, too. Sam's married, and Tess is half his age. A little bit of a trophy thing going on there, I suspect. Still, it isn't my secret to keep, so I'll drop him in it when the time is right. In the meantime, I'll be tight-lipped.

The two women I work with are both older than me, in their late forties. Fran, sitting opposite, is constantly moaning, passing over as much of her work as she can get away with, and then some. Surely I'm not the only one who notices the fumes underneath the mouth freshener? The constant headaches, the late mornings, the hand in the drawer to reach for vodka stashed inside a water bottle.

Next to her sits Lisa. Ah, Lisa, the one who thinks she is perfection personified in her smart Next suit and high heels that show off her trim legs. She is beautiful underneath all the falseness but has such an unhealthy interest in young men.

All these things, I've filed for future reference, squirrelled away in my mind. I know things like this often come in handy. Especially with regards to Sam.

Fran stands up and stretches her hands above her head. 'My back is killing me.' She rubs at it and then picks up her mug. 'Drink, anyone, while I'm offering?'

'Tea, please. I'm gagging for it,' Lisa says.

'Just the tea?'

'Cheeky mare,' she laughs. 'And bring the chocolate biscuits in with you. I got us some more after the finance section nicked our last pack.'

'Coffee for me, ta.' I pass my mug over to Fran.

As she scuttles off, Lisa leans in close to me. 'Has Sam been giving you grief again?'

'No more than usual.' I know she's after the gossip but I'm not going to give it to her. Some things are best kept secret, in my opinion. Or lied about.

'He's a wily one, is Sam,' she continues. 'He's had more women here than hot dinners. I'd be careful if I were you, if you were ever thinking of going there.'

She stares at me pointedly, so I shrug. I'm sure I disappoint her but there's nothing I'd share anyway.

Report finished, I switch off my computer. My work is up to date, and I have an appointment of my own to go to this afternoon.

CHAPTER FOUR

When I first arrived back on the Bennett Estate several months ago, I'd stood at the top of the path, this time staring at a house that had been the making of me from the age of ten until seventeen. Or was that the breaking?

The house is the same, although more weathered due to lack of maintenance. Old wooden window frames, single-glazed windows, and a front door that hasn't been refreshed with paint since I'd gone.

I scan the garden, the grass and hedges overgrown. It's such a mess in the tidy street that it sticks out like the proverbial sore thumb. I'd hoped to clean it up but found there was too much ill-feeling within its walls.

My nan had come to the door then, arms outstretched, and I'd run into them, feeling the familiar comfort of her touch. I'd tried not to cry at how thin she was, how aged she'd become, and what was in store over the next few months. It had been tough to go through, but Jean had taken care of me during my time in need, so I felt duty bound to do the same. Not that I'd begrudged her too much. It was Derek I'd been dreading coming back to.

'Ms Mansell?' the man waiting at the front door asks as I step onto the path now. In his mid-twenties at a push, he's all shiny – suit, hair, shoes – with a bouncy demeanour. He's wiping the dirt from his brogues on the slabs in front of the window.

'Clara.' I glance at my watch. He's fifteen minutes early. 'We did say two-thirty?'

'Ah, yes, sorry about that. The last viewing was cancelled because the sellers accepted a higher offer than the asking price for a quick sale. I was only a few minutes away so came straight here. It gave me a chance to check around outside the property, though. Quite a nice size garden you have.'

I groan inwardly. Sales patter already. The *garden* is a tip back there, too, along with several mounds of rubbish that need to be removed. He's going to have his work cut out to sell this house.

'I'm Mark Lowndes.' He holds out a hand that's never seen a day's hard labour. Manicured nails, I reckon. He thinks he's a real bobby-dazzler. I bet he has a wife or partner who is high maintenance, too. I know his type.

I reluctantly shake it, not wanting to show disdain. Then I open the front door and welcome him inside.

His face is a picture as he goes into the lounge and through to the kitchen, eyes flitting everywhere while he makes notes.

'Have you lived here long?' he asks, scowling when he opens the door for the downstairs toilet.

'I left Stoke when I was seventeen, but my grandparents lived here all their lives. They bought it as part of the Right to Buy Scheme.'

'So it hasn't been modernised at all since then?'

What do you think? 'Not really.'

He turns to me with an inquisitive expression.

'New bathroom. Ripped out the old pampas suite for a white one, but that was years ago.'

We make our way upstairs. I try not to think about what went on in the hallway before I ran away.

It takes Mark all his time to even cross the threshold into the three bedrooms and bathroom. His grimace is of pure disgust. Rage bubbles up inside me. Who does he think he is, judging me like that?

'I suppose I don't need to tell you that I can't offer it for much,' he says to me finally. 'In the current climate, it will probably be snapped up by a builder for peanuts. It's not in a desirable area either, if you don't mind me saying.'

Yeah, I do mind, you patronising git. I might hate the house, but you don't have to look down your nose at me so blatantly.

I refrain from speaking my thoughts out loud. 'I want a quick sale, so I guess you'll do what you have to. I assume my commission fee is as good as anyone else's.'

'Oh, of course.' He gets out a business card, writes down some numbers, and hands it to me. 'I wouldn't go any more than that to start with, although if you emptied it and then cleaned it, it would get far more interest. People like to see the... space. If that's acceptable, I can go through everything that we do to sell the property.'

I take the card from him. The figure is far less than I want, but what does it matter? I can't wait to get rid of the house and, despite how low the asking price is, and the selling costs and inheritance tax that will eat into any equity, it's all profit for me as I never expected a penny of it to come my way.

'How quickly can you get the details online?'

CHAPTER FIVE

This week, I make a start on clearing out Roberta Fisher's flat. Her spare bedroom has a lot of tat, and we've been bagging up a little of it. The sense of achievement has given me a bit of a push to do the same at my grandparents' house. Slowly, I've thrown away anything I don't want to keep. Which is most of it.

At first, I found it too personal, intrusive even, being immersed in a life I hadn't lived in for so long. Even though I've struggled at times, I've left that part of me as far behind as possible.

Having reconnected with my nan, I miss her every time I find something that reminds me of the occasions when we'd had fun together. When Derek hadn't been around to spoil it.

I always refer to my granddad by his first name. Derek wasn't a nice man – granddads aren't supposed to be cruel. Granddads shower you with love, give you sweets and pocket money. They take you on day trips to the park for ice cream, to the zoo to see the penguins, or to the seaside to have a paddle in the water.

Granddads don't clout you around the head every time you're within arm's reach. Neither do they shout all the time and make the mood in the house miserable when they're around. They shouldn't put you on edge. They're supposed to love nans and want them to be happy. And they shouldn't be drunk all the time.

Nor should they make their grandchildren get involved with things that no teenager should ever see. I can still envisage the barn, the sawdust thrown on the floor, the men piling in one after the other, ready to jeer and shout. The blood I'd had to clean up.

I push the thought away as quickly as it materialises.

Tonight is the time to tackle the kitchen units. Most of it I can bag up for the charity shop. Some of the mugs, cutlery, and utensils are okay, but things like saucepans have to go.

After filling several black rubbish sacks, I take a breather and then move into the living room. There's only one place to store things in here, and that's the large oak sideboard. I opened the doors last week, and it was so full that most of its contents slid onto the carpet. Overwhelmed, I'd pushed it all back inside and closed the door to do on another day.

That day has arrived. I pour myself a glass of wine, rip two more black bags off the roll in readiness, and get to work.

This time I open the door slowly, holding on to the items that are slipping out again. There is so much crap. Recipes cut out of newspapers. Knitting and tractor magazines. Christmas cards from years gone by. An old ledger that I opened and shut quickly, not wanting those memories to flood my mind.

There is a cardboard shoe box. I lift the lid and to my surprise find a pile of letters that I've written. I pick an envelope and open it. It's the first one I sent to my nan.

Hi Nan,

I thought I'd write and let you know how I'm doing. I ended up in Manchester. I'm living in a small flat with two other girls and working at a bar in the evenings. It's good because I'm going to college three days a week. I'm taking a course that will help me to get a job in law, maybe even a career if I work hard enough. Funny that I should choose that after all that's happened. But I want to make something of myself, and I can't do that if I don't get a qualification.

I'm sorry for what I did, but I'm glad I'm not too much like my dad. I don't think there was a nice streak in his body at all. Sadly, I now know he gets it from Derek as he is a bully. I never realised when I was younger how controlling he was, until I had to come and live with you.

So I'm doing okay. Isn't it easy lying to other people when you have to? I've made up a whole new back story for myself. Nothing shady about me now. I am scared, though, in case it happens again if I get angry. Because I can feel something dark inside me waiting to get out. I try to keep it under control, but I know it will be my undoing one day.

There are so many memories of Nan in the house, some I don't want to think about. I refold the letter and put it back in its envelope, not wanting to read anymore.

And then I find a pile of scrapbooks. When I was younger, I loved to collect things, and Mum would often buy one for my birthday or Christmas. I thought they'd all gone once the house was cleared after the deaths. Derek had said there wasn't room in their house for too much stuff so most of it had been taken away.

I open the first, the corners on the flimsy cover curling up. A huge smile erupts on my face. It's my *The Wanted* stage. There are so many photos of the boy band, in particular of Tom Parker. I was devastated when he died in 2022. Tom was only thirty-three, with a beautiful wife and two gorgeous kids. How could something like that happen to someone so young? But cancer doesn't distinguish when it comes to age.

The next scrapbook is full of hearts and 'C loves T' written throughout in swirly writing. I must have had it bad.

Expecting more of the same, I gasp when I open the third scrapbook. It's photos of me as a child. Many of them have been taken with either one parent or me with both.

A sob escapes when I turn the page to see myself at the seaside with my mum. We're sitting on a bench on the promenade. I have the remains of a candy floss in one hand, my mum's arm around my shoulder as she draws me near. We're smiling into the camera. I must have been about four or five, although I can't remember the trip at all.

Another one of my parents catches my eye, causing me to bring the album in closer. I'm the spit of my mother, so much that it pains me to see. I run a finger over her image and then flick it at my father's face. If only I hadn't inherited his vicious streak as well as his dark hair, lean figure, and blue eyes.

I snap the album shut and shove it into a black sack. I never want to see my father's face again. The images I can remember of him in my mind are bad enough.

An hour later, the sideboard is empty, and I have three further sacks of rubbish to get rid of. A sense of peace engulfs me, almost as if I'm cleansing myself of my past. Which is ridiculous, really.

I drag the bags into the kitchen and dump them in a pile.

Four hours later, I get out of bed, retrieve the photo album, and take it upstairs. I pop it inside the box of stuff I've yet to go through for fear of bringing back painful memories of happier times.

CHAPTER SIX

The following week, I arrive with time to spare to see Roberta. I'm halfway up the stairs when voices in the hallway stop me in my tracks. A man and a woman if I'm not mistaken. The deeper one is gruff, aggressive.

'Are you stupid? I told you that last week. Why don't you ever listen?'

Curiosity getting the better of me, as the door to flat two opens, I peep over the banister to get a better view. I'm in time to see the man push the woman with so much force, I wonder if she's able to stay on her feet.

'Do as you're told and get inside,' he says next.

I hold my tongue for a moment, then think better of it. I want to see what the bully is made of, and to check if the woman is okay.

'Hi, there,' I say.

The man sees me first, his eyes widening in surprise. He smiles, looking me up and down. Any other woman might have felt uncomfortable by his actions.

He doesn't faze me one iota.

'Well, hello,' he says, finally.

'I'm Clara.' I go down a couple of steps so I can see them both. 'I'm visiting Roberta.'

'Ah, the old bat.' He sniggers. 'I hope you can get through the front door with all that crap up there.'

I wonder who he is to Roberta. She clearly trusts him enough to let him inside her flat. Behind him, the woman cowers in the doorway. At least she is on her feet, but she's rubbing at her left arm. When she sees I've noticed, she drops her hand quickly.

'I'm Wayne,' he goes on, 'and this is my worst half, Shelley.'

'Hi.'

Shelley's voice is quiet, unassuming. They're an odd-looking couple. Wayne seems to be in his late thirties and has stereotype stamped all over him. A gym fanatic, fake-tanned skin, tattoos and piercings, shaved head. He only needs a large bulldog, and he's the epitome of a thug.

Shelley, meanwhile, seems meek and mild, a few years younger than him, I reckon. She barely wears any makeup, her blonde hair tied in a high ponytail. Her skin is pale, as if she doesn't get out much, which, judging by the snippets of conversation I've overheard, must mean he wants her to stay at home so he can play man about the house when he gets back.

I've seen their sort before, been just like them, too. Shelley, unable to be heard because she is dominated by Wayne. Wayne always poking fun at Shelley, putting her down in front of others.

I leave them to it, making a mental note to find out more about what's going on in flat two.

. . .

Shelley watched Clara, returning her smile shyly before she went upstairs. Wayne followed her, too, until she was out of sight.

'What are you waiting for? Get inside,' he snapped.

Shelley turned quickly and hurried into the kitchen area, at the back of the living room. Wayne flopped onto the settee, kicked off his boots, and pressed the remote for the TV.

'Get us a beer,' he said, without turning her way. 'I expect tea will be late now you've spent a while talking to Clara.'

Shelley said nothing. She got his drink and took it to him. Snatching it from her, he farted and scratched his balls in an exaggerated manner.

'Shift out of my way, will you?' he muttered.

Not for the first time, Shelley wished they'd rented somewhere that had a separate kitchen so she could at least feel she had some space of her own. Then again, living open plan meant she had nowhere to hide, but equally, she always knew when Wayne was creeping up on her.

He didn't need a reason to have a dig at her. It was always something and nothing, and if there wasn't anything, he would make it up.

But then he'd been sent to prison. Three years she'd been on her own, and it had been heaven. At the time, she'd hoped he wouldn't even try to see her, but when she'd opened the door to go out one morning not long after he'd been released, he was waiting for her. Like he'd never been away.

That was a year ago; he'd worked his way back into her life, and now she couldn't get rid of him. She'd cursed herself every day for not leaving the area. Why hadn't she been strong enough to think he wouldn't do this again? She was hoping Wayne would get bored and move on.

'Can't smell anything cooking,' Wayne barked.

Shelley jumped at his tone. She switched on the oven, praying this would be over soon. If only she was strong enough to get her freedom back.

CHAPTER SEVEN

Despite the ongoing saga with my supervisor, I'm looking forward to work this morning. I'm pleased that I'm getting on well with Roberta, as after seeing the hovel upstairs, I'm going to be spending a lot of time there.

It must have been hard for her to live with all that muck for so many years. No wonder she wants to get it out of the way.

As part of Stoke Helps Out's services, a large skip has been ordered. I'm going to get rid of a few bags of rubbish of my own, too. Yet, although I've been doing the same at my grandparents' house, it's been strange going through Roberta's belongings, to decide what to keep and what to throw.

As I park my nan's clapped-out car on the road outside Cedric House, I can see the skip has been delivered. Inside, Roberta is waiting for me in the hall. It seems she's as keen as I am to get things sorted out.

'Morning,' she greets me. 'I'm so pleased you're here.

I can't wait to get started emptying the rubbish now I have that big thing stationed on my drive.'

'It's going to take some filling, especially going back up and down those stairs.'

'Which is why I've been bringing boxes downstairs already. I may be in my seventies, but I pride myself on not being a weakling.'

'Good on you.' I hadn't anticipated that. I thought I'd be the one getting rid of everything. 'Let's make a start, then.'

An hour later, we're taking a break in the now half-cleared living room. I can see a nice space appearing and say so.

Roberta agrees. 'I'm glad we started in here first. I genuinely can't believe how much rubbish he held on to.' She reaches for a box from the floor and places it in her lap. Peering inside, she pulls out a handful of beer mats. 'There must be hundreds in here, what on earth would he want these for?'

'Reminiscing?' I suggest. 'Are they places he's visited?'

'No, he got them from the local pub. He used to bring handfuls home with him whenever they were given promotional ones from the brewery. Said they'd come in handy when we sat out in the garden. But when we did, he'd never use any of them.' Roberta sighs, her shoulders drooping. 'He was a silly old soul.'

I rest back in the chair for a moment, wondering what it would be like to love someone for so many years, and then to lose them. I have to admire Roberta. It must have hurt so much when Bill died.

I wince. After cleaning all morning and running up

and down the stairs to the skip, my lower back is beginning to protest. So it seems the perfect time for a fact-finding mission.

'I bet you miss him so much,' I say.

'I do.' Roberta holds one of the beermats to her chest. 'Are you married?'

'No, I haven't found the right man yet.' It's fine to bend the truth, I think.

'Ah, any children?'

'No.' And I don't want to talk about that.

'Are you all right?' Roberta's voice is full of concern. 'You seem fit to drop.'

I sit up sharply. I've had another restless sleep, plagued with nightmares from my past, but I don't want that to be a focus.

'No, I'm fine.' I smile. 'In fact, I'm ready to go again, for another half hour.'

'No time like the present,' she replies cheerfully.

'If you're up for it, I can give you the whole morning tomorrow. Say, from ten until one?'

'That would be wonderful, thank you so much.' Roberta clasps her gnarly hands together.

'I used to love this house when I was at school,' I say then. 'It was on my school route. I often wondered who lived here.'

'Really?' Roberta's face breaks out into a smile. 'Thank you.'

I nod. 'I dreamt of owning something like it myself one day. You know, as you do when you're a child.'

'Yes, we all need something to aspire to.'

I pause, wondering whether to voice what I've been thinking about. Surely it won't hurt to ask.

'I was...' I begin. 'You said you'd like to rent out flat four. My flatmate has a partner now and, well, you can imagine. I feel like I'm constantly in their way, so I'm after somewhere else to live.'

Roberta grimaces. 'It's a mess. There's a lot of Bill's stuff in it, remember me saying?'

'We could empty it at the same time as your flat, a little bit each visit.'

'I suppose it will do no harm to show you first, to see if you like it.'

Yes! This is like taking candy from a baby. I wait for Roberta to locate the key and then shuffle across the landing. Even though she prides herself in her agility, I notice she isn't good on her legs at times.

'The door was a bit stiff the last time I went in,' Roberta tells me.

'Here, let me help.' I take the key, turn it in the lock, and push. The door gives after a moment, and we step inside. Dust motes float through the air, a musty smell coming at us.

'It's a tip,' Roberta warns. 'I couldn't face coming in here after Bill died.'

'But as I've seen your flat, I can envisage what it will be like. The bay window at the front will let a lot of light in. The kitchen window is quite big, too.'

I stride along the passage and into the open-plan space, peering down at the view. Just as I thought. I can keep an eye on the front entrance from here, see everyone coming and going. I turn to Roberta with a huge grin.

'I'd love to live here. The furnishing will come in handy, too.'

'It's so old,' Roberta protests.

'I'll be able to replace it little by little.' There's no need to say I might not be staying around here long enough.

'I'd rather see how you feel once all these boxes have gone. Although, I must admit, it would be nice to let it to someone I know.'

I turn back to the window as something catches my eye. Down below, I spot Wayne rooting through the bags in the skip, cheeky git. After a few seconds, he gives up and comes inside the building.

I wait until I know he'll be in his flat before leaving with Roberta. He isn't someone I want to see. He reminds me too much of my past.

CHAPTER EIGHT

In Wedgwood Street, I sit on the settee, staring at the wall in front of me. It's been over a decade since I left, and yet in some ways it seems like yesterday. Yet even so, I wasn't prepared for the rage that has resurfaced, being back in my childhood haunts.

At half past eight, I can't bear to be in the house any longer, so I pull on my coat and go out into the night. For January, it's quite mild, and dark enough so I can hide in the shadows.

It's a quick walk to Dresden Street. I've stopped twice on the way, watching families through open curtains, seeking a slice of other people's lives. Sneaking, watching, enjoying.

When I reach my destination, I sit on the bench inside the bus shelter and study the house opposite. The dickhead never closes his curtains, so I can always see straight into his house.

He's done well for himself, a ncat semi with two cars

in the drive, a large garage to the rear. It's homely, welcoming. Tonight he's with his wife. Misha seems quite nice from what I've seen of her. It's a pity she has a cheating husband who doesn't think of her or his two kids.

The ongoing traffic slows, and the night grows quieter. I tap my feet on the ground, my legs beginning to numb through staying in one place for so long.

A light goes on in an upstairs window. I watch a man carry a small child who seems to be asleep. He goes out of view for a moment, and reappears without the child, closing the curtains on the night.

The room dims, and I imagine the door onto the landing staying open for comfort.

Then he is downstairs again, flopping onto the settee next to his wife.

His wife.

It's a pity he doesn't take his wedding vows seriously. It was only last month we'd been fucking on that very settee. Misha had gone to stay with her mum for the weekend, taking the kids with her. I'd spent a wonderful day and night with him. I hadn't wanted to leave. It felt as if I belonged there, with him in his home.

And then he tells me on Monday morning that it's over between us. Just like that. Discarded with as much thought as a used Durex.

Now he's switched his focus to the temp.

Walking home half an hour later, I call in at the off-licence on the main road to pick up a bottle of wine and some snacks to finish off the night. After collecting the items, I stand behind a man at the counter while I wait my turn. While he packs his bag, he drops one of his gloves, and I bend down to retrieve it. But when he smiles as I hand it to him, I pause. His face seems familiar.

'Clara?' he questions.

'Yes.' I frown inquisitively.

'Brody. Brody Arington.'

'Brody! Hi.'

'How are you?' Brody steps to one side so that I can pay for my shopping.

'I'm good, thanks.' I force out a jolly voice, taking the bag from the assistant with a thank you. 'How about you?'

'I'm good, grand in fact. I've recently become a father for the third time. Emily Mae, born last autumn.'

'Congratulations!' My heart almost breaks in two. He has kids, and a partner. And yet here I am with a life in ruins and no one to call my own.

'I haven't seen you around since you stood me up,' he jokes.

'Yeah, sorry about that. It was a long time ago. I was in a bad place. I'm fine now, but I was a horrible teenager.' I laugh to hide my embarrassment. 'You were well shot of me, I can tell you.'

I've known Brody since junior school. If I'd been impressed back then by how the young boy morphed into a manly teenager, it's nothing compared to how he is now. He's tall, with jet-black hair and has class written all over him. I can tell everything from his snazzy haircut to his leather brogues are expensive. He's polished, well-presented, and oozing money. I want to know how that happened.

'So, you're married now?' I ask.

'Yes, to Kerry Simons. Can you remember her? We had some lessons together at school.'

'I remember – I think.' Ah, the bully with the face I quite enjoyed punching. I wonder what she's like now.

'That was, what? Ten years ago?'

'Eleven, half a lifetime away.'

'You should call in and see her. She has her own nail and beauty business, on Leek Road by Staffs Uni. She's doing really well, quite the influencer on the socials, too. I'm sure she'd be happy to see how you were going on.'

I doubt that very much. 'Thanks, I might do that, if I get the time.' I change the subject quickly. 'Where are you living now?'

'On the Hulton Estate. A new build. Only been there a few years. It's nice. How about you?'

'Back in Wedgwood Street temporarily. My grandparents have died, and I'm clearing the house.'

'Oh, sorry to hear that.'

'Don't be. I left ages ago because of them. It is what it is.'

We walk out of the shop together, and he stops at a Porsche Cayenne.

'Nice wheels,' I can't help saying.

'Thanks. Can I drop you anywhere?'

I point to a vehicle with a new registration number. 'This is mine,' I lie.

'Well, it was good bumping into you. I'm glad things turned out well.'

'Likewise.'

I stay there as he starts the engine, wave when he

reverses, and then I storm off. That's all I need, my past coming back to rub its nose in my failures.

As soon as I get home, I fill a large glass with wine and take that and the snacks and go to sit in my bedroom. I want the alcohol to block out the disappointing evening.

I used to stay in here for as long as possible when I was younger, and even after all those years away, I still find it a comfort. I sit in the faint shade of the light bulb and draw my knees up to my chest.

Sometimes it can be too much. The pain, the deceit, the loneliness of my life. I wish I could rid myself of all the anger. Despite my nan lying to me for years, there is one night I never want to remember. Seeing Brody has brought back memories of it, the last time I left Stoke when I was seventeen.

All I want is what Brody has, and if I hadn't had to leave that night eleven years ago, *I* could have been his wife. *I* might be living with him in a new build.

I can picture myself with him. We would have made an attractive couple, with gorgeous kids. Instead, Kerry Simons is able to wake up to him each day.

Why can't I find someone decent to settle down with, a man who'll make sure my happiness is his priority? I'm not a bad person really. All I need is someone to love me unconditionally, and to feel safe in his arms. It isn't too much to ask, surely?

Without realising it, Brody has made me feel even more of a loser, emptiness seeping into my every pore. What have I done in my life? What can I be proud of?

I really shouldn't stay in my grandparents' house.

There are too many emotions that could make me free fall. I'm not sure it's good for me to stay in Stoke too long either.

Still, at least I might have flat four, Cedric House, as my safe space until then.

CHAPTER NINE

'Do you need a hand with that?'

I'm carrying a large box downstairs and can barely see my feet, never mind who's addressing me from below. I pop my head around the side of it to see Tom and smile.

'I'm fine, but thanks for offering.'

He waits while I join him at his level. 'You're doing a great job. I can't believe all that stuff in the skip came out of the one flat.'

'Oh, that's only half of it. Did you know flat four was full, too?'

'It wouldn't surprise me.' Tom shakes his head. 'I always saw Bill coming in with something in his hands. He would show me his latest collection, and I'd be polite but, to be honest, most of it was just... junk.'

'He seemed to like a lot of it.' I place the box on the floor and pretend to wipe my brow. 'It's hard work but it's rewarding seeing it all come to fruition.'

'Have you been here long today?'

'About three hours so far. Roberta has a doctor's appointment and has left me in charge.'

'Do you have time for a coffee?' Tom points to his flat. 'I'm working from home and switched the kettle on before I came out to collect the post, so it should be boiled by now.'

'Sounds good to me. Let me take this outside and I'll be with you in a moment.'

I throw the rubbish onto the pile and swipe my hands together, hoping to get rid of a little dust. I've no time to consider what a mess I might be because I'm in the flat in a jiffy. I've been dying to get inside and have a nosy around.

The layout is the same as Roberta's, a living room with a bay window and a small kitchen-diner at the back, two bedrooms, a bathroom, and a storage cupboard. Where Roberta's is all browns and beiges with the odd hint of burgundy, Tom's colour palette is cream walls and a topaz leather settee with mustard scatter cushions and rug. Next to it stands a bookshelf with a mixture of middle grade and adult books.

'This place is amazing,' I compliment, watching how the winter sun lights up the living space. A gas log-burner-effect fire gives out a fair belt of warmth, and there are several family photos in frames sitting on an oak shelf above it.

Immediately, I spot Tom's wife. She's pretty, with long brown hair, a wide smile, and the same blue eyes that have been passed to his daughter. It must have been hard for Tom when she was taken away so young.

'Her name was Sasha.'

I turn to Tom with a faint smile. 'She looks nice and

relaxed in that photo. You can tell what a person is like from images such as this one.'

'Yes, I suppose you can.' Tom glances at it for a moment. 'But what I can see is how she was before the cancer took hold. And that's all I try and remember. Would you like milk and sugar?'

'One sugar, black, thanks.'

I check out the books on the shelves, the wooden model of a Volkswagen Beetle, and a pile of tangled beaded bracelets, before he rejoins me.

Tom places two red mugs on coasters and urges me to sit on the settee while he takes the chair.

'Is it nice living around here?' I ask. 'Roberta has a flat upstairs that she's thinking of renting out once the rubbish is cleared, and I said I'd be interested in it.'

'Yes, it's a quiet area, and the schools are great, too. Isla's enjoying being in year six but is excited about secondary school. I can't believe she's growing up so fast. Time is all but a blur some days.'

'Do you have any help with her?' I pull a face. 'Not that I'm suggesting you're doing a crappy job or anything.'

Tom laughs. 'She has lots of sleepovers at both sets of grandparents'. Other than that, the two of us muddle along. It helps that I only have to be at the office in school hours for the most part, so I can be flexible when it comes to childcare. I catch up a lot when she's gone to bed.'

'What do you do?'

'I'm a marketing executive for a local estate agent, Buckleys. I take the photos and set up the sales pitch accounts online, design brochures, and keep the website and social media up to date. They've been really good since Sasha died. I took a month off and gradually eased myself back into it. They let me work from home a lot at first.'

Thank goodness I didn't choose *that* estate agent to sell my grandparents' house.

'That was good of them,' I reply. 'It must be great to have a career. I've always gone from job to job, but I do enjoy what I'm doing at the moment.'

'Roberta said you're with a charity that helps vulnerable people. That's very commendable. Have you lived in Stoke all your life?'

'Yes and no. I left when I was seventeen.' *Don't ask me to talk about that time.* 'Then I came back last summer. I cared for my nan – she passed with cancer, too, a few months ago. I hope you don't mind me saying.'

'I'm sorry to hear that.'

'Don't be. At least she lived a long life.'

'It is a terrible illness. When Sasha died, I did wonder whether to move, to give me and Isla a fresh start. I thought perhaps she'd find it hard to be here. But after chatting it through with her, we decided to stay for a while. If either of us couldn't settle, or if it was still too painful to do everyday things with the memories all around, then I'd find somewhere else.'

'And how is that going?'

'For now, everything we have of Sasha is here. I can't remember a time without her, and there are some memories I don't want to leave behind yet. I can still feel her in every room, sense she's in the shadows watching over us. It's... weird, I know.'

'But it comforts you, so that's okay. I feel the same

about my nan.' But definitely not Derek. And yet, he's there in every room, too.

'Yes, so far so good.' Tom sips at his coffee. 'Are you with anyone? I know it's hard to deal with it all on your own.'

'I'm divorced. No children, though I'd like some eventually.' I change the subject quickly. 'The people in Cedric House seem nice to have for neighbours. Although I'm not sure about the fella across the way. Do you know what the story is with Shelley and Wayne?'

'I don't like to gossip, but he's a nasty piece of work.'

'I've only met him once and I got that impression.'

Tom pauses. 'Okay, you're perhaps better knowing anyway. Wayne went to prison for assaulting a guy during a fight. It was nasty by all accounts.'

'What? No way!' I feign shock, even though my instincts have been correct.

'He got five years for beating him to a pulp.'

Another one with a temper. 'Were they living here then?'

Tom nods. 'He and Shelley were always arguing. We heard them a lot, and when he was sent to prison, I sensed she was happier without him. But then, once he was released, he came back. I've called the police a couple of times when it's got too rowdy across there, hence Wayne not being a fan.'

I find it quite sweet how he sometimes talks as if he's still in a relationship.

'I met them both the other day, that's why I asked. I sensed Shelley wasn't happy. I hope she doesn't have too much trouble with him.' I drain the rest of my drink.

'I'd better start again, or I'll get too cosy here. Thanks for the coffee.'

'Thanks for the chat,' Tom says as he shows me out. 'It's been good to have some company. Between work and Isla, and well, the grief of it all, there hasn't been much time to go out with friends. Most of them don't feel comfortable since our two became one anyway.'

Out in the hall again, I think how much it makes a change to meet someone like Tom. He clearly loved his wife so much and is doing a great job of bringing up his daughter without her. I wish I could find someone who spoke about me the way Tom does about Sasha. He deserves to find happiness again.

My gaze lands on the door to flat two. Once I've moved in upstairs, I'll try and get to know Shelley better, see where the land lies with her and Wayne. Maybe I might be able to sort out whatever's going on behind that door.

CHAPTER TEN

I pull in the collar of my coat against the bitter wind that's swirling my hair around. It's half past five, I've finished work for the day and am on my way to the church hall for my anger management meeting. I'd almost decided not to go, but as I can sense things building up inside, I feel it's best to make the effort.

I step out of work this evening, and notice Sam walking to his car, an arm full of files. Now would be the perfect opportunity to collar him.

I grab his arm. 'I want a word with you.'

Sam's free hand goes to his chest. 'You made me jump, you stupid cow. What are you doing, creeping up on me like that?'

'We need to talk.'

'I think you've said enough already,' he snaps.

'I'm far from finished.' I step nearer to him. His closeness overwhelms me, and for a moment I'm tempted to lean forward and kiss him. After all, it hasn't stopped him doing the same with the temp.

But then my rage ignites as I remember the way he's treated me.

'I saw you,' I say. 'With Tess. Having a nice little tête-à-tête in your car. I thought you didn't have time for another woman in your life.'

It's fun to see him pale as I continue.

'Did you tell her you were fucking me until a month ago? You ended things between us because you said you loved your wife, and you felt awful cheating on her, and the next minute you have your tongue down someone else's throat.' I point in his face. 'Don't think I won't say anything to Misha. I know where you live, remember? I've spent the night in your bed.'

Sam drops the files in the boot, takes hold of my arm, and marches me out of sight around the side of the building.

'You'd better not say anything,' he seethes.

'Or else what?' I laugh. 'You're pathetic. I don't know what I saw in you.'

'I could say the same myself. You threw yourself at me day after day, and a man can only resist for so long.'

I gasp. '*You* asked me out for lunch, and *you* gave me a lift home via a back lane we could park up in. Was that because you thought I'd be easy?'

The affair started almost as soon as I arrived at Stoke Helps Out. I promised myself I wouldn't get involved with anyone while I was back, that I would be there for my nan, sort out the house and then be on my way again.

At first it was Sam being helpful, showing me how to work the systems, complimenting me on my skillset, and buying coffee if he went out. It gradually increased to more intimate conversations, the usual chatter about his wife not understanding him anymore.

Of course Fran and Lisa noticed, but I ignored them, and their friendly advice not to fall for his charms.

As time went by, and I was enjoying getting to know him, he made his intentions clear. I decided I'd be safe having a fling, and that it might be nice to have some good loving, too.

It was fun, sneaking around at work when no one was looking, Sam often giving me a lift when I left the car at home, and that wonderful weekend when I'd stayed with him overnight.

And then, just like that, Sam said it was over. Well, I wasn't expecting that at all. His wife deserves to know what a cheating rat her husband is, one way or another.

'Leave me alone,' Sam snaps. 'Or I'll be sending an email to HR to ensure you won't be bothering me anymore. Remember, we didn't have to employ you.'

Clara laughs at this. 'The only reason I'm working here is because I've done time, and therefore I'm cheap labour. Or is it that you were attracted to me during my interview? I think HR would be interested if I mentioned harassment, don't you?'

He stands with fists clenched. I can almost hear the expletives going round in his head, but in the end, without a word, Sam walks back to his vehicle. Moments later, it screeches out of the car park.

My work done, I make my way to the church hall. At the entrance, I wait for Andy, hoping he'll turn up this week. He was nowhere to be seen the fortnight before. I've messaged him several times, but he hasn't replied, so I'm not holding out much hope.

I like Andy. He helped me the first time I attended a session. In a better life, I would have enjoyed having him as a friend.

Andy is twenty-nine and was brought up in care after the death of his parents. They'd both overdosed unintentionally at the same time, leaving toddler Andy to find his own way in the world.

When he was seven, he'd been placed with an adoptive family who were kind and supportive, but Andy had given them hell. He freely admitted to ruining their lives and skipping out on them when he was sixteen to give them some peace.

In a lot of ways, Andy reminds me of myself. There have been so many missed opportunities, missed years even, when I think back to my life after I left Stoke. I suppose that's why I get on with Andy so much.

But it doesn't seem like he's going to show this evening. I glance at my watch. With two minutes to go until the meeting begins, I go inside, annoyed with Andy. But then again, when have I ever been able to rely on anyone?

The meeting isn't too bad, even when it comes round to my time to talk. I've been expecting it, this being my third visit without saying anything. All I'd had to decide before going in was which version of the truth I'd treat them to.

'Are you ready to share your story with us, Clara?' Matthew, the session leader, asks me.

I clear my throat. It's going to be emotional.

'My mum and dad were murdered when I was ten.'

CHAPTER ELEVEN

Now back at my grandparents' house, I throw myself onto the settee, ugly sobbing as I try to separate myself from my ten-year-old mind, until I can cry no more.

The memory came at me so vividly on my drive back from the meeting, as if it were only yesterday that my whole life changed. I've managed to shut off a huge part of my earlier years, but talking about it brought it all back in technicolour. My mum with her face bashed in and blood all over her tummy. My dad, a knife in his chest, sitting next to her.

When I rang the emergency services, the lady on the phone kept talking to me, and then I saw blue lights flashing outside the front door. I tiptoed to it and peeked through the letter box. Two police officers walked up the path, a man with a shaven head and a woman with red hair.

'Hello.' The woman bent to my level. 'It's Clara, isn't it?'

I nodded.

'My name is PC Karen Amison, and this is PC Phil Wood. Would you like to see our warrant cards?'

'Yes, please.'

Karen held up a shiny badge on a black leather cover, Phil doing the same.

'Do you think you could let us into the house?'

I didn't really know what I was looking for, but I could see small photographs on them, one with a man's face and one with a woman's.

I opened the door. They were putting on blue plastic gloves as they came inside. The lady called Karen took me into the living room.

'You sit there for a moment, poppet. I'll be right with you.'

I did as I was told. Karen wasn't gone for long. She smiled before sitting down next to me.

'Clara, do you have any brothers and sisters?'

'No.'

'How about grandparents, aunties, uncles?'

'My nan and granddad.'

'Do you know where they live?'

'Twenty-five Wedgwood Place, Tunstall.'

'Do you have a telephone number for them?'

'There's a list on the noticeboard in the kitchen.'

'I'm going to get someone to call them, and then you and I can chat a little more.'

'Are my mum and dad really dead?' I wanted to know.

'Yes, sweetheart. I'm so sorry, but they have both died.'

I burst into tears. 'What's going to happen to me?'

'Nothing for now. You're safe.' Karen handed me a

tissue. 'Are you able to tell me what went on before we arrived?'

I shook my head fervently.

The man who was with Karen popped his head around the door. 'Could I have a word?'

Karen went out to him. I could hear them talking but couldn't make out what they were saying. All I wanted to do was go in the kitchen.

Karen came back in and sat next to me again. 'We've found the phone number for your grandparents. I'm sure they'll be here soon.'

'Can I wash my hands?' I held them up.

'I'm afraid not right now. But we can get you changed soon.'

I glanced down at my pyjamas, most of which were covered in blood.

My knees when I had dropped to the floor.

My arms where I had hugged my mum.

My hands where I'd touched Mum's face to see if she would wake up.

I shudder now as I chase away the images. The anger management classes I've been referred to are free sessions once a fortnight in the church hall, but often I'm too afraid to join in. My fear is I'll become explosive just by the nature of listening to others beforehand. In a group such as this, there aren't many women who attend. In fact, so far, I've been the only one. And that can be an issue in itself.

Some of the stories I've listened to make me angrier, and compared to my own are so traumatic. Other times, I hear someone ranting about how unfair life is, and yet they have no real reason to react the way they did. But then people are different in their responses, so I can't blame anyone.

The thoughts running around my head often make things worse. So I surprised myself when I'd blurted out what had happened to my parents. At the end of the meeting, Matthew had taken me to one side and suggested I might benefit from some one-to-one sessions. He explained there was a huge waiting list on the NHS, and even in some private clinics, but if I have the means to pay, then he could recommend someone I might like to see. The first session was free so I could make my mind up after that.

Perhaps talking about myself and my issues in private is the only way I can deal with them.

Once I'm calmer, I make myself toast and pour a glass of wine. Then I check how much money is left in the large envelope my nan gave to me. There's plenty spare for a few sessions.

If tonight is anything to go by, it will be tough reliving my past, but if it helps me to create a better future, then I have to go back to the beginning to piece myself together again.

Before I can change my mind, I ring the number on the card.

CHAPTER TWELVE

Tom was stirring pasta when the doorbell rang. He turned to Isla who had her books spread out on the dining table.

'Will you let Giselle in, please?' he asked, tasting the sauce to see if he needed to add anything to it.

Isla slid off her chair and stomped to the door. She was back in seconds, followed by a woman in her early thirties.

'Hi!' Giselle arrived in a cloud of sweet-smelling perfume. She was wearing the tightest of skinny jeans, a white shirt, and black leather biker's jacket. She smiled as if she'd already had the best night ever. Her blonde hair was styled in a sexy up-do, tendrils hanging down either side of her face.

She came over to Tom, planted a kiss on his lips, and gave him a quick hug. 'Missed you,' she said.

Tom glared at Isla as she rolled her eyes dramatically. It was Wednesday. He'd only seen Giselle at the weekend. Had he missed her? He wasn't quite sure.

'How're things?' He extricated himself from her grip to see to the food.

If she was annoyed at his lack of emotion, Giselle didn't comment. But then again, she mostly thought of herself anyway. They'd met a couple of months ago. Tom had been on a rare night out, a fortieth birthday meal with one of the guys from work. Giselle was his cousin and had been seated across from him. They'd started chatting, and at the end of the evening, they'd exchanged numbers.

It had been Giselle who had done the chasing. She'd messaged him, and then they'd spoken on the phone. Eventually she'd asked him out and they'd gone for dinner.

The first time they'd slept together had been good, but so painful. Being with another woman only brought on memories he'd closed away for now. Comparisons to Sasha, embarrassment at not feeling into it. Agony afterwards knowing it would never be Sasha again.

The second time they'd slept together had been better, but Tom knew he didn't want to do it again. The problem was, Giselle wouldn't take the hint. He would have to let her down gently soon, though. He enjoyed her company, but there was no future for them.

Besides, she wasn't fond of sharing him with Isla, which didn't go down well at all. Giselle was always suggesting weekends away, saying Isla's grandparents would love to spend time with her. And while he didn't disagree, the thought of spending forty-eight hours alone in Giselle's company didn't fill him with excitement.

Still, he'd better make the most of the evening. And hope that Isla wouldn't play up, because the two females didn't get on.

The meal was quite pleasant, Giselle making small talk with Isla about things she thought a ten-year-old might be interested in. Which Isla clearly wasn't. It was laughable if it wasn't so sad.

'We have a new visitor to Cedric House,' Isla threw into the conversation when they were seated around the TV an hour later. 'Her name is Clara, and she's really nice.'

There was so much emphasis on the last two words that Tom couldn't help a snigger escaping. Giselle threw him a look, and he put his face back to neutral.

'And how old is Clara?' Giselle wanted to know.

'About your age,' Isla replied. 'I think she likes my dad.'

'Right, that's enough, young lady,' Tom interjected. 'Time to change into your pjs, and I'll make hot chocolate while you do.'

With a sigh, Isla left the room.

Tom glanced at Giselle to see her arms folded and a deep frown on her face. He groaned inwardly.

'She is never going to like me,' Giselle pouted.

'She needs time, that's all.' It wasn't an ideal answer, but he didn't know what else to say.

'She *needs* a good talking-to.' Giselle blinked a few times, as if she was getting ready to cry.

But Tom wasn't in the mood. 'Isla is ten years old, she lost her mum a year ago, and you're the first woman I've brought into our home since. Give her a break.'

'She'll never like me unless you say something to her.'

'Like what?'

'Like... I don't know.' She stopped. 'She wants to split us up, doesn't she?'

Tom raised his eyebrows. 'You got all that from her behaviour this evening?'

'No, I got that from the minute she mentioned Clara. Has she been in here?'

'For a quick coffee, yes.' The red flush creeping up from his neck startled him a little.

'Is she attractive?'

Clara had invaded Tom's thoughts a fair bit since that morning. She was a slight thing, a few inches smaller than his five foot ten. He pictured her face, lit up by a beaming smile, her dark hair hanging down as she lowered her eyes at times. Yet she had an almost bouncy disposition. She hadn't been able to sit still without her knee bumping up and down or tapping her fingertips lightly on the arm of the chair. But he wasn't going to tell Giselle any of that.

'That's a bit shallow,' he said instead.

'Well, is she?'

'Yes.' There was no point in lying. And if it made for Giselle leaving him alone, then it might work in his defence.

'I think I should go.' Giselle stood up.

'Okay.' Tom stayed put.

'Will I see you at the weekend?' She shrugged on her jacket. 'Perhaps just the two of us?'

'What would you have me do? Lock Isla in a cupboard when you want to see me?'

'I wouldn't put it that harshly, but it would be nice to spend some quality time together.'

He pinched the bridge of his nose. 'I'll message you.'

'Right.' She leaned down for him to kiss her. 'I'll see you soon, then.'

He brushed her lips with his own. 'See you.'

No sooner had the front door closed, he heard what sounded like an elephant charging down the hall.

Isla popped her head around the door. 'Has she gone?'

'Yes, she has.'

Isla raced across the room and jumped on the settee next to him. 'Cool, can I read another chapter of my book before I go to sleep?'

Tom laughed under his breath, but then he stumbled a little. Isla was so much like her mother that, at times, a glance from her could floor him. God, he missed Sasha.

His eyes welled with tears when his gaze fell upon one of the photos on the fireplace. It was of their wedding day. Over the years before that, they'd been invited to so many large weddings and vowed to make theirs as small and as intimate as possible. They hadn't wanted a church ceremony so had chosen a Friday afternoon slot at the local registry office.

There had been ten of them. Both sets of parents, friends Ade and Jules, and Sasha's two brothers. It had been perfect in every way, so completely understated.

Afterwards, they'd had a meal in a local restaurant, got very drunk, and were home for seven. Tom had almost dropped Sasha when he'd picked her up to carry her over the threshold. But he'd managed to stay on his feet long enough to fall with her onto their bed and then remove her dress.

Losing her so soon meant all his hopes and dreams for the future had come to a halt. The first diagnosis had taken them by surprise. Isla had been four, and they were trying for another baby. A recent blood test when Sasha had complained of stomach pains had led to further tests and scans, eventually showing up a growth on her bowel.

An operation, as well as chemotherapy and radiotherapy, had killed the beast that time. And the second, and the third. But eventually, on the fourth diagnosis five years after the first, it had become terminal. Sasha had died three months later.

Those three months had been the worst of his life. Watching his beautiful angel fade to nothing, wondering in the end if today would be the day she'd leave them. Having to explain to Isla that Mummy wasn't going to come out of hospital this time.

And then all the things that had to be done after the death. Luckily Sasha's family and his own parents had helped him a lot, and he hadn't felt alone for the first couple of weeks. But once the funeral was gone, and the flat was void of his wife, that was when he'd cracked. In the dark, lying in their bed without her, trying to contain his sorrow so that it wouldn't affect Isla.

His phone went with a message from Giselle.

Sorry for being a grump. Can we meet this weekend, and I'll make it up to you?

Tom sighed. Even unused to this dating lark, he knew he wasn't being fair. He would finish it permanently soon. It was heartless to dump her over the phone, but she was making things awkward by not taking the hint.

He decided not to reply now, though.

'Right.' He clapped his hands together and stood up. 'Hot chocolate for two, coming up.'

CHAPTER THIRTEEN

It takes all of two days to resist the urge to see which house Brody and Kerry Arington live in. During this time, I've become obsessed with checking him and Kerry out online. As well as baby Emily-Mae, there's five-year-old Joshua, and Nancy, who is three.

The pictures of the five of them together show a happy, idyllic family. I understand people mostly putting the best of their lives on their social feeds, because let's face it, who wants to read about someone moaning and groaning? Everyone has problems to deal with. But seeing these photos makes me long for the same kind of security, real or fake.

I'd first searched out Kerry's business, a mile from where she and Brody live. Kerry has won awards locally and nationally for the work she does in the community, offering pampering competitions to the vulnerable and needy, which to my mind is a nifty way to gain good publicity. I don't know whether to applaud or stick my fingers down my throat in disgust.

Then I'd flicked through Kerry's photographs on her Facebook page which is set to public. Oh, how much fun she and Brody have with their kids. There are photo albums about holidays, one for each of the children, and then of special occasions.

Their last one, two months ago, is celebrating at a birthday party with family and friends. They seem so happy together. It makes me feel guilty about what I got up to with Brody the night before I left.

Brody has also made a name for himself, setting up his own insurance company, mainly dealing with sports personalities. He has several staff working for him and offices in town, where I remember the old Dorothy Perkins shop used to be.

Next had been their address. I bring the road up on Street View again. The estate, as Brody calls it, consists of one long road with three cul-de-sacs each side. There are six exclusive properties in each, with names rather than numbers. There are also two for sale.

I click on the links again and spend a miserable few minutes going through the photos of each one. Imagining myself sitting on the settee in the palatial living room, surrounded by flowers, beautiful smells, and textured wallpapers.

Lying in a bath in the luxurious suite, soap suds and champagne bubbles.

Going to sleep in a master bed with Egyptian cotton sheets, wearing silk pyjamas.

Cooking a meal at the kitchen island with its granite tops and a large bank of windows overlooking the garden.

Each home is priced around six hundred thousand

pounds. How can they afford this while I am destitute? Surely it isn't all to do with a poor start in life. Then again, I have made a *lot* of mistakes and met some nasty people who tricked me into all sorts.

On impulse, I grab my car keys and take a drive out. I park on the main road a few metres from the turning. Nan's car will stand out, and there's no way I'm letting either Brody or Kerry see me in that.

I step out into the dark and cold evening. At least I can be inconspicuous at this time of year. All I hope is that his car is in the drive. Otherwise, it will be a wasted journey.

I walk up each small street, checking for it, but with no luck. For all I know, maybe he doesn't follow the other posers who have their cars on show. Porches, Mercedes, Beamers, Jags, and Rovers, all with new number plates. Perhaps Brody puts his away each night in a garage.

I imagine how good it would feel to be living in one of these homes. Of course I know everyone isn't happy behind closed doors, but the advantage of luxury surely must temper any pain a little.

I go back to my car and wait for a while, watching each vehicle that turns into the road. By then, I've tortured myself with images of Kerry and Brody in their mansion, and checking out Kerry's social media posts for that day.

But then I spot a car which might be his. When it indicates to go into the estate, I know it's him, so I start the engine and follow, hoping to keep it in my sights. Taillights are on in the distance, and when I see it turn into a cul-de-sac on the left, I park up quickly and get out.

Doing my best Agatha Raisin impression, I sneak around the corner of the first house's privet hedge. Brody is getting out of the car. He's parked on the drive of the second house down. I wait for him to go inside and then cross over the road to be a little closer.

I can see his shadow through the hall window, but the living room curtains are drawn, so I lose sight of him. I curse under my breath. But just then, the front door opens again, and I dive behind a car. Shit, I don't want to be seen here.

It isn't Brody who comes out. It's Kerry. I'm dismayed to see she hasn't changed much. She's still the tall blonde with legs up to her armpits. Done up to the nines but far more subtle these days. Considering she owns a hair and beauty salon, her features are understated rather than pumped up, tattooed and enhanced in every way possible. But then, she's always been a natural beauty.

Kerry is wearing slouchy clothes and fluffy pink slippers, dressed down but still immaculate. Has she made an effort for Brody's return, or does she dress like this all the time? Didn't Brody say she'd not long ago had a baby? She looks amazing, so refined, and so... rich.

Kerry presses the key fob to unlock Brody's car and reaches in the back seat. She pulls out a briefcase, presses the fob again, and goes inside.

Once the coast is clear, I run back to my car. I switch on the engine and screech away. When I get back to the house, I pour myself a drink and drop onto the settee, tired and emotional. I squeeze my eyes shut tightly, hoping to rid myself of the images, but they keep coming at me.

I imagine the scene in Brody's house as if I'm there. I'll be in the kitchen dishing up a delicious home-cooked meal for my man. Brody will shower and change, check in to see the kids in their beds before coming down to relax with me.

And then afterwards, we'll remove each other's clothes and make love while we have the evening to ourselves. There'll be nothing wrong in our perfect lives. We will have no money worries.

But daydreaming about Brody and his home isn't the answer to my problems. Why can't I have a chance at being happy? Why can't I have what they have? I'm twenty-eight, with nothing to show for it except a criminal record and a failed marriage.

Although I don't need one to feel complete, I can't even keep a partner for long. My insecurities make that impossible, my temper always getting the better of me, and then the real Clara shows up. No one in their right mind would like that insecurity.

But I am lonely, and I have changed, haven't I?

Then I admonish myself. Why am I being so down all the time? And no one knows what I've been up to before coming back, nor why I left. I can pretend to be whatever, or whoever, I please.

I curse. No amount of positive thinking or affirmations are going to get me what I want. *Stupid bitch. You don't deserve a home like that one. No one would want to share that with you. You deserve everything you get. Stupid, stupid, stupid.*

I pinch the flesh on the inside of my upper arms until tears fall from my eyes. There'll be bruises tomorrow, easier to hide when the weather is cold. They'll disappear before too long, leaving me with the urge to do it again. Pain I'll inflict on myself. Pain I'll feel, that will never fade.

CHAPTER FOURTEEN

It's only taken four weeks to get Roberta's flat to an acceptable level, but she's been so pleased with the result. I have, too. The flat feels much bigger, and tidier, always a bonus in my eyes.

Roberta mentioned she was going to ring the office to praise me, but I managed to talk her out of it. I don't want to give Sam any inkling that I've been spending so much of my time there.

I've been clearing out some of flat four, too, enough that I now think it's fine to inhabit. Roberta finally caved in about me taking on the tenancy, so, bit by bit, I've been bringing across my belongings – not that I have much to my name.

More importantly, the flat is the perfect place for me to hide out in until my grandparents' house is sold and I'm ready to leave. The estate agent has been in touch several times, saying there's been interest but mostly from buyers who want it for almost nothing. I've told him to try for another month and then I'll reassess those offers or put it up for auction to attract the highest bid. It isn't *that* bad.

I got the keys to flat four a few days ago, so Cedric House feels a little more like home. The photo of my mum I found in a box in my nan's bedroom stands proudly on top of another sideboard, but this one is an antique. I've picked up a cream throw to hide most of the settee and scattered multi-coloured cushions across it.

With the money my nan gave to me, I'll be able to pay the rent until the house is sold. I can't afford to live on the salary I get from Stoke Helps Out. And if things don't work out as planned, I can always do a moonlight flit. Not that I want to as I've grown quite fond of Roberta.

The only drawback I can see so far about living in Cedric House is bumping into Wayne. Every time I see him, he makes a beeline for me, and I swear my skin almost crawls when he reaches out a hand to touch my arm. It gives me the creeps, and if he doesn't stop it soon, I'm going to have words about it.

I go to the front window and gaze down out onto what will soon become my new view. It's so pleasing to see the greenery of the park. Several dog walkers are ambling along the path inside the railings, a few groups of teenagers on their way home from school.

I wonder if Isla will be among them one day. Will she, when she's older, be allowed to walk on her own, or will Tom pick her up in the car? It's a difficult age, I know, and a different environment from when I was ten, even without all my trauma. There were no social media predators, for starters.

The entrance door slams, and I spot Wayne leaving. It gives me the opportunity to slip downstairs and see if Shelley is in. I grab my keys quickly.

Shelley is surprised to see me when I open the door.

'Hi!' I beam somewhat manically. 'I'm on the beg for a bit of sugar.'

'I don't think I have much to spare.'

'Not literally.' I step past her. 'I just wanted to come and say hello. I'm moving into flat four tomorrow.'

'Oh, that's nice.' Shelley smiles. It seems sincere to me.

'I'm looking forward to it,' I go on. 'I've not long split up with my fella.'

'Sorry to hear that.'

'It wasn't working out.' I shrug, nonplussed. 'That's men for you. Hey, you and I should have a girls' night in once I'm settled.'

'Oh, Wayne doesn't like me having people round.'

'I'm sure you could persuade him to go to the pub.'

'Well, yes, but—'

'I'll bring wine.'

Shelley is about to protest, but then suddenly she nods. 'Okay. I could cook something?'

'Super! Does he go out on any particular nights?'

'Most of them, but always Fridays.'

'Then let's make a date for next week. How about you take my number and message me when he leaves? If you prefer not to tell him, that way he'll never know.'

For the first time since we've met, I get a beaming smile from Shelley.

Perfect.

. . .

After a walk around the streets checking out my favourite families, I find myself sitting in the bus stop opposite Sam's house again. It's pouring with rain, and I'm shivering despite my thick jacket and scarf, but I don't want to spend the evening at my grandparents' house, not now I have the flat to stay in from tomorrow. Besides, it's easier to walk to Sam's from there rather than Cedric House.

Due to visiting Roberta first thing, I'd been late for work yesterday, and Sam gave me grief about timekeeping. Well, I think it was about that because I tuned out after a few seconds. But he got my full attention when he then said he wanted to see me next week for a six-month appraisal. I suspect it's something he's made up so he can intimidate me. He can try, the loser.

I've been here for about ten minutes, leaning on the side of the bus shelter, when the door to his house opens. Sam strides down the path, glaring at me while he waits for the traffic to pass and then jogs over.

I stand up, ready to face him. This might be fun.

'What is your problem?' he cries, raising his hands, palms up.

'Er, I might be waiting for a bus.'

'Oh, yeah? Where to?'

'Mind your own business.'

'But you have a car.'

'So?'

'You're staring right into my house!'

'Close the curtains then.'

'Why are you doing this?'

'I told you, it's a bus stop.'

'You're so infuriating.' He stares at me in exasperation. 'You need to back off. Your behaviour isn't fucking normal.'

'Says the man who shags everyone alongside his wife, after giving them the sob story that they're no longer getting on.'

Sam glances around quickly, but there's no one around.

'Scared the neighbours might hear something they shouldn't?' I snigger.

'You're mad.'

'I might be.' I pose another question. 'Shall we make an agreement? How about you leave me alone at work, forget the appraisal, and stop being so nasty in general, and I won't say a word to your wife about anything you've – we've – been up to that could ruin your beautiful home arrangements.'

Sam runs a hand through his hair, pacing the pavement in front of me. He groans loudly before the slightest of nods.

'Also, leave Tess alone, too.'

'That's got nothing to do with you.'

Unbelievable. I raise my eyebrows.

'Okay, okay!'

'Good, I'm glad that's settled.'

I watch him walk back across the road into the house, giving me one last warning glare before closing the door. Then I smirk. What a gullible idiot.

But my gloating doesn't last long as I walk around the streets again for an hour, peeping into as many homes as I can. It makes me feel low, isolated.

I call at the chippie for a quick bite to eat, find I'm

not hungry so, after a few mouthfuls, I ditch the food underneath the nearest hedge.

It's late when I finally lock the front door behind me, sighing heavily. Minutes later, sliding into bed, I let my tears fall. The house is so depressing, not good for me at all.

One more night, and perhaps I'll only have to come in here a few times until the property is sold. Now my only hope is I leave the demons of my past behind here, too. I definitely don't want them to follow me to Cedric House.

CHAPTER FIFTEEN

I haven't told anyone that I'm going to see a therapist. As far as I'm concerned, I'm doing this for myself, to make things better. Since my release from prison, I've been willing to do anything in my power not to go back there.

Emma Tweed is in her forties and lives on the outskirts of the city in a detached house with a sweeping drive and landscaped gardens. I cringe when I park my nan's old Fiesta next to a gleaming black Mercedes, its number plate only two years old.

But Emma couldn't have been more welcoming. She shows me into the hall and through to a side room. A desk and computer take up one wall, and there are two comfy chairs and a small table in a large bay window with a view of a lawned area. She makes coffee from a machine hidden in a tall cupboard and ushers me to sit in the chair on the left.

'Now, make yourself comfortable,' she tells me. 'I'll sit for a while and listen to what you have to say, and hopefully we can get to the crux of the matter. I'd like to try and find your trigger point as soon as I can. The episode which started things going wrong in your life. Sometimes it isn't the event you think it is. It can be something much deeper. We can build from that and, hopefully, make you feel better about coping with the world as it is now.'

For some reason, whether it's the environment I'm in, or if it's Emma herself that gives out a calming quality, I find it easier than I'd imagined sharing my background. We speak about it in detail for forty minutes, and then Emma gives me a piece of paper.

'I'd like you to complete this and bring it to your next session. But before you go, now that we've spoken a little about your past, what is your aim for these sessions?'

There is no hesitation in my reply. 'I want to stop feeling so angry all the time.'

'Is there any particular thing which makes you feel that way?'

'*Everything.*'

Emma smiles. It reminds me of my nan. A lump appears in my throat.

'I'm going to give you some exercises you can do,' Emma goes on. 'Are you happy to meet once a week for the next month?'

I nod. I might as well put Derek's money to good use.

That evening, I think about the night my grandparents collected me after my parents had died. I had still been in the living room, sitting with the lady police officer when I'd heard voices outside the window.

'I wonder if this is your nan and granddad,' Karen had said. 'Will you be all right while I go and see?'

I'd nodded, although I wasn't sure. It seemed ages since the police had arrived, and all I wanted to do was go back to bed, wake up in the morning, and hope that what had happened had all been a dream.

How could my parents be dead? My beautiful and kind mum. What was I going to do?

I recognised Nan's voice straightaway, listening as she spoke with Karen.

'You can't come into the house,' Karen told her.

'Why not?'

'It's a crime scene. I also don't want this to be the last vision you have of your son and daughter-in-law.'

There was a silence, but I listened intently.

'Is she in there?'

'Yes. I'll get her for you. I must warn you. I've changed her out of her pyjamas, and they've been taken away for forensics, but she still has blood on her hands and a little on her face.'

'You haven't let her wash?'

'I'm afraid not. Once we get her to the station, we need a few samples, and then you can take her home when we've asked her some questions.'

'It's nearly midnight.'

'I understand, and we'll be as gentle as we can. I know you'll want to comfort her, too, but there may be evidence on her. I'm sorry, but it's procedure. Will you be accompanying her to the station?'

'Yes, of course.'

Karen came back into the room. 'Your nan and granddad are here, Clara. Let's get you with them, and then we can go to the police station. It will only be a short trip.'

I saw my nan outside, her arms outstretched, and I rushed into them, bursting into tears again.

'My poor child,' Jean said, over and over.

My granddad was sitting on the wall with his head in his hands, staring at the ground. He didn't come over to us. I hoped he wasn't blaming me for what had happened.

At the police station, we were shown into a room where another lady officer wiped a tissue over my hands and put a thing like a cotton bud into my mouth while I was with my nan. Little bits were clipped from my fingernails.

Then we went through into a different room, with a settee, an armchair, and a coffee table. There was hot chocolate for us. I managed to drink some of it, but my eyes were droopy. All I wanted was to go to sleep. I curled up next to my nan.

'I'm sorry, Nan,' I whispered. 'It was so messy.'

'Now, you listen to me. This is not your fault. You've always been a good girl.'

'But I—'

Karen came back then, with another woman.

'Clara, my name is Allie, and I'm a detective.' She smiled at us. 'I'm so sorry to hear about your mum and dad. I know you've told officers what happened earlier, but I would like to ask you a few more questions. Would that be okay?'

I nodded. She asked me lots of things, but I was so

tired, my eyes closing of their own accord. A few minutes in, she stopped.

'Okay, we'll leave it there. You can take her home, and we'll get a specialist to come and talk to her when she can handle it. She's going to need help to get through this. I'll allocate a social worker in the morning.'

'We can take care of her.'

'It's standard procedure in cases like these.' Allie smiled reassuringly.

I held on to my nan as we went to the car. Granddad was in the driver's seat, but he didn't speak to me. I fell asleep almost as soon as the engine started.

I shudder now. Even after all those years, it's painful to think about.

When I'd gone home with them, Nan had settled me into the spare bedroom, tucking me in before kissing me goodnight.

'Get some rest,' she'd said. 'You've had a terrible shock, but I'm here for you. I want you to know that.'

I was so afraid, but I nodded so that I could be left alone. It was then that my tears started. Unfamiliar shadows scared me. I'd never liked staying there when my granddad was home, only when Nan was on her own.

And then I'd heard them talking on the landing.

'I don't want her staying here. The last thing we need is a child living with us.'

'Derek, have a bit of heart. Clara is all we have left, and she's traumatised after what's happened.'

'Maybe, but—'

'*I won't let anyone else take care of her. Clara's staying with us.*'

'*You're not the boss of this house.*'

Now, almost certainly mirroring my ten-year-old self, I bring my knees up into a foetal position. Back then, I often wished I could go to sleep and never wake up, because I didn't want to live like that. But maybe now I'm talking about it, things might look up for me.

They surely can't get any worse.

CHAPTER SIXTEEN

Fully settled in Cedric House, I'd nabbed a notebook from work that afternoon and am now doodling all over it, the TV on low in the background. Thinking back to my session with Emma, I turn over to a new page and write three words.

What is love?

I pause, wondering why I've written that. Then I let my mind wander as I begin to write again.

Does anyone really know what it is? It can show itself to you in lots of ways, even without anyone saying I love you. It doesn't have to be about sex. Love could be staying with the same person until you're old and grey. It could be sorting out his pants and socks the way he likes it. It could be a smile, a hand on an arm. A kiss on the forehead. A rub of a shoulder.

Love could be cooking him his favourite meal when it's not something you enjoy. Or watching a scary movie when you'd rather enjoy a romcom. Of course, that works the other way round, too.

So what do I want love to be? I want something uncondi-

tional, and a commitment that he'll stick with me forever. I want him to know everything about me and not turn away in disgust. I need to feel protected by him.

In return, I would give him the same and—

Shouting stops me. I reach for the TV remote and lower the sound. The noise is coming from downstairs. An angry male voice, a distressed female. It takes me back to my childhood, and I shoot off the settee and rush downstairs.

The second I bang on the door of flat two, the noise stops.

The door opens, and Shelley pops her head around the frame. Her hair is a mess where Wayne has no doubt pulled at handfuls of it, and there is a red mark visible on her cheek.

I pretend not to see either and smile brightly. 'Hi, I wondered if I could beg some milk from you. I've just dropped mine all over the kitchen floor and I don't really want to go out again. I'll bring you a fresh bottle tomorrow in return.'

'Wait a moment, and I'll see if we have one.'

I follow her in regardless. Wayne is lying on the settee, face like thunder.

'What brings you here?' he says.

'Had an accident with spilt milk, so I'm on the cadge. You don't mind, do you?'

''Course not.'

I take the opportunity to sit down across from him. 'Anything good on?'

Wayne looks at the TV screen which is showing a YouTube clip of a car chase across the US. 'Naw, not really. It gets boring sitting around, though.'

'You're not going out this evening?'

'Can't be bothered. You?'

I shake my head. 'I have lots to do since moving in the flat.'

'Yeah, seems strange you living upstairs. I bet you can hear a lot,' he says pointedly.

'Not really. I always have the TV on for background noise. Don't like a quiet room.'

Wayne thinks about what I've said before nodding. He turns back to the screen.

Shelley comes in with a milk bottle, a quarter full. 'I don't have a spare, but will this do you until tomorrow?'

'It will, thank you. I owe you one.'

Shelley smiles and perches on the arm of the chair next to me.

'So, how long have you two been an item then?' I ask, no intention of leaving anytime soon.

'Too long, if you ask me,' Wayne remarks.

'Oh, sounds like fun... not.'

'Why don't you mind—'

'Would you like a coffee?' Shelley gets to her feet abruptly.

I know she's trying to get me to leave, but I nod anyway. 'Yes, please, that would be great.'

Wayne sighs and turns up the volume on the TV.

'Don't be rude,' I say. 'I think it's nice to get to know neighbours.'

'I'm not your neighbour.'

'I thought you lived here.'

'I have a flat.'

'And where might that be?'

'Doulton Crescent.'

I know of it, twenty minutes by foot and a dive of a street. Worse than the one I grew up in.

Wayne stares at me. 'I expect you know I've not long come out of prison.'

'No one's told me,' I fib. 'Although I'm interested in why you were locked up.'

'GBH.'

'Ah, bad-boy vibes?'

I'm teasing him, yet gleaning information at the same time. But I sense Shelley, still beside me, and realise I'm making her feel uncomfortable. I give her an apologetic smile.

'Mine's black, no sugar please,' I say.

'Would you like one, Wayne?' Shelley offers.

Wayne stares at her before sighing loudly. 'I think I will get that pint.' He pulls on his boots, discarded next to the settee, and stands up. 'See you tomorrow, Shell, and don't forget what I said.'

'I won't.'

Both Shelley and I stay still until the door closes behind him. Then we sigh with relief.

'Are you okay?' I ask. 'I heard him having a go at you, so I thought I'd come down and see if I could stop him.'

'He's been in the pub most of the afternoon and was asleep when I got in. Of course it was my fault because I woke him. He scares me when he's so angry.'

'Did he... hit you?'

Shelley shakes her head. 'No, because you came down. Thank you.'

'Anytime. If I can get Wayne to stop when I hear

anything, make him realise that someone knows what he's doing, it might make him think twice.'

'I doubt that, but thanks anyway.'

'What does he do for a living?'

'He's a plasterer by trade, but he doesn't get much regular work because of his habit of going for a pint during his lunch break and not coming back. I do split shifts at Clarkson's Factory, in the warehouse, so he comes and goes.'

'And does he live here? He confused me when he talked about Doulton Street.'

'He stays with one of his brothers, Neville.'

'Is the lease for this flat in your name?'

'Yes, we changed it when he went to prison. Roberta insisted. She wasn't impressed when he came back, hence him staying in two places. But he's mostly here. I told Roberta how much I've tried to keep him out. She became my lookout then. It was kind of her. As it is of you.'

'So you have two fairy godmothers watching over you.'

'I do! Now, coffee? I'm sorry I haven't got anything stronger.' Shelley smiles shyly.

I return it confidently. 'Coffee will do fine.'

Later that evening, I think about Wayne. He reminds me of Derek, a Jack-the-lad with an overexaggerated opinion of himself. An idiot who probably has his hand in lots of illegal stuff, petty crime, and things off the back of a lorry. I'm sure he's up to something, so I need to get into the flat when he isn't there and have a snoop around. I also need Shelley out of the way, too.

How can I get a key?

Maybe I can lift one, get a copy cut and replace it before either of them notices. But I'll have to search for it, and I can't if either one of them are there.

No, there must be a better way. It will show itself to me eventually. Although, I'm very good at thieving as a last resort.

CHAPTER SEVENTEEN

Letting myself into Cedric House with my own key now is always a joy, but I'm especially glad to see it this evening. Sam has been on my case all morning, to the point I'd snapped at him, and he'd tore into me even more. He's trying to get me fired, I'm certain. So as long as I play along while I'm there, it will be fine.

He just doesn't get it, does he? How in control of his life I really am. It would take one visit to his home when his wife is in, and his marriage will be in trouble.

Of course, I'd taken the perfect selfie in bed with him, when he was asleep. Photos like that have been my saving grace, and if he carries on the way he is, I'll show him what I'm capable of.

So I'm glad it's Friday and that I'm going to see Shelley. Not too far to travel, I muse. I decide to have a small glass of wine while I wait for a message to say that Wayne has gone out.

I relax back on the sofa. Well, as much as I can. It's

so stiff, like a board, not at all comfortable. But at least I feel calm there. Going back to my grandparents' house now always makes me feel apprehensive. I'd been able to bond with my nan a little in the weeks before she'd died and was annoyed about all the wasted opportunities I'd had to come and visit. But Nan kept on insisting I should stay away. It was cruel of her, but I can understand her reasoning now.

I remember the last time Jean had visited me in Manchester. We'd met in a café near to Piccadilly Station. The place was heaving, and my eyes scanned the room for a pair that were familiar to me, similar to my own. I saw a hand go up at the back of the room and made my way through the tables towards the woman who had been sitting but was now getting out of her chair.

'Clara! Oh, Clara, it's so good to see you,' Jean cried, arms outstretched.

'Nan.' I buried myself in them, the scent of her both comforting and distressing.

We smiled at each other and sat down. Jean had ordered me a cappuccino and a Danish pastry. I hadn't the heart to tell her I didn't enjoy the pastries, but I'd got myself into the predicament that because I'd faked my enthusiasm for the first one she'd bought many years ago, Jean always ordered me the same thing.

Not that there had been many meetings between the two of us. I could count the occasions on both hands, but Jean did always prompt one most years. She'd message me countless times until it wasn't polite for any more excuses. And she always came to Manchester.

The first thing I noticed as we chatted was how much weight Jean had lost. At seventy-two, her skin always looked tired, but this year there was something more. Something underneath, I assumed.

'How are you, Nan?' I ventured. 'You seem a little peaky to me.'

'Old age, Clara.' Jean chuckled. 'There isn't anything you can do to stop it either.'

'So you're okay?'

'I've been having a few tests for chest pains, but everything is coming back clear. That's great to rule out a lot of things, but it means I still haven't got a diagnosis.'

I reached across the table to hold her hand. It was the first contact I'd had with a person in a long time.

'Anyway, I'm not here to talk about me.' Jean added some sugar to her drink and stirred it. 'Tell me how you are getting on. Anything good on the horizon?'

I smiled. Even though I only saw her once a year, Jean always asked the same question, which was in the guise of: Do you have someone to love you yet? Are you getting married? Will I be a great-gran soon?

Whenever she'd rung me, I would give Jean a version of my life that was as far from the truth as possible. I'd told her that I'd been to college, and then university to study law. After that came a job as a legal assistant at a solicitors. Then I'd gone to another firm under the premise of becoming a PA to the managing director of a law firm.

Occasionally I forgot what job I was doing, but still. I wondered if Nan had ever guessed. If she had, she'd never said. I hadn't told her about Evan Mansell either, and was glad after what had happened between us.

Today I'd dressed smart even though I was going to my shift as a cleaner for a major hotel chain that morning. Nan still thought I was working in the law firm. I'd fielded questions by learning a few statements on the internet to impress her with, knowing that Nan wouldn't ask anything else as she'd barely understand.

Yet it was important for me to give a good impression. Because of how I'd left Stoke, and never gone back, I had to show I was surviving on my own. With no intentions of ever returning.

'Nothing new to report,' I told her. 'I'm still working at the law firm, still enjoying my job, and I've moved into a flat in a much nicer area. Lots of bars and restaurants nearby, that I visit with my friends.'

Jean reached across this time and gave my arm a squeeze. 'I am so proud of you, love. You took a horrible experience and turned it into your advantage. I don't think I'd have been so successful!'

That's because it's all lies. 'And how is Derek doing?'

Jean's smile slipped, along with her demeanour. 'Your granddad is still the same selfish bastard he's always been. I'm still at his beck and call, but well, because of what happened, I don't have an alternative to looking after him myself.'

Sure you do. You could put him in a care home or suffocate him. My smile is faint. 'You're a saint for doing it all this time.'

'You're still best being here.'

Would I have stayed away so long if I'd known the

truth, I wondered now? It's a thought that haunts me night and day.

My phone beeps, interrupting my thoughts, and I reach for it.

Ready when you are!

On my way! I type, promptly putting my thoughts back in the box they've escaped from. Time for my recce event.

CHAPTER EIGHTEEN

Downstairs, Shelley is waiting at the door, slippers on her feet. She seems exhausted behind her smile. Makeup can only cover so much, and I'm glad to see she's put some on this evening.

I hold up a bottle of wine. 'Hope you'll help me to demolish this.'

'I'll have a teeny bit.' Shelley presses her thumb and index finger close together.

'Hmm. I don't think so!' I shoo her in and follow behind. Inside I find the table set and the smell of something delicious in the air. I sniff in appreciation.

'It's only jacket potato with a bolognese mix,' Shelley says.

'Sounds good to me. I'm starving. How have you been since I last saw you?'

'Good, thanks.' Shelley brings the food across to the table and dishes it out.

'And Wayne?'

'He's not been around much, thankfully.'

I smile and sit down across from her, pouring the wine.

'So, you go first. Tell me all about yourself,' I prompt, once we're settled.

'Not much else to say. You know I work at the factory, that I've been with Wayne for far too long, and that I've lived here for six years.'

'And do you like it here? Tom and Roberta seem good to get along with.'

'Yes. Although it's one house, no one is ever intrusive. We say hello, how's the weather, and maybe have the odd coffee together here and there. But that's enough to feel welcome.'

'And of course, there's Isla to brighten things up. She really is a tonic.'

Shelley smiles. 'She's the sort of daughter I'd love one day.'

'Me, too. How about your family? Are they in Stoke?'

'Yes. My parents are over in Longton, and I have an older brother. He lives in Weston Coyney with his wife. They have twin boys, six, who are adorable.'

'Do you see them often?' It's all I long for, a large family to socialise with, and to care about me.

Shelley pulls a face. 'Not as much as I'd like to nowadays. When Wayne was in prison, they'd call round lots, but that's changed since he got out. My brother has threatened him a few times – punched him once – but he never gets the message. He's like a leech, and he makes it so awkward, as if he owns the place. So I go and see them whenever I can.'

'And he's here waiting for you on your return.' I roll

my eyes in dramatic fashion and smile to show I'm being sarcastic rather than facetious.

Shelley nods.

'What's his background?'

'His parents were alcoholics. Dad died when he was in his forties, used to beat them all apparently. Wayne has two older brothers who ended up in prison long before he did. There's a sister who's done well for herself, though, Gina. She's the head of drama at the local college. I like her but I don't see her often now. She won't come here because of Wayne, and I can't see her because Wayne would say I was going behind his back.'

'That's nuts.'

'Gina went the same way for a while but then straightened herself out. I wish Wayne would. He's okay for the most part when he's sober.'

'*I* wish there was something you could do.' I think for a moment. 'Did you change the locks when he was in prison?'

'Yes, but he wheedled a new key out of me. And even if I hadn't given him that, he would have waited outside then, or followed me to work. He's done both before, when I've tried to finish things with him.'

Hmmm. Perhaps I can make him leave of his own accord.

'I bet you don't go out much without him checking in on your phone.'

'No, but mobiles are good for that. I'm trying not to be weak. I had so much fun when he wasn't here. I wish he'd get bored of me and disappear.'

'But then you'll always worry if he'll come back.

Some things need to be permanent to make a difference.'

'What do you mean?'

'Oh, nothing. More wine?'

'Not for me.'

'It's the start of the weekend. Do you have work in the morning?'

'No.'

'Neither do I...'

Shelley holds up her glass. 'Go on, then.'

I top it up, mine, too, an idea springing to my mind. 'You know what you should do? Give me a spare key. That way if you're in any danger, I can let myself in and—'

'Oh, I don't know about that. If he finds out—'

'I'd feel better knowing I could rescue you if you get hurt. Or if you need me as a friend. Men like him don't know when to stop.' I pause. 'My parents had a terrible marriage, and I was brought up around domestic violence. I know how terrifying it can be to want to get out and not be able to.'

'Are your parents still together?'

'I don't see either of them now. Too many bad memories.' Well, that's one way of putting it.

'Ah, that's a shame. I love my mum.' Shelley pauses. 'But if your dad was anything like Wayne is at times, then I don't blame you.'

'It was the undertone of it all that affected me most. I'd hear them shouting when he'd come in from the pub bladdered and wanting to start a fight. I'd see Mum's cuts and bruises the next day and think "here we go again." But it was the atmosphere that was hard to live in. It was like treading on thin ice. Having to be quiet every Sunday afternoon because he'd passed out on the settee.

'I remember the little things. The looks that were thrown between the two of them, or he'd grab my mum's wrist when she went past. Sometimes it was as simple as his plate wasn't warm enough. I'd be sitting at the table trying not to cry for fear of upsetting him even more.'

Shelley's face drops. 'That's how I feel at times. The slightest thing upsets Wayne. I'd never marry him, or have children with him, but he won't leave me alone. He thinks I belong to him, and I don't. Will you ever marry and have children?'

'Marry, perhaps, and he'll have to be special. I can't put a child through what I endured. And some men change when you get hitched. I read about that all the time. Obsession and love become possessive abuse once the ring is on the finger.'

'Do you think that about every man, or just ones like... Wayne?'

'There are *much* sweeter guys out there for you. You deserve better if he's hurting you.'

Shelley lowers her eyes. I curse under my breath. Me and my stupid mouth.

'I didn't mean to scare you or make out that what you're doing is wrong.' I reach across and touch Shelley's arm. 'Lord knows my mum tried so many times to get away from my dad, but I also know how hard that would have been for her. Especially with me in tow. He earned the money and kept it for himself. That was what most of the arguments were about. Mum was always trying to make ends meet while he was getting drunk in the pub.'

'God, that's awful.' Shelley shakes her head. 'I don't want to live like that.'

'It could be a gamble with Wayne, then. Does he often turn up drunk?'

Shelley nods. 'That's when he hurts me most.' She gets up suddenly and goes over to a drawer in the kitchen. She roots about inside it and then holds up a key on a ring. 'I think I will feel better knowing that you have it.'

I grin when she gives it to me. 'I'll keep asking for supplies if I hear him having a go. At least that might stop the red mist from coming over him long enough for him to calm down and leave.'

'Thank you. It's nice to know that. It makes me feel safer. But I will think on what you said. Because he is ruining my life at the moment, making me anxious in my own space.'

'It's not worth it, believe me.'

Shelley nods again. 'Should I have yours, too?'

'What?' I've gone off thinking about what I can do to help her.

'A key. Would you like to leave one with me?'

And let Wanky Wayne get in my flat? I don't think so.

'Yes, that's a good idea,' I lie. 'I'm bound to lock myself out one day. I'll get one cut and bring it down to you.'

Shelley grins at me. 'Thanks for watching over me.'

I smile back. 'That's what friends are for.'

Kind of.

CHAPTER NINETEEN

The next morning, after a knock on the door, I open it to find Tom on the landing.

'Hello! My first visitor,' I say, beckoning him in.

But he stays where he is.

'I'm really sorry to trouble you,' he says. 'Normally if I have an emergency, Roberta is around to help, but she's gone out for the day and...' He glances at me sheepishly. 'Would you be able to mind Isla for me while I go out for an hour? I need to call in the office to sort something out.'

'Of course, I'd be delighted.' I glance behind him to see he's alone. 'Where is she?'

'I thought I'd ask you first, but also, would you come downstairs rather than me bringing her up? I think she'd feel better about that.'

'Yes, no problem.'

'Are you sure? I don't want to impose on your weekend.'

Like I have other things to do...

'Honestly, it's fine. Let me grab my bag and keys.'

Tom is waiting for me on the landing when I return. I follow him down, and he thanks me again.

'Honestly, it's fine. Does Roberta watch Isla often?'

'She steps in when I have business to attend to. She's been a great backup since Sasha died.'

Isla is sitting on the sofa watching TV when we go into the living room.

'Clara is going to sit with you until I get back,' Tom tells her. 'I promise I won't be too long.'

'Hi, Clara.' Isla pats the seat next to her. 'Do you like dinosaurs? We could watch *Jurassic Park* if you do. Or we could watch something with a mystery.'

'Like *Scooby Doo*?' I sit down next to her. 'You do know who he is?'

Isla turns sharply towards me. 'Everyone knows who Scooby is. And Scrappy, don't forget him.'

'Indeed.' I quite enjoy being chastised. I wasn't sure if a ten-year-old would have heard of the cartoon. It seems *Scooby Doo* is a firm favourite throughout the decades. Excellent news.

Tom gathers his laptop and, along with a manilla file, puts them in his bag. He leans over the settee to kiss Isla on the cheek.

'Don't talk Clara to death, Isles,' he says. 'We have to be friendly to the neighbours.' He smiles at me. 'There's coffee and tea whenever you need it, and chocolate cake in the larder unit.'

'It's not homemade,' Isla explains. 'Dad and I aren't good at baking.'

'Really?' I stare at Tom pointedly.

'Let's just say we've had a few disasters.' A blush appears on his cheeks, and he bites his bottom lip.

Once Tom has said his goodbyes, I nudge Isla. 'Do you have the ingredients to make a cake if I said we could do one now?'

Isla whoops. 'We definitely have everything we need. We only used most things once.'

'Let's have a go then.'

Isla gets to her feet and then stops. 'You have made a cake before?'

I feign hurt. 'Of course I have, although a long time ago.' I reach for my phone. 'And what I can't remember, Mr Google can help me with.'

Within twenty minutes, a mix for a sponge cake has been made, spread over two tins and popped in the oven. While we wait for it to cook, I make myself a cup of coffee and Isla a drink of squash. We sit on high stools either side of the kitchen island.

'Do you like living here, Isla?' I want to know. 'It seems a nice area.'

'It is.' Isla cups her hand over her mouth and whispers, 'I'm a bit suspicious of...' She points a finger towards the ceiling.

I don't understand so I frown.

'Roberta,' Isla whispers.

I'm still none the wiser.

'I think she killed Mr Fisher and buried him in that rubbish.'

I gasp inwardly, trying to keep my face straight at the same time. This kid has a good imagination.

'I never saw anything strange when I was clearing

things out with her,' I say, hoping to quash Isla's thoughts immediately.

'Are you sure?' Isla narrows her eyes. 'Did you check every room?'

'Well, yes, I suppose I did. There was rubbish popped in the skip from all of them.'

'But did you look inside every bag?'

'No.'

'So how do you know?'

'For starters, I think Mrs Fisher is a lovely lady, and for another, she was deeply in love with Bill, and I don't think she would have wanted to harm him.'

Isla sits in silence for a moment. I can almost hear her mind ticking over. How on earth has she come up with such a ludicrous suggestion? Yet, I remember being inquisitive at her age. Before the death of my parents, I had been all questions and learning. My mum was really clever and informative when she was happy. But when I went to live with my grandparents, every-thing changed.

I try to push the images the conversation is gener-ating from my mind. The slaps, the pulling of hair, the cracks across the head as I wasn't quick enough to move out of harm's way.

'I'm sorry, Isla, but I think you've got this one wrong. Roberta is a lovely lady.'

Isla sighs. 'I do like her a lot, and she's been very kind to me.'

'Would it help if we chatted through some of your thoughts?'

'Wait a minute.'

Isla gets off the stool and disappears. She's back in

seconds with a pen and a notebook. 'I've made a list of things.'

I'm taken aback but keep my face straight. 'Okay. What do we know about Mr and Mrs Fisher?'

'They were married for a very long time.'

'Go on.'

'They were always together until he died.'

'Right.'

'Mr F would bring flowers for Mrs F every Friday. I used to wait for him in the window to see what colour they would be. Red ones, white ones, yellow and orange ones.'

'Well, that's a lovely thing to do. Was Mr F nice to you?'

Isla nods. 'He was always showing me his treasures. He said he got most of them on his travels, although I don't think he really went anywhere.'

'What about Roberta? Was she always nice to Mr F?'

Isla stops. 'I think you're right,' she concedes. 'I don't think she would hurt him. Mr Fisher must have been buried at his funeral.'

'Funeral?' I question.

'Yes, it was a while ago now.'

'So all this time you've thought he was here, you've been aware that he's been buried?'

'Yes, but...' Isla shrugs. 'No one saw him after he died.'

'Isla, I can't be sure, but I don't think many people see the deceased after they die, unless they're immediate family, or close friends and partners. Do you know who they are?'

'Mums and dads, brothers and sisters, grandparents. A boyfriend or girlfriend?'

'Yes. They can go to the funeral home and say goodbye before the service.'

'I've seen coffins on the TV, where they are open, and you can see the dead people.'

'That happens, too, but not so much nowadays, I don't think.'

'Roberta never let anyone see Bill.'

'That doesn't mean he wasn't inside the coffin.' I put a hand over Isla's. 'Is this to do with your mummy, Isla? Because if it is, and you find it hard to talk to your dad without upsetting him, you can always talk to me.'

'I never saw her in the coffin. Dad wouldn't let me.' Isla bursts into tears.

'Hey, now.' I move around the table, stopping by Isla's stool to give her a hug. 'It's probably because he wants you to remember her how she was. Dying can leave a person not looking their best. He told me he likes to remember her as she was on the photo above the fire.'

'He did?'

I nod, then I fetch the photo and prop it up in front of her. 'Your mummy was very pretty.'

Isla lets a tear roll down her face. 'I've been silly, haven't I?'

'Of course not.'

'I knew really that Roberta hadn't murdered him. She is the loveliest old woman I know.'

'Yes, she is.' I wipe Isla's cheek gently with my thumb. 'Let's ice that cake before your dad gets in. He should be back any minute. And this can be our secret.'

Isla nods.

Standing upright again, I feel for the girl. It's terrible for one parent to die, let alone two. Even now, sometimes losing mine can be as raw to me as the day it happened.

So when Tom arrives back, I'm torn whether to mention the incident or not. In the end, as he shows me out, I decide I will.

'I wasn't going to say anything,' I admit to him afterwards. 'But if I was her parent, I'd like to know.'

'Yes, it's a weird one,' Tom agrees. 'It explains things a little. Ever since Sasha died, Isla has become obsessed with death. It isn't healthy, but all the medical people say she'll grow out of it eventually. They reckon it's because she's grieving, trying to understand why her mum has gone. I hope it's true, so I don't have to worry about her gruesome thoughts.'

'Are you going to talk to her about it?' I don't want to lose the young girl's trust.

Tom shakes his head. 'But I will keep an eye on her, perhaps broach the subject another way. Thanks for confiding in me. I'm glad she found she was able to talk to you.'

'We all know how much easier it is with someone who isn't close. She's a great kid. You did a good job of bringing her up.'

Tom's cheeky grin widens with pride. Then he laughs. 'After what's she's told you, I'm not so sure.'

'Grief affects us all in different ways.' I stare at him, seeing if he'll mention his wife. But he says nothing else, just nods in agreement.

I go up to my flat, happier than I'd been that morning. It seems Isla trusts me enough to tell me her secrets, and Tom has left his daughter in my care.

And I feel good about both.

CHAPTER TWENTY

The following week, I open the door to Cedric House and am met with Isla sitting at the bottom of the stairs. The door to flat one is open, so I assume Tom is nearby, too. It's something that happens often, and I've started to enjoy seeing her.

Sometimes Isla will be reading. Others she'll be writing in her notebook. Once she had roller skates on, going round in small circles. I suppose it's a bit of independence for her. Isla is on her own but safe in the house when she isn't able to play in the garden due to the weather or the dark evenings.

'Hi, Isla,' I greet. 'Have you had a good day?'

'Yes. We've been learning about the Roman Empire.' Isla holds up a book for me to look at.

I sit next to her on the step. 'I can't recall anything about that. Maybe I wasn't paying attention. Do you like school?'

Isla thinks for a moment. 'I love maths but I'm not

good at art. I like writing stories in English lessons, but I don't like playing sports.'

'I hated sports!' I laugh. 'No one would pick me to be in their team because I was so useless.' I lean closer conspiratorially. 'I played on it, though, because I didn't want to join in. None of them guessed.'

Isla smiles, and then her face becomes serious. 'Clara, do you like Wayne?'

'From flat two?' I feel it's best not to tell her I can't stand the fella. 'He's okay, why?'

'I was sitting here yesterday after school, and I saw him coming downstairs. He had a bag under his arm. I think he came out of Roberta's flat.'

'The bag he was holding, what colour was it?'

'It was brown, like my school satchel.' It's Isla's turn to giggle. 'Is that what they call a man bag?'

'Yes, I think so.' It doesn't sound like one of Roberta's to me. 'Did he say anything to you?'

'He said "hey".' She lowers her voice to sound like a man. 'Then he rushed past me and into his flat. Do you think I should tell Roberta?'

'Don't you worry about that. Maybe I'll play detective, Isla. See what he's up to.' I touch my nose twice and stand up. 'In the meantime, you keep an eye out and let me know if you see him going upstairs again?'

Isla nods.

I leave her to it then, all the while wondering what Wayne is up to. I have to find time to sneak into flat two soon. Take my opportunity when I can.

It comes on Wednesday after work. Isla mentions that Tom is taking her out for a treat straight from school. I race back to Cedric House. Tom's car isn't in sight so, unless Wayne is in, there's only Roberta at home. Shelley has told me she's working until six, so I have a couple of hours. I only need a few minutes.

Upstairs, I change out of my work clothes into comfy sweats, put the strap of my bag over my head, and creep downstairs. I knock on the door to see if the coast is clear. Then again. When no one answers, I pull on latex gloves and use the key to get inside.

It's a pretty apartment. Shelley is as clean as me, which is good to see. Wasting no time, I slip into the living room. I spot Wayne's iPad on the arm of the settee and pick it up. I press the home key and grin when it lets me open it. The amount of people who don't put a password on a device that stays in the home never fails to amaze me. I assume they don't think what could happen if it gets in the wrong hands, if someone breaks into their home. People become complacent.

In my previous years after leaving Stoke, I'd become a dab hand at getting by with other people's money. Now I'll only do it if it's necessary for my survival. For instance, if my grandparents' house doesn't sell quickly enough, I might have to fleece a couple of men to pay the rent. Either that, or let the house go at a lower price than I'd be happy with. Only time will tell if I have to slip back into my old ways. I really don't want to.

It wasn't as difficult to be a thief when I'd been younger. Now there are extra things to trip me up. CCTV, way too many security guards, tags on every-thing. It isn't easy to pick more than one item up at a time, and besides, there are barely any decent shops in town now that lots of the high street favourites have either closed or gone elsewhere. So I stay on the straight and narrow as much as I can nowadays.

Earlier, I'd been thinking about how far to go with Wayne. There are all sorts of unsavoury things I can download and hide in a hidden folder so he might not stumble upon them. For now, I shall tease him. Order some things online for him and hope he doesn't twig. I'd seen him staggering in on Friday night, so he might think he's ordered them when he was drunk. Luckily, Amazon has pretty quick deliveries.

But then I realise that, even if I delete the email about the order, it might go to his phone or another device. He'll be able to cancel it before it's dispatched. He might even blame Shelley and have a pop at her. I sigh. That isn't going to work.

I have a quick scan around and then move to the kitchen and out into the hallway again. There doesn't seem much in the main bedroom, mostly Shelley's belongings. Next, I look around the bathroom, finding nothing much of interest.

In the spare room, I open a wardrobe and bingo! It's full of items in boxes and clear bags. Trainers, branded water bottles, football shorts and socks, T-shirts. They're all designer labels, no doubt counterfeits. I can't see them being the real thing.

I riffle through them. They must be stolen, and a great find for me. I might be back in here for myself at a later date.

There are more personal items in there, too. A set of fountain pens in a box. An array of trinkets in a velvet pouch. These are things I'm sure will have sentimental value. Is Wayne on the take? Are they from burglaries?

At the very back, in the corner, I spot a few jewellery boxes. I reach for one, opening its clasp. Inside is an expensive bracelet. But then I spot another box, one I recognise. I open that, too, and groan. It looks like a watch that belongs to Bill Fisher. I know because I popped it in the storage box that's now on the top of Roberta's wardrobe.

Wayne must have stolen it.

I recall the conversation when we met, when he mentioned all the rubbish in Roberta's flat. I think about Isla seeing him coming out of it with a bag. Has he been helping in the guise of stealing valuable items to sell?

Because if so, what an opportunity I have now to cause Wayne a little grief. I pop the watch and its box into my bag. I'll return it to Roberta without her knowing it's gone. That will teach Wayne a lesson for being such a knob.

CHAPTER TWENTY-ONE

My next meeting with Emma comes around far too quickly. Although I'm still reeling from the week before, I know I have to face my demons if I'm ever going to get better.

'Do you want to talk more about your parents?' she asks once we're settled.

'Not yet.'

'Why not tell me about your school days? I can imagine it was hard to go back after what happened?'

I nod. It seems like a better place to start.

'Before then, I hadn't really been noticed. I kept my head down and got on with my work. I think I just wanted to please people, because I could never do anything right at home.'

'Were there any teachers you could talk to?'

'I didn't dare. I was quite timid as a child. Occasionally one of them would ask me about a bruise, and I'd say I'd fallen over, or bumped into something. More often than not, I went under the radar.'

Until the weekend that changed everything.

'I expect it was quite a shock having to live with your grandparents,' Emma says after I go quiet on her momentarily.

'Totally. It meant a change of address, too. I'd been brought up three miles away, on another estate. I can remember the council housing officers coming out a few times when I'd been home after school. They'd be there about a noise complaint, or they'd come in the guise of a property spot check when they felt a little concerned. My mum would always play it down, though, as if there was nothing going on, that the neighbours were overreacting. But even she couldn't have predicted what would happen eventually. I could, though. I could see it building up.'

I close my eyes briefly. I thought I hadn't wanted to talk about my parents. Maybe I should let my words flow.

'So you'd known for a while things were getting worse?' Emma probes.

'Yes.'

'Do you think your grandparents were aware of the situation?'

'Probably, but I couldn't tell them. It felt wrong to talk to them about it, I guess. I just wanted my parents to be happy, and my dad to be nice to my mum.'

'Was he always angry?'

I recall one particularly brutal incident. It had been a Sunday afternoon, and I'd arrived home after a sleepover at my friend, Amy's, home. The weather had been glorious, and they'd had a barbecue. There been games and a paddling pool, lots of ice cream and fizzy pop. Some of Amy's relatives had come over, too. It had been so much fun.

When Amy's mum dropped me at home, I'd run inside excitedly, hoping to tell Mum all about it. But the house had been silent. There was no one downstairs, and as I'd raced upstairs, I started to panic.

It was too quiet.

My parents' bedroom door was ajar. I crept up to it. If my dad was in there, I'd be in trouble if I woke him up.

But when I peeped in, I saw my mum curled up on top of the bedcovers. She had her back towards me.

'Mum?' I whispered.

'Leave me alone, love.'

I walked over to the bedroom window, looking through it to check Dad wasn't in the garden and going to run upstairs and tell me off any minute. When I was certain it was only the two of us, I turned back to the room.

And burst into tears.

Mum's face was already black and blue, her left eye closed and bulging out like a tennis ball. There was a cut on her upper lip, and I noticed a whole chunk of her hair missing on one side.

How could my dad hurt my mum so much when he loved her?

How could my mum stay when he was so cruel to her?

I kneeled at the side of the bed, resting my hand on her arm.

'Mum?' I whispered, a sob stuck in my throat.

'I'm okay.' Mum's voice was quiet, but it was there.

I raced downstairs and dampened a tea towel. Then I ran back to the bedroom and held it gently to her face.

'You're a good girl, Clara.'

'We have to leave,' I whispered, wiping at my tears.

'We've been through this before. It's not possible.'

'But I'm scared, he's going to kill you.'

'Oh, love, you're not old enough to deal with this. I'm so sorry. One day, we'll get away and never see him again. You'd like that, wouldn't you?'

I nodded, dabbing gently at Mum's wounds. She always defended him. It was the same every time.

It wasn't his fault.

You know he doesn't mean it.

It was something she'd done that had made him mad.

He'd had some bad news and was upset.

'Why don't we live somewhere else without him,' I had asked over and over. But Mum would say there was no point. She said he'd always find us and bring us back, and it wasn't worth the extra pain.

He must really hurt her for her to say that.

'Yes, he was always angry,' I tell Emma. 'I think that's because I'd normally see him when he'd been to the pub. He used to go most days from work, so I'd be in bed when he got in. At the weekends, he'd go out at dinnertime and either not come back until he was kicked out of the pub or else he'd be flat out on the settee all afternoon, and woe betide us if we woke him.

'I don't know why they fought all the time. Amy's mum and dad were so much fun. I was lucky to have a friend like her for a while. I felt safer at her house. Her mum was lovely, giving us treats. I quite often stayed for a sleepover. But I always worried about Mum and what would be happening when I wasn't there. Because I knew that seeing me sometimes made Dad stop and think before he hit Mum again.'

Tears pour down my face.

'So you had nowhere to feel safe and have some fun, really?' Emma asks, her tone hushed as she passes me a tissue.

'Only when I went to Amy's house.' I wipe my eyes. 'I don't want to talk about anything else today.' The session has drained me, and rather than make me feel better as I'd hoped, eager to let some of my past go, dredging it up has been a horrible experience.

And yet, still I continue.

'Everything changed when I went back to school. I don't know why, but Amy was different with me. Maybe she didn't know how to react, what to say to comfort me, but she stopped being my best friend. It really hurt. Amy had been someone I could always talk to, even at that young age. Then I had no one.'

'What about your grandparents? Didn't you feel safe when you went to live with them either?'

My face darkens. 'It was like going out of the frying pan into the fire.'

CHAPTER TWENTY-TWO

After finding Bill Fisher's watch, I don't want to keep it for too long. Knowing my luck, Roberta will notice it's gone and I'll be found with it, and that will never do. For once in my life, I'm not the one doing the thieving, so I don't want to get caught red-handed with something that would give the wrong impression. I have to visit Roberta and see if it's hers before going any further.

I knock on Roberta's door.

'I bought some cakes; thought you might like some company over a mug of tea?' I throw a thumb over my shoulder as soon as Roberta answers. 'Although you're quite welcome to come over to mine, if you prefer?'

'No, come in. I have cakes, too.'

I follow her into the living room where I can see the kitchen table is laid out for four. There are two cake stands, layered with small pots of jam next to scones, dainty sandwiches, and slices of caramel shortbread, miniature Victoria sponge cakes, and chocolate-covered marshmallows. A large tub of cream sits in between them.

'Afternoon tea!' Roberta clasps her hands together in front of her chest and sighs. 'And it's all down to you.'

'Me?'

'I'm a member of a book club.' Roberta waves a hand in a circle. 'Not much talking about the books goes on, though. It's more a meeting of old minds and a catch-up on the gossip. There are four of us who have kept in touch since we worked together in Woolworths. We meet each month at one or other of our homes. I obviously haven't been able to host for such a long while, but now my flat has so much room in it, I can have them round to tea.'

I suddenly feel all warm inside. Roberta is happy because of me, and it's the most wonderful feeling.

'I'm so pleased,' I reply. 'And it all looks very inviting. When are your friends arriving?'

'Not for another hour, so we have plenty of time to put the kettle on. I'm going to enjoy myself so much today. So many cakes!'

While Roberta makes tea and I put my cakes on a plate, we chat about day-to-day things. It makes me feel a bit sneaky as I then rush into her bedroom later, when she is freshening up in the bathroom.

It's much tidier without Bill's paraphernalia, and it only takes me a few seconds to reach up and pull down the storage box on top of the wardrobe. I place it carefully on the bed and quickly check inside it.

I was right. Bill's watch is missing. That sneaky bastard Wayne!

I check to see Roberta isn't going to come back at

any moment, then I get out the watch from my bag. I hear water running from the flush of the toilet, and know I have only seconds to spare. Quickly, I glance around. I'll have to put it somewhere safe in case Wayne comes after it again. Somewhere he won't be able to find it without searching the whole flat.

I race through to the kitchen, my eyes scanning the best place to leave the watch for now. I open the sink unit to find a plastic box full to its brim with tea towels. I take one out and wrap the box in it. Then I push it out of sight, into the crease behind the sink overflow.

I hope Roberta doesn't find it missing before I have time to sort Wayne out. But if she does, I'll tell her the truth and pray she believes me. The last thing I want is the police involved.

I go back into the living room and sit down where Roberta last saw me. The bathroom door opens just as the buzzer goes off for the entrance door.

Despite my flushed face, I can't help but smile when there are cheery hellos, followed by raucous laughter. Four women troop in, Roberta first. They remind me of The Golden Girls, all bright and bubbly, and I smile.

'This is my tenant, Clara,' Roberta introduces me. 'She lives across the hall. We've just been putting the world to rights over a cup of tea.'

'Is this the lady who helped you transform your home?' A woman steps closer and beams at me. 'I have to congratulate you on doing such a great job.'

I smile with gratitude. 'It was a joint effort. I think Roberta did as much as me. I just got the ball rolling.'

'Which charity do you work for?'

'Stoke Helps Out.'

'My son-in-law works there. Richard Mortimer. Do you know him?'

I shake my head, keeping my cool. Does this woman know me, or even worse, my family from years gone by?

'I don't think so,' I reply quickly. 'But I might know him by face and not name. There are a lot of people there.'

'There are, and they do a great job. I'm Nita, by the way.'

I sigh with relief after I'm introduced to the other two women, Pauline and Marji, without further mention of the charity.

'Well, I'd better make myself scarce now,' I say. 'I know you have a lovely afternoon tea to enjoy, over your book discussion, of course.'

All four are still chattering when I leave. What a lovely sound it is.

Over the next couple of hours, I think long and hard about how to get Wayne back for what he's done. At the moment, no real crime has been committed because he thinks he has the watch.

Although another thought strikes me. Is he going to blame the theft on me if it comes to light? Maybe Roberta will immediately blame me, despite not knowing of my background. I can't risk that.

It's all what-ifs and maybes really, but it has my heart racing at the thought of Roberta thinking ill of me. Perhaps I should ask Tom for advice. It will give me a reason to call on him at the very least. But then, I don't want anyone to catch me with the watch and think I'm the thief.

I cast my mind back to the first time I stole something. I'd been barely twelve years old, asleep in bed when a loud bang had woken me up around midnight. I'd sat up, listening in the dark.

It had been two years since my parents died, and yet I still felt on edge when Derek was around. He was always going on about how lucky I was to have family to take me in. He said I should be grateful I hadn't gone into a children's home with nasty boys and girls. Most of the time, I wished I *hadn't* come to stay with them. Because Derek was as mean as my dad had been.

My nan took care of me as best she could, though, and sometimes Derek did behave better when she was around, as long as he hadn't been to the pub. Thank goodness she was all right to me. It made living there just about bearable but, as soon as I could, I was going to leave. I had plans. I wanted to go to college and then on to university, move out of Stoke so I could get away from my past.

Although that in itself was a problem because Nan would get the brunt of everything then, just like my mum had. Could I leave Nan alone with Derek? I wasn't sure I'd be able to.

The voice of Frankie Valli with the Four Seasons burst out of the living room. The house reverberated from the sound, the volume up as high as it would go. I put a pillow over my head, hoping to drown it out. What was wrong with him, the old fool?

Since I'd come to live there, I'd realised where my dad had got his mean streak from. Derek would lash out at me and Nan quite often. Mostly we were in bed when he came home drunk. And if not, we had to creep around while he was asleep, trying not to wake him for fear of retaliation.

Last month, he'd been rushed into hospital and had to have his appendix removed. The mood in the house had lifted, until he'd come home and everything had reverted to normal. He expected Nan to wait on him, tend to his every need. It wasn't fair that the women in the Cooper households should be treated as slaves.

But I could understand my nan keeping the peace, too. Derek was calmer if nothing antagonised him. One day perhaps I'd understand how men and women were supposed to act when they were together. One day, I hoped to find a prince and have a fairy-tale wedding. We'd live in a big house and have five children. They would all look after each other and be close-knit.

The music stopped for a second until the next track started. I'd be wrecked in the morning at this rate. Derek was already in a drunken stupor, snoring his head off on the settee. He often did that, leaving the record on repeat and sleeping right through the noise.

Ten minutes later, the music still blaring, I threw back the duvet and tiptoed downstairs. The living room door was open and, sure enough, Derek was asleep in the chair.

Taking a deep breath, I tiptoed slowly over to the chair where he'd flung his jacket. I slipped a hand in and reached for his wallet. Inside it were two notes, a ten pound and a twenty. I took out the ten and then put the wallet back. All the time, Derek snored.

Folding the note so that it was small enough to hide in my fist, I sneaked over to the music centre and reached for the volume button. I knew better than to switch it off, dropping the room into silence, as it might wake him. Instead, I switched it down second by second until it was much quieter. Then I legged it out of the room.

Nan was halfway down the stairs when she saw me.

'What are you doing up?' she whispered.

'He woke me.'

'Is he asleep?'

I nod. 'I couldn't stand the noise any longer. I'm tired.'

'Get back to bed and I'll sort him out.'

All tucked in again, I laughed with relief. I'd got away with it. Derek probably wouldn't remember how much money he'd spent on a night out. Tomorrow on the way home from school, I would treat myself to a large bar of chocolate and a 50p pic 'n' mix. I'd take the sweets to school and share them out, but I wouldn't give any to Kerry Simons. See how she liked being left out of things.

Of course it hadn't stopped at that one theft. And even if it was Derek's fault that I learned how to do far worse later in life, I'd been grateful that it had at times been to my own benefit.

CHAPTER TWENTY-THREE

Even though my friend, Andy, hardly ever turns up for the anger management meetings, I'm in the habit of waiting for him outside the entrance until the very last minute. So I'm surprised to see him sitting on the low wall as I approach it.

Andy waves when he spots me, puts out his cigarette, and stands up. He's over six feet tall, bulky with it but not overweight, and his crew cut hairstyle is left over from his days in the army. He's wrapped up warm against the cold.

'Hello, stranger,' I say, trying not to show my annoyance at his recent absence. 'To what do I owe this pleasure?'

'I've only not made the last two sessions.' Andy looks surprised. 'Have you missed me?'

'No.'

I have, funnily enough, but I'm not going to tell him that.

'You have!' He grins. 'Moaning Marian on the late

shift has been off sick and I've been covering for her, so I couldn't come. But she's back now, so... here I am.' Andy shrugs. 'How are you?'

'Okay, ta.'

I'm not going to be won over that easily. People are always making up excuses. I need this group, though. It's my saving grace. Andy should be more aware of that.

I pause. This isn't about Andy. This is about routine and keeping everything under control.

I nudge him. 'Got anything to say this week?'

Andy's face drops. 'Not that I want to share with the group. But... I've been a dick, if I'm honest. I lashed out at Darren when he was being nice. I can't help myself at times. I don't know how he puts up with me. He didn't do anything wrong, and there I am, spoiling things. Do you think we're wired to destroy everything that's good in our life?'

Yes.

'I don't know,' I say instead. 'Maybe.'

'I like Darren. I love him, Clara, and yet I hate him, too. He makes me feel too normal, too safe. That's why I want to sabotage what we have. It's so wrong, but I don't know how to be any different.'

'I know the feeling.'

'Oh... have you met someone?'

'No, but if I had I'd be scared I'd fuck up as usual.'

'Ah, you won't know until you try.'

'I suppose. But you and Darren seem to do okay and—'

'I'm not a good example. My parents were rough with each other. I never knew how much it rubbed off on me. I mean, I saw them scrapping. My mum gave as much as my dad, and then they'd make up. So when I get angry with Darren, I punch him on the arm and expect something back, and when he doesn't respond I get upset. I think he doesn't love me then. How warped is that?'

Yes, how warped is that? Because I know exactly what it means, and it's happened to me lots of times.

'So why don't you do something about it?' I say, knowing that I never did.

'I'm here, aren't I?' Andy falters. 'Don't lecture me.'

'Sorry.' I grin. 'Let's go inside.'

Later, when I'm asked if I want to say anything, I know people will think I'll say no, or want to talk about my parents, but there's something puzzling me, and what better place to air my thoughts about it than here.

'Do you believe if we have the opportunity to surround ourselves with pleasant things and good people, that we can become more positive?' I say to Matthew.

'I do, yes,' Matthew replies. 'However, it's not as easy as that, especially in a working-class city where there are less opportunities than in more affluent ones.'

'So why isn't wealth distributed fairly?'

'Because people are greedy,' Andy joins in. 'There will always be the haves and the have-nots.'

'I don't mean that.' I go on to explain. 'Say, for instance, you go to college and get further education, despite your upbringing, and then you get a good job.'

'Around here?' a voice from the back quips up. 'You're having a laugh.'

I ignore him. 'Say you started a business then and could be your own boss.'

'That would be a nightmare, a whole bundle of stress,' someone else says.

'Okay.' I sigh, my attention waning. 'How about if we grew up in a shitty environment, didn't do well at school, and could only get a dead-end job? But then we moved into a better area with lovely people. Would that eventually rub off on us and make us nicer?'

'We are nice!' Andy admonishes.

'You know what I mean. Would we forget our past and our demons and be able to start afresh? Or would one simple thing we didn't like in our new surroundings begin a knock-on effect of bringing us back down to earth, reminding us of where we've come from and putting us back in our place?'

'I'm not following you, Clara,' Matthew says. 'Can you explain better?'

I shrug. 'I'm not sure I can. I suppose it's a nature versus nurture question, but surely if someone like me mixed with pleasant people, had a lovely home and a loving partner, with no money worries—'

'Living the dream.' A man further along rolls his eyes, but he does smile.

I pay no heed to him. 'Would I still get angry? Or would I be happy again because of my situation?'

'No one can be cheerful all the time,' Matthew responds.

'It would help to have spare money, bills paid, decent food in my belly, and a roof over my head that I owned so I didn't have to worry about it,' Andy says. 'But that's never going to happen.'

'Why not?'

Andy thinks for a moment. 'Nature versus nurture? Maybe I don't think I deserve it.'

I sit back as the group begins to chat my question through, but eventually I shut off from their answers. All I want is for one of them to say that it *is* possible to change if the circumstances suited.

Because I'd like to be happy while I'm at Cedric House. It has a warm feel to the building and, apart from Wayne, everyone is lovely. Surely it will make for better mental health, coming home to somewhere like that every evening? Or is there only me in this room who believes it's possible?

Afterwards, I nip to the pub with Andy. I wonder why I like him so much, seeing as he's just like my father. Maybe it's because we've been through similar childhood traumas, dragged up rather than brought up.

Sometimes it helps to talk to someone who's been through similar to what I have. Who has inflicted pain on others just because they could.

'What was all that about, in the meeting?' Andy asks, when we're both seated with drinks. His is a glass of Coke. He told me once that even the sniff of alcohol will get his anger revving up.

I take a sip of my wine, ignoring the fact I used to be the same. 'I wanted a little light in a dark day, I suppose.'

'So you believe all that bollocks?'

'I have to. Otherwise there's no happy ending for me.'

Andy laughs, then realising I'm being serious,

straightens his features. 'I guess everyone deserves a second chance.'

'I wish I could be a kind and thoughtful person. But I'm always afraid I might hurt someone I care about again. I can't put anyone through what I fear might happen. There has to be a way to stop the violence from exploding.'

Andy blows out a breath. 'If you find it, please tell me what it is. I'm tired of living like this. Feeling the anger that builds up in me for no reason. The broken relationships because of it. The sense that I'm living on a knife edge, just waiting for something to erupt. It's not good.'

'Then *change* it.'

'How?'

'I don't know, but there has to be a way.'

We drink in silence for a while.

'I don't have answers, Clara,' Andy says. 'I wish I did, for both of us. I guess we must learn to live with it, sense the signs that it's going to start and try to stop it before it's too late.'

I nod in agreement. Pity no one told my father that.

CHAPTER TWENTY-FOUR

I'm balancing at the top of a stepladder while I hang new curtains at my window. Tom has offered to fit a pole for me and, wanting any excuse to spend time to get to know him better, I take him up on it. As well, anything to rid myself of the horrible brown ones that have been there since I moved in. I've found a decent-priced pair in the local market.

It's beginning to be a habit, coming home with the odd thing for the flat. Items that make it look homely but individual, hence the Seventies swirl-inspired curtains that are mustard, pink, and beige. I've bought six *Game of Thrones* mugs which I saw online at Amazon, and a lamp that stands in the corner of the room. More cushions for the settee and a few canvas prints. I also treated myself to a small flatscreen TV, as the one at my grandparents' is ancient. All in all, it's beginning to feel like my own space at last.

'You said you're divorced when we first met,' Tom says as he packs away his tools in a box. 'May I ask why?'

'He wasn't the man I thought he was.'

I'm glad he can't see my face as I have my back to him. Because that's an understatement if ever I'd heard one. So I think it's best to give him a little information.

'At first we were good together, but then he became violent.'

Tom stops what he's doing. 'God, Clara. I'm glad you got away from him.'

I sigh. 'He brought out the worst in me, too.'

'What do you mean?'

'Oh, nothing more than I became a shell of my former self.' Curtains hung, I step down to the floor again. 'He was controlling, and I was so scared of him at times that I worried for my safety. It was easier to behave, so to speak, and keep the peace. I didn't like it, and often thought I was letting myself down. We were a bit like Shelley and Wayne. Evan, that's my ex, he always wanted to have the last word. That was usually in an argument he'd started, typically over nothing important. He liked the sound of his own voice way too much.'

It's a long time since I've said his name out loud, and yet it feels as if it was yesterday that we last spoke.

'How long were you with him?' Tom wants to know.

Too long.

'Four years on and off.'

'You split up once?'

'We were separated for a few months, yes.' Now that's what I call bending the truth.

'Don't tell me. He promised to treat you better and he didn't.'

'Something like that. It was fine for about a month, and then it all went back to normal. In the end, he went too far, and I'd had enough. I left and went to stay with a friend until I found my own place.'

'Wow, that's intense. At least you're rid of him now. When was the last time you saw him?'

'Several years ago. He lives in Manchester. He stopped trying to find me when he got another woman. I pity her but I can't blame myself for her being with him. He could be very charming, weaving you into his web. He made me do a lot of things I'm not proud of.'

I'm suddenly back to a night when I'd gone out hustling. As evenings go, I'd had worse. The man had met me as arranged in the lobby of the hotel. I'd put on my most revealing yet sophisticated dress and felt good.

He'd spotted me right away and waved.

'Suzanne?' he asked.

'Yes, hi. Charles?'

'Please call me Charlie.' He leaned forward and kissed my cheek.

I caught the scent of his cologne and inhaled its manliness. Not too overpowering but very stated.

We chatted for a while, and for once, I began to enjoy his company. Which was a shame really. Still, I would hazard a guess that he might treat me better than the last man I'd hooked up with.

'I've booked us the best room,' he whispered, leaning a hand on my thigh. 'We can go up now if you like?'

'I think that would be good,' I purred.

The sex was average, nothing kinky, and I enjoyed it for the main. It made a change to be with a man who wasn't so drunk, or angry that he couldn't get it up, who wasn't double my age and who thought of my needs, too.

So when I slipped a sedative into his drink while he was in the bathroom, I half felt sorry for him. Later, snapping a photo with him laid out naked on the bed was a moment of disgust, but a necessity. Then while he snored lightly, I searched through his pockets, taking his credit cards.

I slipped my shoes on, then applied my lipstick again. Popping it in my bag, I was ready. I blew Charlie a kiss and left as quietly as I'd arrived. He'd told me he wasn't married, but who used a hotel room if there wasn't anything dodgy going on?

A cloud of melancholy cloaked my shoulders. Sometimes being on the take was good, others not so. This was one of the good occasions. But beggars couldn't be choosers. And I was thinking of leaving Manchester in a couple of days, so he wouldn't find me.

I never managed to leave any of it behind. Not Evan, not Manchester.

Until my hand was forced.

'How about you?' I say to Tom. 'Have you always lived in Stoke?'

'Yes, born and bred a potter.' He sniggers. 'Never set foot in a potbank, actually. I was better at numbers than art, and yet I became a designer. I love marketing.'

'Where did you and Sasha meet?'

'She was on a hen night, and I was on a stag do. I bumped into her, literally, as she was coming out of the loo in Wetherspoons. I apologised and walked off, only to have her following me. The groups we were with were standing near to each other. We smiled at the coincidence and got chatting. When everyone went to the next pubs, we stayed put.'

'I wonder, in the grand scheme of things nationwide, how many couples met in a Spoons. It must be in the thousands.'

'I bet it is. And you. Where did you meet your ex?'

'I was coming out of Tesco, and my bag burst,' I say. 'He helped me to collect all the apples that rolled everywhere, even though I would never have eaten any of them. I said thanks and went on my way. Over the next two weeks, as creatures of habit, we bumped into each other, and I found myself waiting to see him, so I made sure I was there at the same time. On the fourth occasion, he asked for my number. I wish I hadn't given it to him, but that's another story.'

'And now, do you like it here in Cedric House?'

'Yes, because I have lovely, friendly people around me. It feels great to come home, even if we're living in separate rooms, it's one big house, really.'

'I never thought of it that way, but you're right. I'm still in two minds whether to move out and start afresh, but every time I find a property, there's always something that puts me off. I know I'm making excuses. Perhaps we'll stay here for a few more years. I'll see how Isla feels when she's in secondary school.'

'Sounds like a plan.' I enjoy spending time with Tom. He has a wicked sense of humour and is always willing to put himself out for others. 'Thanks so much for helping me fit the new pole. I'll close the curtains with glee this evening. I like those that brighten rooms more when they're drawn than when they're open.'

'And those sure do make a statement.'

I beam at him, thankful to see he's teasing.

'I've been thinking,' Tom goes on. 'Maybe we should have a roast lunch, all of us. We could get together in the one room, perhaps in my flat. Nothing too fancy. Just the five of us, or six if Wayne can be bothered to show up. Not that I'd want him there, but he and Shelley are an item, I suppose.'

'More's the pity.' I smile. 'But yes, that would be nice. Thank you.'

'For what?'

'For listening and not judging. And for inviting me to lunch. I'm looking forward to it already.'

CHAPTER TWENTY-FIVE

I hate lying to Tom. But how can I tell him the truth about how I really met Evan? It doesn't bode well to say it was while I was out shoplifting. I think back to the first time Evan spoke to me.

'I've been watching you for a while, miss,' he said, grinning at me.

'I'm sorry?'

'The box of perfume you put in your handbag. I take it you're not going to pay for that?'

'I don't know what you're talking about.' I turned to leave, hoping the man wouldn't follow me. Most of the security guards were in uniform. How had I missed him?

He reached for my arm, and I pulled it away sharply.

'I'm only messing with you.' He held up his hands. 'I don't work in the shop, but I have seen you stick something in your bag. So either remove it and let's get out of here. Or bring it with you and I'll bring my stash, too.' He pointed to a bulge in his trousers. 'I am pleased to see you, but that's not all I have tucked down my pants.'

I stared at him. I hadn't seen him around before, but I knew from his accent that he was a Mancunian. He had slate-grey eyes, twinkling as he grinned. His hair was black, close cut, and his skin either tanned or dark, I wasn't sure which.

I took a quick glance around the shop. No one was taking any notice of us, so I nodded.

'I'll buy you a drink if we get out in one piece.' He grabbed my hand. 'And if we get collared, we can run!'

I walked with him towards the door. We weren't stopped so we carried on down the road. I glanced at him surreptitiously. His hand felt good in my own. I was intrigued to say the least. But I was furious, too.

'You bastard!' I hit him in the chest when we were far enough away from the shop to know we weren't going to be collared. 'You almost gave me a heart attack back there.'

'Better me than the security guard.' He laughed. 'I saw what you were doing a mile off. You were lucky there was no one around at the time.'

'I knew because I'd seen the security guard go off for his break minutes earlier. What do you take me for, an amateur?'

'Well, I wouldn't have put you in the professional league. I'm impressed.' He pointed to a coffee shop up above. 'A hot drink or a cold one in Spoons?'

'Coffee will do, thanks.'

'I might even stretch to a slice of cake if you're lucky.'

'Aren't you the charmer?' I teased. Because now we

were away from the shop, and he still had his hand wrapped around mine, I felt I wanted to spend time with him. At least I could find out his name.

'Evan,' he told me once we had coffee, two slices of Bakewell Tart, and a table in a quiet corner.

'I'm Clara,' I said, for once fine with using my own name. I had a feeling I'd be getting to know Evan better, so it was good to be straight from the get-go.

'Do you live around here?' I asked casually while I stirred my drink.

'Deansgate. Been there all my life. You?'

'Salford. Came when I was seventeen and forgot to leave.'

'You don't like it?'

Did I like it? Because nothing had told me to move on. I'd lived in different areas as I'd gone from flat to flat. It was far enough away from the city centre not to be drawn to it every day, and yet easy to get to when I was short on cash.

'It's home, I guess.'

'But you're not from here. Is that a Liverpool accent mixed in with a bit of Manchester?'

'No.' Outrage was clear in my voice. 'I'm from Stoke, but I do get accused of being a Liverpudlian every now and then. I guess it's a difficult accent to pinpoint.'

'So why here and not Stoke?'

'Felt like a change.'

'What do you do?'

'This and that. You?'

'That and this.'

I returned his teasing smile. It was fun to banter

with someone of the opposite sex without trying to fleece them. Although I couldn't help noticing the watch on his wrist and wondering if it was fake. If it was, it was a good copy.

He followed my gaze. 'It's real.'

'You would say that.'

'I guess you're right. How long have you been on the take?'

'Since I don't know when. I do it when I have to get by, or when I'm in between jobs. I don't do it for a thrill, just for necessity.' I frowned. 'You're not going to tell me you're an undercover cop, or something, are you?'

His laughter had people turning around.

'Nothing of the sort. I'm Fagan to your Nancy. I only saw you today because you're on my patch.'

'I suppose you're going to teach me how to pick a pocket or two?'

He smiled and leaned in closer. 'I'm not sure I can teach you any tricks. I bet you know them all. But you do know that two heads are better than one?'

'I prefer to work alone. Easier not to let myself get duped.'

Evan clutched his chest. 'My heart is broken at your insinuations.'

'Sorry, I don't trust many people nowadays. I find it hard to let my hair down.'

'Well, maybe we can do something about that.'

He ran his thumb over the back of my hand, and I gasped inwardly at its intensity. I was determined never to get too close to anyone, but at the same time I wondered if I was going to fall for him right there and then.

Could he see that? And if so, would he still be interested? There was only one way to find out.

I leaned across and kissed him.

That kiss sealed my fate. Had I not met Evan that day, how would my life have turned out? Would I have found someone like Tom, someone decent to rely on and love? Would I have been able to carry a child full term with another man, or was the fault mine? Would I not have gone to prison?

Ifs, buts, and maybes.

Which is why I bring it up during my next session with Emma.

'Do I attract a type?' I ask.

'I'm not with you,' she replies.

'Am I never meant to meet someone decent because I mix with the wrong people? Do I have a way about me that says either "here comes trouble" or "she can be manipulated"?'

'Do you think you do?'

I dislike it when Emma bats a question back to me. But it always opens up a discussion, even when I don't want to look into things deeper.

'I must do. If I hadn't left Stoke in a hurry, I'd have probably been shacked up with a scrote off the estate, claiming benefits, on drugs, and scrounging whatever I could get.'

'Do you really see yourself like that?' Emma questions.

'You only know half of my story so far. You might feel differently when I've told you everything I've done.'

'The past can't be changed, Clara. But we can work on the present to make you a brighter future. Because you are worthy of love, and of someone special loving you. I think you're hard on yourself because you need something to blame. You hold your parents and grand-parents responsible for your lost childhood.'

'Rightly so.'

'I can understand that. But even now, you seem to pop yourself in a box that's labelled "misfit" because of it. You can choose to change right now, leave all that behind.'

'Can you see me doing that?' I scoff, wondering if these therapy sessions are a waste of money after all. 'Because I can't.'

CHAPTER TWENTY-SIX

I've been in the office for most of the afternoon, and at five-thirty I'm done for the day. I log out of my computer and say my goodbyes. Sam hasn't been in since two o'clock, so I've enjoyed the afternoon much better than usual, sitting looking busy.

I'm buckling up the seat belt in my car when I see him pull in two spaces away. He mustn't have spotted me, so I decide to wait until he's gone.

The door to the building opens, and through the rear-view mirror, I watch Tess run across to Sam's car and gets in. He reverses out, and I see Tess laughing as she fastens her seat belt. When they're out of the car park, I start up my vehicle and follow them.

He takes her to a pub a few streets away, one that I've been to with him several times. To all intents and purposes, they look like a couple of friends, but I know better. How can Sam do this to Misha? His children?

My blood boiling, I sit stewing. He obviously doesn't believe me when I say I can ruin his life. Perhaps now is the time to make it clear. I get out of the car and go inside.

The pub is a popular eatery, and there are people milling about everywhere, getting food and drinks. It doesn't take me long to spot the two of them, at the back in a corner. Out of the way so as not to be seen.

I stand by the bar, watching them fetch food from the carvery, and then sit down. I sidle over to them. Sam's face is a picture when he spots me.

'Having a good time?' I smile sweetly at them both.

The expressions on their faces are comical.

'What are you doing here?' Sam stutters.

'I'm taking photos of the two of you together. Like I warned you I would if you didn't stop playing around.'

'We're just having a meal after work,' Tess says. 'There's no harm in that.'

'I don't doubt it. Still, once his wife sees what I caught you up to, she can make up her own mind.'

Tess frowns at Sam. 'You told me you were separated.'

'What, that old chestnut? He's lying to you. He did the same to me.'

'You utter bitch.' Sam stands up, fists clenched.

'What are you going to do in a room full of people?' I tut. 'It wouldn't be wise to do anything really. And it's not entirely a good look for HR, is it? Out with one of the temps? Again?'

'What do you mean, again?' Tess questions.

'Ignore her,' Sam mumbles and sits down.

'Yes, ignore me.' I point to Tess. 'But not you, Sam. Because I have the evidence I need to ruin you and I'm about to act upon it if you don't tell her to leave right now.'

I watch Sam's features go through every set of emotions. Eventually, he sighs in resignation and turns to Tess.

'You have to go, babe.'

Tess gasps, eyes wide. 'You can't be serious.' Sam says nothing, so she rounds on me. 'But he was going to give me a lift home.'

'I can do that, if you're stuck.'

'I wouldn't be seen dead with you.'

'Ah, okay then, it will be a taxi ride. Make sure he pays for you.' I beckon for Tess to get out of her seat. When she does, I sit in her place. 'That's better. I'm starving. This smells divine.' I glance over at Sam. 'Tuck in, don't let it get cold.'

'I'm not leaving.' Tess folds her arms.

'No, I am,' Sam says.

He stares at me, and I stare back at him. Well, this is childish.

'If you want to wait for a lift, I suggest you find yourself a seat,' I throw at Tess, without looking her way.

'You're such a bitch.'

'Really?' I shake my head. 'Didn't your mum ever teach you good manners? He's married.'

'It didn't stop you.'

'Honeytrap, my love,' I lie. It's time to reveal my trump card. I get out my phone and show the screen to Sam. The photo I took of him lying next to me in his bed while he was sleeping.

'It was a good night, that.'

Sam snatches for my phone, but I move it before he can get at it.

'I told you what would happen if you went near Tess again.' This time I stand up. 'I'm going now. It's okay, I wouldn't leave you to find your own way home. Besides, you're welcome to him.' I lean over and pinch a roast potato from his plate. Then I knock over his pint, into his dinner and all down his trousers.

'Oops.' I titter before leaving. I'm probably going to pay for that in the morning. But right now, I couldn't give a toss.

Back in my flat, I drop back in the settee, feeling drained. What on earth am I playing at? I overreacted in a matter of minutes. But seeing Sam with Tess pushed all my buttons.

I go out again, this time on foot, cursing myself for being unable to stay in because I'm restless. It's only half past seven, earlier than usual, so my walk in the dark is through busier streets.

My feet take me to KA Nails and Beauty, the business Kerry owns. It's a thirty-minute walk, a nice distance for me. Mostly, I prefer the quiet of the night to the busyness during the day. And if anyone comes near me, I carry a knife in my pocket. I'm not that stupid.

It's sad I have to think along these lines, but my mind is clearer when I can walk. Now it keeps going over and over the scene in the pub.

Kerry's business is at the end of a row of shops, which include a convenience store, a post office, and a craft shop. The salon has a late night each Thursday, so I sit on the low wall surrounding the car park, far away enough not to be seen.

I idly watch the traffic going past, wondering if everyone is going home to their loved ones. To spouses, partners, friends to share good times with. To chill out over a meal, watch TV shows, or relaxing in a bath together. To catch up with children and share stories of their days.

I turn the other way and watch as Kerry finishes her last customer. There are three people who work in the salon, tidying up around her.

My eyes brim with tears when I see them all stopping to chat, then laughing raucously. Envy shoots through me. Have *I* ever had fun at work?

When Kerry comes out and gets into her car, I walk away. There isn't much else to see, nothing I can torment myself with.

Nothing to stop the guilt from what I've done earlier to Sam and Tess from crushing me. I was supposed to be getting better, not worse.

But, as ever, I am so unpredictable.

CHAPTER TWENTY-SEVEN

Now I'm settled in my flat and my work with Roberta is finished, I have time to go and visit some of the other clients I've been helping. That's one thing I hadn't anticipated when I started working for the charity. The job isn't challenging, but I grew attached to some people more than others.

Over the first few weeks out on site, I learned who I liked and who I didn't. Most are lovely, a few downright rude. One man, Arthur, is a nightmare. He's a groper. I can't tell you the number of times I've removed his hand when it's rested on my arse. He has me spraying my clothes with a body mist every time I come away from his home, or else the inside of Nan's car ends up smelling like stale chip fat.

My first visit today is to Graham. He lives in the third bungalow in a row of six. There's a large green in front of it, and he's constantly shooing the kids away, stopping them from playing football. I reckon they'll have a nickname for him. It's something I did when I was younger, playing up the old people, and now feel embarrassed about it.

Graham is a widower, his wife having died two years previous. I don't have to do much cleaning because the place is always spotless. He makes me coffee and buys me chocolate digestives.

I sit and chat with him for half an hour, knowing he enjoys the company. He seems much perkier than he was during my last visit when he'd told me his stomach was playing up. Now, looking at him sitting across the table from me, no one would believe he's in his eighties.

I'm reluctant to leave when it's time, but I don't want to miss out on seeing Nellie. She lives a few streets away, in another row of bungalows, this time the second one along.

Nellie has been housebound since having a car accident several years ago. Her bed is in the living room so she can look out onto the streets she's lived in since birth.

I tidy up for her while she tells me of the local goings-on. She never misses a trick from that window and has me in stitches with the antics the neighbours get up to.

Once I'm finished, I make a mug of tea and place it on the table next to Nellie's bed. It will take her through to when the carers come to give her lunch.

'Pass me my bag, love,' Nellie says afterwards.

Here we go again. I hand it to her. Nellie struggles for a moment with the clasp but eventually reaches in it for her purse. She holds up a twenty-pound note.

'Treat yourself to something nice.' She smiles. 'I really enjoy your visits.'

I wag a finger at her. 'Now, you know I can't accept gifts.'

'And I'll be offended if you don't.' Nellie thrusts the note at me.

'And I'll be sacked if anyone finds out.'

'I won't tell them.'

I gently push Nellie's hand away. 'It's a lovely thought, but I like coming to see you, and that's enough for me.'

Nellie pouts, but the note is returned to her purse. We go through the same thing each visit, and I'm proud of myself every time I refuse the offer.

Once those two visits are done, my time is my own, although my next stop will be somewhat emotional. I drive to Carmountside Crematorium.

As a child of ten, it wasn't my favourite place, but it's kept so well that it reminds me of a country estate within a busy residential area. I drive past the chapel where a service is being held. There are so many mourners that some are outside, crowded around the door. I wonder what it's like to be so popular. There'll be no one at my funeral if I die right now. Poor me.

The weather is fine, a hint of spring in the March air. The sky is a cloudless blue, but it's still cold. I indicate right and follow the one-way system. I drive past graves that have been recently filled, then I park and pick up the small bunches of flowers I've bought earlier.

Once out of the car, I take a deep breath and then spend some time reading a few messages on headstones nearby, to gauge a date so that I can find the one I'm looking for. It's the first time I've been to the cemetery since my nan died. I find it too painful after all I learned from her.

It always makes me sad to see the lives of people who have been lost, especially the ones where there's been hardly any life at all. The babies, the children and young teens.

I walk the length of two rows until I find what I'm after. I stand in front of it for a moment and then stoop to place a bunch of flowers at the base of the stone. Hands clasped, I read some of the message inscribed on the stone.

In memory of Sasha Simson
15th August 1993- 28th June 2024
Loving wife of Tom, mother to Isla.
Daughter to Ivan and Teresa, sister to James and Michael.
Taken too soon, missed so much.

I was surprised to find out Sasha had been buried. In years gone by, burials were the done thing, but now lots of people are cremated. And it's becoming even more acceptable to have a designer funeral, one without a service at all. It all sounds so morbid but perfect.

The headstone is gleaming, and there are fresh flowers and a pot with a rose plant. The bright-yellow ribbon around it has clearly been put there recently as it's spotless.

I haven't wanted to visit my grandparents' graves since I buried my nan, still too angry about everything.

Today I head to where my parents are laid to rest. It's typical of Derek to allow them to be together, cruel, too.

I can remember my parents' funeral as clear as anything. Everyone's eyes on the ten-year-old child walking with her grandparents either side, my nan holding my hand. The church service drew a lot of attention, from media and press as well as nosy neighbours and friends. I recall Derek muttering about some being there for the show of it all. At least there isn't TV footage I can torture myself by watching over and over.

I walk along the gravel path until I pass the second bench. Then it's the fifth row back, three graves down. I place the second bunch of flowers on the headstone base and stand back again.

'I miss you, Mum,' I whisper.

What would my life have been like if that night hadn't happened?

I stand silently. Then I wipe away the few tears that have spilled and set off back to my car. I still can't face seeing my grandparents.

CHAPTER TWENTY-EIGHT

On Sunday at midday, I take a deep breath and knock on Tom's door. My palms are ridiculously sweaty. When he mentioned arranging lunch for everyone, I thought it was just a thing he'd said, so I'd been delighted when he set a time and date. I run a hand over my hair as I wait for him to answer. In my other is a strawberry cheesecake. I haven't made it myself, but I've chosen a local patisserie for a fresh dessert.

The door opens, and there he is. My stomach flips over.

'Hey, Clara.' Tom smiles. 'You look lovely.'

Blushing furiously, I thrust the box into his chest. 'I bought cheesecake!'

'You didn't need to, but it's much appreciated.' He takes it from me and holds the door open. 'Come on in.'

'Clara,' Isla cries when she spots me. 'I got an A in English on Friday, for that story you gave me the idea for.'

'Oh, that's wonderful news.' I am delighted. Last

week, I'd come home from work to find Isla sitting on the stairs. She was writing in a notebook. I'd stopped to talk to her, expecting her to be playing detective again.

'What are you up to?' I asked.

'I'm trying to think of a story for my homework.'

'Do you have a topic?'

'Home.' She pulled a face. 'It isn't very inspiring.'

I held back a smile. Isla sounded so grown-up.

'How about something about this house? Choose four different people behind each door and invite them to tea.' I sat down next to her. 'You could say before they met, they didn't really know each other but they all got on well and wanted to do it again.'

Isla put the tip of the pen to her lip. 'I could give one of them a dog, too. I'd love a beagle, but Dad says I have to wait until I'm older.'

'What a spoilsport. I'm sure you can work your charms on him eventually. Dogs are great company.'

I'd left her then, deep in her notebook again, writing away. But I hadn't thought for one moment she'd then go on to use my idea. A warm feeling rushes through me.

'And what idea was that?' Tom queries.

'I gave her a prompt. She did the rest herself. She's very clever.'

'Takes after me.'

'So modest.' I roll my eyes in jest.

Tom sniggers. 'We're waiting on Shelley and then we'll start. Help yourself to wine, juice or water, whatever is your poison.' There's a knock on the door, and he disappears for a moment.

'Roberta, I hear you've been planning a holiday,' I say, sitting across from her at the table.

'I'm going to see my sister in Brighton. I thought I'd stay for a week or so. It's been a while since I've seen her socially, and a bit of sea air will do me good.'

Clara smiles. 'I'm sure it will. I'll keep an eye on the place for you.'

'You're so kind.'

If only she knew. But this is different. I want to be helpful rather than rob the place.

Once Shelley is settled with a drink, Tom dishes out the food. He's prepared a roast chicken, and we all tuck in with relish. The wine flows as well as the chatter.

Tom relays a tale about Isla when she was a small child, and I listen with glee. I'm right about what I said to him. I haven't felt this happy in a long time. These people here could almost be my family. Roberta my grandmother, Shelley my older sister, and Tom and Isla? Well, they could be my husband and child.

I stop, a little freaked about where my thoughts are going. It's as if I'm finding out for the first time what it's like to spend time having lunch with family. It *does* feel like I belong here. Like I was meant to meet Roberta, help her out and come to live in Cedric House.

There's a knock at the door, and Tom pauses for breath. 'Grab another bottle of wine from the fridge, Clara, while I get this.'

'Are you expecting anyone?'

'Not really, but it can only be Wayne.'

I've just popped the bottle on the table when there are raised voices coming from the hall. Suddenly Wayne appears in the room. He stands wide-eyed, glaring at each one of us in turn.

'This is all nice and cosy.' He staggers slightly, his speech slurred. 'I can't remember getting an invite.'

'It was a last-minute thing,' Tom fibs.

'And you told me you were working, anyway,' Shelley says quietly.

'What, in the pub?' I scoff.

An awkward silence drops on the room.

'Would you like a piece of cheesecake, Wayne?' Isla breaks into it.

'Quite the family gathering, isn't it?' Wayne sneers. He walks towards the table, banging his hip on the corner of it.

'Hey, watch it.' I reach for my wine glass that is teetering.

'Come on, time to go,' he says to Shelley. 'I can see I'm not wanted here, so you're not staying either.'

I glance across at Shelley who looks scared to death. She says nothing as she gets to her feet.

'Leave her be,' I retort. 'We haven't finished yet.'

'It's got nothing to do with you.'

Tom touches Wayne's arm. 'She doesn't—'

Wayne turns and punches Tom in the face. 'Mind your own business, *neighbour*.'

'Daddy,' Isla screams and gets out of her chair to go to him.

I step between the men. 'Stop it!' I shout.

'Fuck off, you meddling cow. She wouldn't have been here at all if it wasn't for you.' Wayne points his finger in my face. 'I know your game. You're trying to turn her against me. It won't work. She knows where her bread is buttered. And that's with me.'

'I wouldn't see a future with Wanky Wayne as anything to be excited about.'

Wayne's features crease up. Then, once my words sink in, he lunges at me next.

I block his fist and throw one back. It hits him in the mouth, taking him by surprise. He comes at me again, and I punch him in the stomach. Then before he can gather his breath, I pull his arm behind his back and march him out of the room. He struggles, but I manage to open the front door and push him out into the hall. He falls to his knees.

I stand my ground while he gets back to his feet. But I've clearly made an impact on him as he's even more unsteady.

'I'd leave right now if I were you,' I say. 'Perhaps come back when you're sober and ready to apologise.'

Wayne wipes at the blood that's coming from a split lip. 'You have a mean punch.'

'Plenty more where that came from.'

'I don't think you'll be trying it again. Not when I'm sober.'

'Weren't you leaving?' I wave at him sarcastically. 'Bye-bye.'

Once he's out of sight, I go back into the flat, dreading to see the others. Tom is sitting at the table with a bag of frozen peas held up to his face. No one says a word.

But they all stare at me.

They all hate me.

'Are you okay?' I ask Tom.

'I'm fine.' He rubs at his jaw where a red mark is appearing. 'A bit shocked. Where did you learn to fight like that?'

'I took self-defence classes a while ago,' I lie, flexing my fingers a couple of times. 'Didn't think it would hurt that much, though.'

Roberta starts laughing. I grin, and as first Shelley, then Tom joins in, I laugh, too. Isla giggles, and before long, the wine is flowing again, along with the conversation. And lots of cheesecake is consumed.

But the inquisitive looks coming from Tom make me realise that I haven't entirely got away with my excuse. He's going to ask me about it later, I'm sure. And then what do I tell him?

I'll have to decide that at the time.

CHAPTER TWENTY-NINE

'I punched someone on Sunday,' I tell Emma as soon as we're sitting down for my next therapy session. I quickly run through what happened with Wayne. All that time, Emma stays quiet until I finish.

'Do you think he deserved it?' I ask finally.

'I believe violence may be necessary when it's used for self-defence purposes,' Emma replies. 'Do you?'

'Yes, and I'd do it again if he came at my friends.'

'And you were trying to protect one of those friends. People who you've become close to. I think an element of that would have been natural instincts.'

'Really? Then why didn't Tom hit Wayne? He told me he was terrified.'

'Because he's not used to it?'

'Well, he didn't grow up with drunk and abusive family members who he had to defend himself against.' I smile to show I am at ease. 'But it wasn't that. I was more annoyed that it made me stand out.'

'Because you lost your temper?'

'Yes.'

'Or because you stood up for friends using violence?'

I'm not certain where Emma is heading. 'I don't follow.'

'We can view this from two ways. A positive is that you helped someone. A negative is that you hit out as if it was the natural response. Can you recall what age you started hitting others?'

'I was fourteen.'

'Was it because you felt inferior?'

'Not really. I don't think I knew any better then.'

'Did people goad you, push you, or were you always looking for trouble?'

I remember an incident when I'd been on my way home from school. It had been bitterly cold, and yet I was dawdling. Derek was on the early shift, finishing at two o'clock. Most of the time, he'd go straight to the pub, meaning I'd get the house to myself until Nan came in from work at half past five. But sometimes he was there when I got in, and I hated being alone with him in the house.

Even so, I was minutes from home, having just rounded the corner onto the estate when I heard thundering footsteps behind me. I glanced over my shoulder to see Kerry Simons and two of her cronies, Natalie, and Amy, my ex best friend. I sigh inwardly, not in the mood for any of them.

'Cooper!' Kerry cried. 'I want a word with you.'

I continued walking.

'Oi, don't ignore me.'

A heavy punch in the middle of my back stopped me

in my tracks. This time, I turned around, all three girls level with me.

'What is wrong with you?' I questioned.

'I heard you've been chatting up Brody. He's my boyfriend, so keep away from him.'

'He wouldn't go out with a slag like you,' Natalie joined in.

Ah, so that's what this was all about. Kerry felt threatened by me. Well, so she should, but someone was lying.

'I haven't seen Brody in weeks,' I said truthfully.

'Liar!' Kerry screeched into my face.

I could almost see her tonsils. What a weirdo to make such a fuss over a boy.

'I don't even like him.'

'Why, what's wrong with him?'

'Nothing.' I sighed. 'I'm going home now. I suggest you do the same.'

I made to leave, but a fist to the side of my head had me reeling. The girls jumped me, one pulling my hair. Another dragged my bag from my shoulder and threw it to the ground.

Kerry slapped my face. 'I said don't ignore me.' She pointed a finger in my face. 'My Brody wouldn't look twice at you, so you must have thrown yourself at him. I'm only warning you once. If I see you so much as glance in his direction, I'm coming after you again.'

'Hey, what are you lot up to?' a voice shouted. 'That's not a fair fight, leave the girl alone. I can see you, Kerry Simons, and I know your mother.'

Kerry stopped. 'I'll get you at school tomorrow, bitch,' she taunted me before walking off.

But those few words had forewarned me. In fact, they egged me on. They nestled in my mind and settled in for the long run. All that evening, I tried to keep my temper on an even keel, but angry thoughts burned inside me. How dare they do that to me.

By the time morning came round, I couldn't leave the issue. Once at school, I searched out Kerry. I found her standing with her crew, pointing at some unfortunate sod who was the butt of their latest snide remarks.

I strode over, pushed Natalie and Amy out of the way and, before any of them could react, punched Kerry full in the mouth.

Kerry's lip split. She gasped in shock. Then she screeched at the blood she saw on her fingers.

It didn't stop me. I hit Kerry twice in quick succession and, as she put up her hands to defend herself, I punched her in the stomach.

By this time, other kids in the playground had stopped to see what the commotion was and were crowding around, urging each of us to fight. But I'd done what damage I needed to Kerry, and now it was time for the other girls.

Natalie took one look at Amy, and they both ran. Bloody losers.

'If you can't stand the repercussions, then don't give it out,' I shouted after them.

Then I glared at Kerry, who was still clutching her mouth. 'Stay away from me or I'll do more than that next time. I hate bullies.'

I walked off feeling ten feet tall, straight out of the school gates, and went home for the day. It was worth the week's detention I received because, funnily enough, Kerry never bothered me again.

'I think it was all of that,' I say now. 'Sometimes I'd react to a situation. Other times, I'd be the instigator. I suppose it depended on how much attention I was after.'

Emma raises her eyebrows, urging me to go on.

'I always felt like the child no one wanted. Then when I had a chance for things to turn out better, I got the wrath of Derek.' I pause. 'In some ways, when I was older, I realised why my dad turned out the way he did. Derek made him into a bully because he was cruel to him when he was a child.'

'Did your dad ever talk to you about it?'

I shake my head. 'No one told me. I deduced that from living with them. There was such an angry vibe in the house. I used to hate going in, so I built up a wall to protect myself.'

And that's why I want to find a safe and loving home of my own.

CHAPTER THIRTY

The next evening, I'm carrying a bag of shopping upstairs when the door to flat one opens and I see Tom.

'Need a hand?' he asks.

'No, I'm good.' I smile. 'I wanted to say thanks again for a great time on Sunday. Lunch was lovely, despite the little interruption.'

'It was nice.' Tom pauses. 'I did worry about you, though, after you... sorted Wayne out. Are you okay?'

'Yes, why?'

'You seemed so angry when you lashed out.'

'That's because he hit you first!'

Tom grimaces. 'I suppose I let myself down by not reacting. I've never been in a fight since I punched a boy in nursery when I was five. Even then he hit me twice as hard, and I ran off telling tales.'

We smile at each other shyly.

'Coffee?' he asks.

'Are you alone?'

'Is that a proposition?'

'No, you eejit.' *Well, it is if you want it to be.* 'Is Isla at school?'

'She is.'

'Then come up to mine and I'll make you one.' Now I hand him a bag to carry.

'You've got this so nice,' Tom says, looking around a few minutes later. 'I quite like seeing how we've all made the same flats individual.'

'I don't have much to call my own at the moment, so it will have to do.'

While he stands at the front window and the kettle is boiling, I wonder whether it's time to be straight with him. Well, in as far as I'm willing to be.

'You asked why I was so angry when Wayne hit you?' I speak.

Tom faces me with a wry smile. 'I guess you never learned to fight like that at a self-defence class.'

I don't smile back. Instead, I point to the settee, and we both sit down. I hope I'm not going to slip up, what with all the lies I've been telling everyone lately, but I want a chance to explain to him. Make him understand that it won't happen again.

'It was because of my parents,' I tell him.

Tom frowns. He waits for me to continue.

I take a deep breath and begin, knowing even now that I can't tell the whole truth. But I see Tom's demeanour soften towards me. I don't need to will tears to fall as he sits there showing such compassion.

Afterwards, he reaches for my hand. 'That must have been awful to go through, and at such a young age. Did you have anyone to stay with?'

'My grandparents. They lived in the bowels of the Bennett Estate, but they're both dead now.'

'So you have no family at all?'

I shake my head.

'That must be tough.'

'It is at times. Others I'm so used to being alone. Which is why it's great to live in Cedric House. We're respectful to each other – all except Wanky Wayne, of course.'

Tom, who is taking a sip of his drink, almost spits it out at my remark. He swallows quickly.

'Wanky Wayne suits him. Although I'd better be careful I don't say it aloud in front of him, or Isla, come to think of it.' He laughs. 'That's really cheered me up.'

'Happy to help.'

Tom glances at his watch. 'I need to go. It's nearly time to collect Isla.' He pauses for a moment. 'Would you like to join us for tea tonight? We eat early, though. At five?'

'I'd love to.'

'Great!' He stands up and takes his cup to the kitchen sink, rinsing it quickly before leaving it to drain. 'Thanks for the coffee.'

'I'll see you soon.'

I close the door and lean on the back of it, a gentle sigh escaping. If I haven't misread the signs, I might say there's a little awkwardness between us. Tom has at least understood my need to lash out now we've spoken about my past. So if Wanky Wayne does mention it, he has no leverage.

I make a promise never to do that in front of Tom

again. *If* there is going to be more between us, then I want him to see my better side. The person I really want to be if the darkness can be kept under control. Perhaps with the attention and love of a good man, I can behave.

Yeah, you keep telling yourself that, Clara.

I have a pleasant time with Tom and Isla. We eat chips and a burger apiece, and there's angel cake with mugs of tea afterwards. I end up staying until Isla is ready to flake out and am surprised when she asks if I will put her to bed.

Isla's bedroom is decked out in pinks, lilacs, and silver. I wonder if Sasha designed and furnished it before she died or if Isla helped her dad to do it afterwards. Either way, it's charming.

I recall my own room in Wedgwood Street, thin cord carpeting and flimsy curtains that let in the light. Worn bedding. Woodchip wallpaper that was put up to be painted over annually to keep it fresh, and yet never had been. I covered the walls with posters out of magazines to stop it looking so dreary, making it a tad more individual. Nevertheless, it hadn't mattered much as I never brought friends home.

Isla flicks a switch, and a row of fairy lights shine above the bed as she climbs under the covers. I tuck her in and say goodnight. She seems so tiny with only her head visible.

'I really like you, Clara,' Isla says.

'I really like you, too,' I reply, a huge smile erupting on my face. I sit down for a moment.

'Why don't you have any children?'

'I'm a bit young yet, I suppose.' It's the best answer I can come up with.

But it doesn't fool Isla.

'How old are you?' she asks next.

'Twenty-eight.'

'My mum was younger than that when she had me. I think you shouldn't leave it much longer.'

I don't know whether to laugh or cry. I've wanted a child for years, but since I miscarried, the circumstances haven't been right. Or the timing, or whatever else. All the excuses. Looking back on it now, it's been a blessing. But it still doesn't stop me from hoping that one day I will hold my own child in my arms.

'Will you kiss me goodnight, Clara?'

'Of course.' I plant my lips on Isla's cheek.

'I think you'll make a good mummy,' Isla speaks quietly, before her eyes close.

I wipe the hair from Isla's face, pushing back tears that are threatening to fall. One day, I hope my dreams come true. And if I do have a daughter, I'd like one as sassy as Isla.

I rejoin Tom in the living room, and a few minutes later I decide to call it a night. Yawning loudly, I sit forward on the settee.

'I'd better be going,' I say. 'Thank you for tea.'

'Isla hasn't put you off calling again, has she? I swear she goes to bed saying something, and the minute she wakes up, she continues where she's left off. She doesn't stop talking.'

'It's sweet. You're very lucky to have her.'

'I know.' Tom shows me to the door. 'Thanks for popping in. We both love to see you.' He moves forward, not enough to crowd me, and kisses me lightly on the cheek.

'I've had a great time,' I reply, wanting to draw him in close so I can kiss him properly.

'Isla is having a sleepover on Friday evening with a friend from school. Would you like to go out for dinner? It would be nice to see you somewhere outside Cedric House.'

'I'd love to.'

'Great!'

Tom's smile lights up his face. His beautiful, gorgeous, scrumptious face.

'I'll message you closer to and we can sort out where to go.'

I almost float up the stairs. This thing with Tom? Somehow it feels right. Like it's meant to be. So I'm not going to resist him, even though it might be temporary.

Surely, I deserve a little fun?

CHAPTER THIRTY-ONE

I know I won't be able to escape the wrath of Wayne for long after what I've done to him. But he's kept his distance from Cedric House, much to Shelley's joy. Which means I can relish thinking about what had happened, and what may happen, between me and Tom instead.

I can't wait for Friday evening, and as ever, the week drags on. So I'm excited to receive a call from the estate agent on Wednesday morning while I'm in the office. I hope someone has put in a decent offer this time.

'Hi, Clara, it's Mark. I went to show a potential buyer around your property this morning, but it's been broken into.'

'Oh, for... but there's nothing worth stealing!' I leave the room and go into the corridor for privacy.

'I suppose the opportunistic thief might not know that,' Mark goes on. 'A window has been broken in the kitchen door. When was the last time you were there?'

'Sunday.'

Just after dinner at Tom's.

'I can't say for sure if anything is missing, but I think you might want to secure the property. The buyers were put off by the break-in. They are a young couple who wanted a fixer-upper. Shame, I thought I had it in the bag with this one. I'll keep trying.'

I disconnect the call and kick the skirting board with the toe of my shoe. Has someone in Wedgwood Street noticed I haven't been around much? What a pain this is going to be to sort out, and I've lost the potential house sale, too. As quickly as possible, I arrange to meet a locksmith there at four p.m.

I arrive a few minutes before him, going round to the rear to see what damage has been done. The door seems to be untouched. The small pane of glass that's broken allowed a hand to get through to unlock the door from the inside, so I might not have to change the locks. Hopefully just the glass will have to be replaced. If it's kids, I'll need to keep them out, though. I don't want the place to look any worse than it already does.

I step inside. Mark's right. Someone has been looking around as cupboard doors and drawers are open. In the living room, the old TV is still there, alongside the radio and a crabby CD player. There isn't much mess because I've thrown away most of the stuff in the sideboard. A fool can see there's nothing worth taking. Perhaps whoever it is gave it up as a bad job after the kitchen.

I go upstairs quickly, checking the other rooms until coming to my own. And then I see someone has been in there. Drawers are open, my bed covers lifted to show the mattress. The envelope I left there purposely with two hundred pounds of emergency money is gone.

I pick up my pillow that's been thrown to the floor, place it over my face, and scream into it. I need to let my anger out somehow. Why does this have to happen now?

But at least none of my personal possessions have been stolen. I took them all to Cedric House when I moved in. I can't begin to think what might have happened if my work notepad had gone missing. It has all the details of the vulnerable people I've been helping.

'Hello!' a male voice shouts up the stairs a few minutes later. 'Hope you don't mind me coming in, but I knocked twice on the back door with no reply.'

I step out onto the landing to see a man in his forties, wearing jeans and a thick checked shirt. 'Hi, you must be Steve.'

'The very one.' He smiles. 'Made a mess in here, haven't they? Do the police know who it is?'

I shake my head, knowing full well I'm not going to report it. 'I suppose the For Sale board is a draw.' I go downstairs to him. 'I'll just have to hope it sells soon.'

'You're not living here?'

'In this hovel?' I shudder dramatically. 'My nan's died and left it to me. I can't wait to get it sold.'

'Okay, I'll get the back door sorted and perhaps put on a bolt top and bottom of the door, unless you want to secure the front door, too?'

'The cheapest option, please.' I stop. 'Actually, on second thoughts, change that, too, please.'

'Right, then. I'll get started.'

An hour and a half later, Steve has gone, and I'm left with new keys for the front and back doors and a window that's secure enough for now. I know it isn't ideal, but it won't be for long. Hopefully. I'm sad that I've lost a sale, but there will be someone else along soon.

Maybe I should spend a couple of nights here to put off anyone else trying to break in. But, then again, what's the point? I can leave a lamp on instead. Perhaps that will be enough to fool most crooks.

I really don't want to spend the night here because it could make people at Cedric House curious, suspicious even. They might worry about me, and how will I explain where I've been?

I lock up and leave.

When I park in front of Cedric House, Wayne is sitting on the wall. He takes a drag from his cigarette and throws the end to the floor. I glare at him, but he doesn't pick it up. Instead, he puts out his arm for me to walk down the path first. Then he follows me into the hall.

'Going to see Shelley?' I ask.

'She's not home yet. Thought I might surprise her.'

'Quite the romantic, aren't you?'

'Quite the fighter, aren't you?' he bats back. 'I wonder where you got that from?' He raises his eyebrows.

'From hitting idiots like you.'

He snorts. 'I suggest you leave Shelley alone. You pack a mean punch, but that was when I was drunk. You wouldn't mess with me when I'm sober.'

'What is this? Are we age ten in the playground?'

'You started it.'

'*You started it*,' I mimic. 'No, you barged into Tom's house playing the hardman. But men like you don't bother me.'

'Men like me?'

'Evil shits who think beating up a woman makes them hard. You're pathetic.'

'I'm warning you. Keep away from me, or I'll come after you, and you don't want that. Not with your new beau. Spending a lot of time in flat one, aren't you?'

'That's nothing to do with you.'

'Let's keep it that way.'

I storm upstairs. My first assumption about the burglary is that he had something to do with it, and I thought he'd come to gloat. But if it's not him, why is he hanging around like a bad penny all the time? He has the potential to spoil everything. Haven't I got enough to keep in order? I wish I could punch his lights out permanently.

But maybe there is a better way. Along with Bill Fisher's watch, which he clearly hasn't noticed has gone, and the other items I suspect Wayne has stolen, perhaps it's time *I* followed him, to see what I can find out.

For now, it's better not to lose my temper and show him what I'm really capable of. Because that will ruin everything.

CHAPTER THIRTY-TWO

'You seem bright this week,' Emma says to me.

'My neighbour, Tom, has asked me out for dinner,' I tell her. 'I don't think it's a date as such, but I'm going to play it by ear, though.'

'Sounds like a plan, but it also seems to me as if you're afraid of committing to a relationship. Are you?'

'Yes and no. I think he's too good for me.'

'In what sense?'

'He's too pure. I'm scared I'll ruin him.'

'Ruin him?'

'Like I do everything.' I sigh. 'My temper gets the better of me, and I fire off with my fists.'

'How many times have you done that with men you've been in relationships with?'

'Several.'

'So that makes you think it will happen again?'

'Yes, because I always screw everything up. Besides, Tom's wife died a year ago, and I'm worried he's on the rebound. And he has a daughter, Isla. She's ten.'

'Have you talked this through with him?'

'A little,' I lie. I haven't mentioned any of it.

'What did he say?'

'We should take it slowly.'

'That's good, isn't it?'

I nod. It is if it were true, but I still can't be sure I wouldn't hurt Tom.

'You mentioned you were married,' Emma says next. 'When was this?'

'Nine years ago. It lasted on and off for four years.'

'What went wrong?'

'We were too young, impetuous. I thought I had a new start, being Mrs Mansell. I thought I could leave my past behind with a new name, but nothing changed.'

'How old was...?'

'Evan? Two years older than me. Life with him was *always* a roller coaster. When we first met, I spent so much time at his flat that I ended up moving in with him after a month. We'd been together about six months when he asked me to marry him. It wasn't romantic, down on one knee or anything. It was just "let's get hitched."' I snort. 'I thought I hadn't heard him properly at first and I didn't believe him until he said it to me again. He gave me some twaddle about wanting to spend the rest of his life with me.'

'What answer did you give him?'

'I stated the obvious at first, that we didn't even have a place of our own. The flat wasn't very nice, more like a squat, the state of it. And it was rented, so we could get kicked out any day.'

'So home has always been important to you?'

'Yes, I wanted something that no one could take

away from us. We didn't have any spare money for a wedding either, but he told me not to worry about that. And then he said we do have a roof over our heads.' I snigger. 'He was pointing at the damp patch above the bed, the wallpaper clinging to it for dear life. But then he followed that with crap about having each other and that was enough for him. And I fell for it.'

'Did you say yes then?' Emma asks.

At nineteen, marriage to someone like Evan seemed like a good idea, even if we hadn't been together for long. I nod.

'More fool me. It took just over a month to arrange. We gave notice at Salford Register Office and chose the first date we could. Bob and Trish, the couple in the flat downstairs, agreed to be witnesses. I had to get a copy of my birth certificate as I haven't got a passport.' I stop for a sip of water. 'It was strange seeing my parents' names on it, and it made me think about my mum. It hit me hard that she wouldn't be at the ceremony. Wouldn't be able to help me choose my dress or see her little girl getting married.' I sniff. 'Mind you, there would be no one else either. It was just the four of us.'

The day of our wedding dawned with heavy rain, but by the time our appointment came around at two-thirty, the dark clouds had cleared, and even though it wasn't particularly warm, the four of us took some photos in the park across the road. We had a meal at an Italian restaurant and afterwards went back to the flat.

'And how did it feel to be married to Evan?'

'To be honest, I'd never been so happy. I belonged to someone at last, someone who loved me, cared for me and, even if we didn't have a conventional life, so what?

Evan was all I needed.' I swallow, not liking the memories this session is bringing up. 'But it didn't last long. We fought a lot. Making up was fun, but it got to the point where fighting was all we were doing.'

'Was your relationship always volatile?'

'I suppose it was. Evan was often looking for evidence that I didn't really love him. It was as if he expected to find it, and then he was angry when he believed he'd proved himself right. I...'

There's a silence, an uncomfortable one for me.

'Go on,' Emma encourages.

'I got pregnant, but I miscarried. I'm glad now, but at the time I was devastated that the life inside me had died.'

'That must have been terrible to go through.'

'It was.'

I try never to think about those black days. Evan had been so pleased when I told him. We'd made plans, told friends after twelve weeks when we thought it was safe to do so. Two weeks later, it was all over.

'I always thought there was something wrong with me,' I say. 'It was my body rejecting our baby.'

'Did you ever try again?'

'No, because six months later, Louise moved into the flat across the landing from us.'

CHAPTER THIRTY-THREE

Later that evening, I run through my session with Emma again. Emma never judges, so the more I visit, the more it becomes easier to say things to her. I wonder if I'm talking about my past mistakes because I need to clear my conscience, so that I can start over with a clean slate.

Because since then, I've been thinking about Evan as much as Tom. About how damaging Evan has been to me, and how, thankfully, he and Tom are opposites.

I didn't want to mention Louise to Emma either, but now the woman has got stuck in my head, too. We'd got on when she'd first moved in. I liked having her around. We were the same age and shared lots of similarities. We even worked close to each other, so would often walk together to our relevant shifts.

Usually I'm the thief, so it was the first time I'd run into someone who stole from me. Because Louise had been after Evan the minute she'd set eyes on him. One particular evening when I'd been working overtime, I'd got in exhausted, tired, and hungry, shortly after nine, only to find Evan and Louise sitting on the settee, their feet on the coffee table.

It could almost have been me, as Louise and I were so alike in looks and stature. Except Louise had beady eyes, wary eyes that followed me all the time, as if she was trying to read my mind.

'This is cosy,' I retorted, throwing my jacket across the chair.

'Lou needed a hand with some furniture she wanted to change around. I mentioned I was about to watch this, and she came across. You don't mind, do you?'

I wanted to watch that film with him, and he said he didn't fancy it. 'Not really. Are there any cans left?'

'We had the last two.'

'Yeah, sorry, Clara,' Louise said.

She wasn't sorry at all. I made myself a quick bite to eat and sat down at the kitchen table. The two of them laughed, Evan nudging Louise and then pointing to the screen. All the while, no one spoke to me.

It was half an hour before the film finished, and Louise decided to leave.

'See you tomorrow, Clara,' she'd said as she grabbed her keys and phone from the coffee table. 'Evan has invited me to go clubbing with you. He thought you might need a hand.'

'Doing what?'

'Hustling.'

I didn't say a word until Louise had gone. But then I rounded on Evan.

'What was all that about?' I stood in front of him, blocking him from seeing the TV screen.

'What do you mean?' He shooed me with his hand. 'Get out of the way.'

'We don't invite anyone else, Evan. It's only me and you. It's *always* going to be me and you.'

'Fancied a change,' he replied.

'Her for me, you mean? Are you two screwing?'

'Don't be stupid. Whatever gave you that idea?'

I could tell by his face that I'd caught him unawares. And that he was now going to lie to cover up the truth. After all, wasn't that what we were both good at?

'I feel sorry for her on her own, that's all.' Evan shrugged. 'She has no friends around here.'

'Then why did she come to this area?'

'You know she got evicted from her last place and could only find this. She told you that when she arrived.'

'And since then you've spent hours helping her out.'

'It's what people do.'

'So if I asked you to slap some paint on the walls in here because I am sick of seeing the same thing day after day, you'd do that?'

'Whatever. Look, can I watch the TV in peace without you moaning the minute you walk through the door?'

I groaned loudly and flounced out of the room. In bed, I waited for him to join me so that I could continue the argument, but he stayed in the living room. When he finally appeared, I'd calmed down and was ready to make up. But what he said then made me angry.

'It's because you sleep with other men that I don't find you as attractive as before,' he told her.

'I barely sleep with any if I can help it!' I retorted. 'I

choose drunks. What's your excuse? Because you sleep with far more women than I do men. Aren't I good enough for you anymore?'

'I don't know. It's not as exciting when it's handed to you on a plate whenever you want it.'

'You bastard.' I punched him in the arm and turned over.

But he hit me back, harder.

I held in tears. I wouldn't cry in front of him, but why did we always end up fighting? He hurt me, but I hurt him, too. A relationship shouldn't be like that. Yet, I soon realised I enjoyed hitting Evan back.

It happened more often when I began to suspect that something was wrong. It was about two months after Louise had moved in. He'd been over to her flat several times to help her out with odd jobs. Attaching a curtain rail, a dripping tap, putting together a flatpack she was struggling with. I hadn't been threatened about it at first. Why would I be? We were married and had been getting along fine until Louise turned up.

I was still hustling men with Evan, out in the clubs. We had an open relationship in that sense of things, because Evan fleeced women at the same time. But we always went home together, with our booty.

Now that Louise was coming along, too, it was a step too far for me. I was almost certain they were having an affair. The signs were all there, and it was one thing to sleep with someone for money, but to think that my husband didn't love me enough to respect that his body was mine, and mine alone, tore me apart.

One night, shortly after Evan had left to go to the pub, I'd spotted Louise leaving her flat, too. On impulse, I decided to follow her. Evan had been waiting for Louise at the end of the street. He kissed her and threw an arm around her shoulder. They walked past the local pub and, after fifteen minutes of staying far away enough not to be seen, I saw them go into the park.

It was half past eight. People milled about everywhere enjoying the last warmth of the evening. It had been a balmy day, one of several in a row, and the British people were relishing a little piece of summer.

I kept Evan and Louise in my sight before watching them disappear behind a wooden hut. Careful not to make a noise, I crept nearer and peeped around the side of the building. Louise was pushed up against the railings, her legs wrapped around Evan. I didn't need to look anymore to see what they were doing.

That two-faced bitch. Only last week, Louise had reiterated there was nothing happening between her and Evan and that I needn't worry. Now she was fucking him in a public place?

I crept back to the path and ran home. My head was spinning. I'd thought me and Evan were meant to be, forever. How could he do that to me? We were married. Didn't I mean anything to him?

I watched at the window for them to come back. Louise appeared first, after half an hour. Evan followed a few minutes later. I couldn't believe it even then. How did they think that would stop them from being caught?

I wondered whether to say anything to him or to keep the news to myself and make him pay. It would depend on if I could control my temper if he acted as if nothing had happened. But there was more than one way to skin a cat. If I had time to think, I might be able to get my own back on them both.

Because my marriage was over. He'd slept with Louise, of all people, and right under my nose. He might as well move in with her across the landing. It made more sense.

Evan was whistling when he came into the living room.

'I didn't expect you back so soon,' I said.

'There was no one I wanted to see in the pub. So I necked a couple of pints and came back.'

Liar!

'Do you want some toast? I'm starving.'

'Yes, please.' How polite I can be. 'Did you see Louise?'

'No, why. Has she been over asking for me?'

As if she needs to. 'No, I just wondered if she was okay. She wasn't well in the week. I might check up on her tomorrow.'

'Cool. She hasn't got many friends, except us.'

Except you. My husband.

My eyes welled with tears. Why didn't he love me enough to only be with me?

CHAPTER THIRTY-FOUR

I manage to park my thoughts about Evan and Louise before Friday evening arrives. I've bought a new dress and a pair of heels, both unusual for me nowadays, and I've splashed out on a bottle of my favourite perfume, too. It makes a pleasant change not to steal it, I muse, spraying it liberally.

It's been wonderful to treat myself to something, having an occasion to look forward to. I even thought about booking in to have my hair cut at Kerry's place, but I chickened out at the last minute and went somewhere else. Still, I'm pleased with the result. My hair is so shiny and is in much better condition with an inch of dead ends cut away.

Tom has messaged me, and we've arranged to meet at seven, so a few minutes past the hour, as I don't want to seem *too* keen, I go downstairs. I'm about to knock on Tom's door when he opens it.

'There she is!' he cries. 'I was coming to get you.'

My eyes drink in the man standing in front of me.

Tom is wearing dark-blue fitted jeans, a pale-cream shirt open at the neck, and a checked jacket. His hair is wet at the ends, and his face is a little flushed, but it's his smile that's the most alluring thing about him.

Or is it his lips?

'I'm not late, am I?' I ask.

'Not at all. I thought I might be, but it's all good.' He kisses me on the cheek. 'You look amazing. Smell nice, too.'

We smile coyly at each other, before Tom points to the entrance door.

'Shall we go? I have a table booked for seven-thirty, and it's a bit of a drive, so we'd best be on our way.'

He takes me to The Railway Inn, crossing over into the Staffordshire Moorlands. The clocks went forward at the weekend, so the sky is clear. Even though it's getting a tad darker each minute, it makes for excellent conditions as Tom drives along winding lanes, our conversation flowing, no awkward silences. I have to keep reminding myself that we aren't on a date. This is dinner with a friend.

The pub is in a beautiful setting, rolling hills and a wooded area to our right. Inside, it's almost packed to the brim with a jovial feel, people enjoying themselves. It's had a recent extension which is fitted out with natural woods, large slate floor tiles, high ceilings, and stylish country accessories. There's a buzz of conversation around the room, a burst of laughter erupting from a table of eight.

'Good job I booked,' Tom remarks when we're shown to a table.

'I can see why it's so popular.' He pulls out a chair for me and I sit down.

We order food and again chat like old friends. Tom tells me about Isla's antics and how she's won a prize for history at school.

'I have no idea where she gets that from,' he says. 'But I'm glad she's able to settle. I was worried about her for a time when Sasha died, but she's been a rock for me regardless.'

I like how he still talks about his wife. She's bound to be a big part of his life for some time yet, but the fact he feels comfortable bringing her up with me is nice. I don't say anything about my nan, though.

The food is delicious. I haven't been out for a meal in such a long time and especially one so expensive. I feel like a princess and don't want the night to end. Sadly, soon it's time to leave.

'I've had a great evening,' Tom says after he insists on paying.

'Me, too.' Now there is a silence, but it's more charged than before.

'I'd like to get to know you, Clara. I know someone has hurt you in the past, but I would never do that.' Tom reaches across for my hand. 'How about we concentrate on the future for now?'

I smile, although it doesn't sit well with me. How can I be happy, with all the lies I've told him? Still, if this is going to be a fling, I can pretend for now.

What I can't mistake is how I feel about being here with Tom. It must be showing on my face, reflected in my eyes. It's nice, exciting. Last week we were friends.

Today? I'm not sure if there's more to come, but I'm excited to find out.

Back at home, I stand outside Tom's front door. 'Thank you. I've had a great evening.'

'Me, too. Can I interest you in a nightcap?' he asks, almost shyly.

I nod, and we go inside. But there's no time for drinks because he pushes me gently to the wall, kissing me with a tender passion.

No, no, no. This is so wrong.

Tom stops briefly for a moment, gazing in my eyes as if to seek permission to continue.

When I pull him close, it's all the encouragement he needs, and as my lips touch his again, I almost sigh with giddiness. I want this to happen. There's something about Tom that makes me feel worthy, like I don't have to be on my best behaviour. That he likes me for who I am portraying. Which is something I'll have to address soon.

Eventually, he opens the bedroom door, and I step inside, my hand in his.

The sex is tender as we explore each other's bodies for the first time. It's been a while since I've felt lust like this. Tom is getting under my skin, and I'm not sure if it's a good thing or totally wrong. Either way, I don't care right now and give myself over to enjoying the moment.

Afterwards, we lie in bed together, me in the crook of his arm, and I wonder if Tom has any regrets. It was spur of the moment, and pretty close to home if anything goes wrong. I glance up to see him staring at the ceiling. The lamplight is low, casting shadows across the room.

'Are you okay?' I ask, rubbing my hand over his chest, revelling in the feel of him under my fingers.

'Yes, are you?'

I stop. He is asking me?

For a long time, I've used my body for my own gains. I wasn't bothered about satisfying myself, and neither were many of the men. Even with Evan, more often than not there was an argument beforehand. He liked to scream and shout at me, slapping me around, saying that the sex was more passionate that way. It wasn't – it was horrid and raw and passionless – and often I'd fought back because of it. Yet I hadn't wanted to give up on my marriage. Be a failure, feel incapable of being loved.

With Tom it's different and, even if I only have this night with him, I will treasure the memory of it all.

'I couldn't be better.' I snuggle into him a little more.

CHAPTER THIRTY-FIVE

The next morning I awake, happy to find myself in Tom's bed, but the man in question is nowhere to be seen. I stretch out luxuriously. The smell of bacon wafts through from the kitchen, sizzling above the sound of music playing low. I smile in appreciation. A nice breakfast will start the day off perfectly.

I could get used to this. Fingers crossed it isn't a one-off thing. Because I want to do what we did last night again.

A few minutes later I get up, stretch, and glance around for my clothes. They're folded up on a chair in the corner of the room. Seeing Tom's shirt that he discarded hanging over the back of it, I pop it on, covering my nakedness but leaving as many buttons open as is decent. I don't want to dress in last night's clothes until the final minute, even though I'm only going upstairs afterwards. Besides, I glance at myself in the wardrobe mirror, I want to be sexy, inviting. Although a shower will be a plus.

Maybe with Tom.

I open a drawer and search out a pair of his boxers and pull them on, too. Then I join him in the kitchen.

'Well, hello.' He raises his eyebrows and grins. 'Tom's café will be open soon. Take a seat while you wait.'

'Can I help?'

'No, thanks. I've got it. You sit back and enjoy.'

I hitch myself onto the stool and sit across from him. The scent of his cologne is on his shirt, ensuring I definitely want him all over again.

And again.

And again.

I watch him lay out napkins, cutlery, and condiments. While the bacon is crisping and the oatcakes warming, he prepares mugs of tea. A minute later, he pops the bacon with tomatoes on the oatcakes and rolls them up. He slides two on a plate across to me.

'Breakfast at Tom's,' he says. 'I hope you enjoy it, miss.'

I tuck into it, and can't help thinking of all the times I've missed doing this. Is this what a proper relationship would be like? Considerate, tender lovemaking, waking up together and sharing a hearty cooked breakfast? Of course I know it'll all be about desire at the beginning, as it was in my earlier relationships. But still, I haven't had much of this in my life until now, apart from the first few months with Evan, and that stopped soon after we married.

'I wonder...' I pause. 'Do you have any regrets about last night?'

Tom stops mid slurp of his tea. 'I'm sensing that you do.'

'Oh, no, not at all,' I'm quick to point out before he gets the wrong idea.

'Good, because I don't.'

'What about us living so close? And what about Isla? When will she be back? I don't want her to find me here in your shirt and pants.'

'Not until midday. But perhaps we could keep things between us for now, until we see where this goes? I'm worried because she really likes you.'

'I like her, too.' I get that warm fuzzy feeling again. 'She's fun – and so clever.'

Tom blushes, which is quite charming.

'I don't want her to suddenly think all sorts about us,' he says. 'Whether it's good or bad thoughts.'

'I get you.' I'm more pleased by the mention of an us. 'There's no need to explain. Slowly, slowly, it is.'

'You can always come downstairs to watch TV, and then we can open the wine when she's gone to bed.' He sniggers. 'It isn't far to walk.'

I laugh, too. I haven't had so much fun in a long time. Tom has reawakened my body as well as my mind. Whatever is happening, I want more of it.

Tom watched Clara while she ate her breakfast. Last night had been crazy. He'd offered to take her out for dinner on a whim, worrying about it ever since in case she got the wrong idea. He wanted to be friends, maybe then move on to more intimacy now that he wasn't seeing

Giselle. But when they'd got to the pub and ordered a meal, sitting across from her had suddenly felt special. It was as if he'd known her forever, and he'd wanted more.

Waking up with her in his bed had been good. She'd slept on Sasha's side, and it had seemed a little weird, but also like a new beginning. A beginning of what, he wasn't entirely sure.

He hoped he hadn't blown it when he'd mentioned taking things slowly. It wasn't on his account. It was all about Isla. His daughter, his pride and joy. He didn't want her to be upset that there was someone in her mummy's place. Being a widower of a ten-year-old at thirty-four hadn't been something he'd ever thought about.

Tom sensed something wonderful might grow in time, but was it wise to get involved with someone so close, living in the same house? What happened if it went wrong?

What happened if it went right?

He decided he would take things as they came, day by day, week by week. This wasn't going to be a one-night stand, but only time would tell if it would stay the course. Isla always had to be his first thought.

'Penny for them?' Clara said, bringing him back into the room.

He stared at her. God, she was gorgeous. He checked the clock on the wall above her head. There were two hours to go until Isla was due. Now, what to do to fill the time...

'Was breakfast to your satisfaction?' He leaned across to collect Clara's plate, stacked it on the top of his own, and stood up.

She snorted. 'It was, kind sir. You certainly know how to spoil a girl.'

'No, that will be now we've had breakfast.' His voice was husky. 'That is, if you'd like a repeat performance of last night.'

Clara pouted. 'On one condition. I need a shower first. Maybe you'd like to join me?'

Tom discarded the plates on the island and followed Clara who was already on her way to the door.

CHAPTER THIRTY-SIX

When it's time to leave, I place my coat and bag over my arm. Tom opens the door, and I step into the hall. But I want another kiss. The electrifying chills running though my body are making me tingle.

'I've had a great time,' I say afterwards.

'So have I.'

I can't stop smiling. Finding Cedric House has been a huge bonus, but what I hadn't reckoned on was meeting Tom. I kiss him one last time, disappointed that he hasn't arranged to see me again. But I won't push him.

The door across the hall opens. I turn to see who it is. Typical, it's Wayne. I wonder if Shelley is in, or if he's done his usual sneaking around when she isn't. He clearly still hasn't noticed the watch is gone, which reminds me. I need to sort that out when I can.

'Well, well, well. What do we have here?' Wayne comes towards us with that ridiculous swagger. 'The local freak and the man with no balls.'

'Piss off, Wayne,' I say.

'Have you told Tom everything about your past yet?'

'I know about her parents, if that's what you're referring to,' Tom replies.

'Oh, there's way more than that, isn't there, Clara?'

'He's teasing, Tom, trying to get us to react. We don't want the likes of him ruining our fun.'

I stare at Wayne as I pass him. He has a smirk on his face that I'm going to enjoy wiping off one day.

Upstairs, I've just stepped inside my flat when Wayne takes me by surprise. He shoves me inside and closes the door.

'Hey,' I cry. 'Get out before I punch you again.'

Wayne holds his hands up in mock surrender. 'Peace, my friend. Maybe we should call a truce?'

'What do you want?'

'To say thanks for the money you left under your mattress. It'll come in handy for a night out.' Wayne chuckles, then stops abruptly. 'I'm sure you wouldn't want your friends to know where you came from, or why you've taken a flat here when you have somewhere to live. Mind you, it is a bit of a dump, the house in Wedgwood Street.'

I glare at him. It *was* Wayne who broke into my grandparents' house? I shouldn't have underestimated him, and yet I have no proof even if I had reported the break-in to the police. He's bound to have covered his tracks.

'That's not enough for you to bargain with.' I curse inwardly. I don't want to give him ammunition to start looking into me. 'Tom already knows,' I lie.

'Everything? Let's see.'

I try to remain calm. I don't want him to see me rattled.

Wayne sits down in the armchair by the front window. 'Mine's coffee. White, two sugars.'

'Would you like it in a mug or over your head? Because if not, you'd better give me my money back.'

More laughter. He wags a finger at me. 'I've met my equal in you.'

I ignore his statement. 'You said you wanted to call a truce?'

'Yeah, because you and I are too alike to trundle along together without getting in each other's way. We've both grown up around this neck of the woods. We're from broken homes, shitty houses with people who didn't care about us. I bet *you've* been in trouble, too. It wouldn't surprise me if you'd done time as well. You can't be all goody two-shoes after being dragged up.'

I say nothing. I'm not going to tell him anything and I doubt he'll find out from anyone. But my reddening skin gives me away.

'Ah, Clara has a past she's not proud of. If you and the boy from downstairs are getting together permanently, I might need a reminder every now and then not to let all this slip.'

'What kind of a reminder?'

'I'm thinking on it.' He runs his tongue across his top lip.

He's so repulsive. I roll my eyes.

'Not good enough for you?'

'You're all talk.'

Wayne shrugs. 'If you won't play ball, then you can

live in fear that I might tell Tom what I know about you. It could ruin a good thing just like this.' He snaps his finger and thumb. 'Oh, and you can leave Shelley out of this from now on.'

'Out of what?'

'I don't want you seeing her anymore. You're a bad influence.'

I yawn loudly. 'I'm bored with this conversation. I suggest you let yourself out, or else I'll be *throwing* you out.'

'Think a lot of yourself, don't you?' Wayne stands up, pointing in my face. 'Leave Shelley alone. I don't want her getting anything you say into her head. She's fine the way she is.'

'If you keep your fists to yourself, then we have a deal.'

'Ah, but the trouble with Shelley is she riles me up and I just love to order her around.'

'She deserves a better life than the one you can give her.'

'Don't push your luck.'

I grab his finger and, in one quick move, twist his arm behind his back. I slam him up against the wall.

'Let me go, you mad bitch.'

'Now that I've got the better of you again? You might break into my house. You might get to find out things about me, but one on one, I'll win every time. So leave me, and Shelley, alone. Or do I have to throw you out again?'

'Okay, okay! I'm leaving.'

I release my grip. 'Off you pop, then.'

He turns, rubbing at his hand before heading to the door. 'I'm not done with you yet.'

Ditto. Because I'm going to steal a lot more than two hundred pounds worth of stuff from his little stash downstairs.

He leaves the door open. I rush to close it, sighing with relief. It won't be over. Wayne isn't the type of man to let a woman get the better of him. But why is it that the first time I've felt settled in a good while, someone has to try and spoil it for me? Despite wanting to stay on the straight and narrow, I'll have to sort Wayne out. I can't let him ruin my happiness.

Thoughts of me and Tom together come to me. Am I feeling good at last? If I stay once my contract is finished at Stoke Helps Out, then I'll be free to start again without any lies.

If only it could be that easy.

Shelley jumped when the front door opened and slammed shut. She sat upright, waiting for Wayne to show his face, praying he was sober. When he stepped into the room, she could see he wasn't drunk, but he was furious about something.

'Hiya,' she cried. 'Want a brew?'

'Got any lager?'

She went to fetch it from the fridge.

'I've just been talking to that friend of yours, Clara.'

Shelley groaned inwardly as she removed the top from the bottle. That was all she needed, Clara winding Wayne up. He'd taken a couple of days before he'd come round, though, which had been a wonderful reprieve. Sadly, it looked as if that was over now.

She handed the drink to him and sat down again. He'd already changed the channel to something she didn't want to watch, but she said nothing.

'Did you know she's shagging tough boy?'

'Who?'

'Tom. I saw her sneaking out of flat one earlier.' Wayne made kissing noises.

Shelley held in her disgust. Secretly, she was pleased and couldn't wait to hear all the details.

'I've been doing some checking up on her, too,' he added between swigs. 'It appears your new friend isn't who she says she is. I've found stuff out about her.'

He said nothing else, leaving Shelley in the dark. She hated when he did that. He wanted her to ask, so he could feel superior with his knowledge. And yet, if she didn't, he'd get arsey with her anyway. Stuff it, she wanted to know.

'What is it?'

'Has she told you much about her past?'

'Not really.' She wouldn't give him any ammunition to get back at Clara.

'Did she tell you that her grandparents used to live in Wedgwood Street?'

She shook her head.

'The house is for sale, so she must own it now. God knows why she's been staying here.'

Shelley frowned. 'That doesn't make sense.'

'Derek Cooper, who I assume will be her granddad as her mum and dad are dead, used to run illegal fights.

Made a ton of money on the side, although he pissed most of it away.'

'What kind of fights?'

Wayne held up his hands, both made into fists. 'Bare knuckles. At Holdcroft's Farm, in the barn. People used to bet on who'd win. It was popular years ago, but it got stopped when one lad was nearly killed. And that was after the real fight.' He chuckled. 'Clara comes from a shit family, just like mine.'

Despite being curious as to what was going on, Shelley didn't like seeing Wayne gloat. She'd grown fond of Clara. She'd enjoyed having her close, keeping in touch with messages and texts, and she always made her laugh. They'd met a few times since she'd cooked supper, and later that week, she was going upstairs to share a bottle of wine. She hoped Wayne being here wasn't going to jeopardise that.

As if he could read her mind, he knocked back the contents of the bottle, burped loudly, and wiped his mouth. 'I'm off to see a man about a dog.'

And with that he was gone. Leaving Shelley with an overwhelming sense of relief, and intrigue to find out more.

Had Wayne just said Clara's parents were dead?

CHAPTER THIRTY-SEVEN

I'm at work updating some of the visits I've carried out when Lisa strides across the floor. She points at the empty desk across from me.

'I've just seen Tess coming out of Sam's office. She seemed really upset. I think she might have been crying. I wonder what that idiot has said to make her feel like that.'

'Have you asked her?' I pipe up.

'No.'

'Why not?'

'It's not really my business.'

'And yet you'll sit here and gossip about her.' I push myself up from my desk and go to find Tess. Since the episode with Sam, we've started to talk a little. It helps ease my conscience to be honest, and this will do even more.

There are only two cubicles in the ladies' toilets. The door is open wide on one, so I knock gently on the other.

'Tess, are you okay?'

'I'm fine.'

'It doesn't sound like it. Has Sam said something to you? Lisa saw you coming out of his office.'

'So you're all talking about me?'

'Well, I left her and Fran to it. Don't care much for tittle-tattle myself.' I pause. 'Look, come out, and we can talk if you like.'

There's silence for a moment, and then the door opens. It's clear Tess has been crying. My heart goes out to her. Because Sam can be a real twat when he wants to be.

'What's he said to you?'

'I suppose you'll be pleased to know that it's over between us now.'

I sigh and give her a faint smile. 'I overreacted when I saw him with you. It was thoughtless and stupid.'

'He's dumped me. He says he wants to make things up with his wife.'

'That'll be a first.'

'It isn't just that. He says my work isn't up to scratch and he's going to let the agency know that he wants someone else in my place.'

'The creep!' I'm on a fixed contract. Tess is covering on a week-to-week basis, whenever she's needed.

'He shouldn't be allowed to get away with this,' I continue. 'It's wrong what he's doing. He needs teaching a lesson.'

'What are you going to do?'

'I don't mean literally. But let's have a think about how to sort this mess out. In the meantime, you go back to your desk. I'm going to have a word with him.'

'What will you say?'

'I don't know yet. How about you tidy yourself up, go and make everyone a coffee, and I'll see what I can do?'

Tess nods, a faint smile appearing.

She's a nice girl underneath, reminding me of how I was at her age. Gullible, taken in by anyone. Used, abused. Discarded. Made fun of, leered at.

I can't let that happen to Tess.

I walk back to the office, stopping at Sam's door. I knock and step inside.

'I haven't said you can come in yet,' Sam says, closing his screen quickly.

'Watching porn, are you?' I snap.

'No!'

'On work's time, too.' I tut.

'I wasn't.'

'Of course you weren't, but I've a good mind to spread that rumour around.'

'What do you want?'

I sit down uninvited. 'I've just been talking to Tess.'

'Ah. The woman *you* harassed the other week.'

'The woman *you* were with instead of your wife, yes. She's really upset about your antics.'

'What's that got to do with you?'

'She's just a kid, and you've used her, like you did me.'

'Not this again.' Sam points at the door. 'Show yourself out, I'm busy.'

'I haven't finished yet. I've told her to make a complaint about you.'

I have his attention now.

'You're making one against her. It's wrong. Her work is good. You only want her to leave because you've had your fun and now she's surplus to requirements. Imagine what HR will think when I add my thoughts to it as well.'

He pales.

'Drop the complaint and write her a good résumé. I doubt she'll stick around much after today anyway, the way you've made her feel.'

'She needs to act like a grown-up, not a child.'

'Like you, you mean? Shirking your responsibilities?' I take out my phone. 'I might get some photos printed. I have several more apart from the bed selfie. They'll be easy to shove through your front door. Or leave on your car overnight. Or—'

'You are such a bitch.'

'Takes one to know one.'

'Okay. Send Tess in to see me.'

'I don't think that's wise. She's really upset at the moment.'

'It's not up to you.'

I raise my eyebrows. 'Come on now. Don't push your luck. Leave the poor girl alone to get over your faux pas. She'll be as bright as a button again tomorrow, knowing she won't have to leave because her arsehole boss has used her and then dumped her. And then perhaps you can keep your dick in your pants and be faithful to your wife?'

'I'm a grown man, and I can do what the hell I like. You don't own me.'

'You're married.'

'And you're jealous because I've moved on from you.'

'It's not that at all.'

He throws his pen down on the desk. 'Isn't it about time *you* grew up and accepted things are over? You won't then have to babysit Tess.'

'You still think this is about me and you?' I laugh as I stand up.

'What else could it be?'

'You being unfaithful to your wife.'

'Didn't bother you when you stayed over.'

'I told you, I did it all purposely. To catch you out.'

'Oh, please. You were infatuated with me. It's not a nice look, and quite frankly, all this is verging on the edge of stalking.'

'Me? I've a good mind to go to the police and get them to—'

'Where were you yesterday morning?' Sam interrupts me.

'I had a dentist appointment,' I fib. 'Why?'

'Saw you in Mount Close. Visiting a friend, were you?'

I freeze as I try to keep my composure. That's Nellie's address. 'I might have been. It's no concern of yours.'

'For all I know you could be seeing another married man.'

'Oh, please,' I mimic. 'We're not all like you.'

'Close the door on the way out.'

'Truth hurt?' I turn and march off. That bloody man. I'm going to get him for this.

CHAPTER THIRTY-EIGHT

After the day I've had at work, I'm glad to be home. I'm really excited about the weekend. Shelley is coming up in about an hour, and then tomorrow I'm spending time with Tom and Isla.

I jump straight into the shower to wash the day away. Even with Sam annoying me, my life is so different from what I'd imagined when I came back to Stoke, and I'm wondering if it's true what I suggested at one of the anger management sessions. If you surround yourself with lovely people in a safe environment, it might just rub off on you.

I'm pouring wine when a message from Shelley comes in on my phone. I go to answer the front door, not wanting to leave it on the latch in case Wayne is around.

Shelley arrives with a bottle of red and a beaming smile.

I hold up my glass. 'Beat you to it. We can save that one for another time. Or we can open it later...' I beckon her in. 'How have you been? Seems ages since I saw you, and yet no time at all because we've been nattering online.'

'Nothing much to tell. How about you?'

'Same. Except that I had a date with Tom last Friday.'

Shelley grins. 'I knew you and him had a thing.'

'A thing?'

'There were hot looks flowing between the two of you when we all had lunch. I would have mentioned it to you – secretly of course – if Wayne hadn't spoiled everything. Sorry about that again. It's left a sour taste in my mouth.'

'Don't ever apologise about him.' I sit down next to her on the settee and place a bowl of crisps on the coffee table.

'But then he said he saw you coming out of Tom's flat on Saturday morning.'

I pout, wondering what else the idiot has told Shelley. It's taken the shine off my good news.

Shelley nudges me. 'Forget about him, tell me about you and Tom.'

I smile then. I can't help it. I run through my week, not going into too much detail, obviously. All the while Shelley's smile widens, so does mine. Tom and I have seen each other a few times since the weekend, with Isla in tow mostly, but it's all been fun.

'Do you think you'll get together permanently?' Shelley pauses. 'Isn't it awkward with you living in the same building?'

'If it doesn't work out, I'll accept that. Besides, I might not be here long anyway.'

'What do you mean?'

I'm surprised to see that my words have shocked Shelley. 'It was only meant to be a pit stop, until my contract runs out at Stoke Helps Out. I think I'll be going back to Manchester then.'

'Is that after you've sold the house in Wedgwood Street?'

My face drops. Wayne couldn't keep his mouth shut, could he?

'It's not how it seems,' I reply. 'I just have things to sort out before I can leave, and it seemed nicer to stay here while I do.'

'Oh, I'm not judging. I think it's great that you're here, but I'm not sure I'm keen on you leaving anytime soon either. Plus you're doing a great job of keeping Wayne away from me. I hope he doesn't come back for good when you're gone.'

Her appreciation is really nice to hear. I want to make her feel safe, too.

'You'll have to make sure he stays away.' I gnaw at my bottom lip. 'Please don't tell anyone about my grandparents' house. I hate going back to it. So many bad memories.'

'Of course I won't. Wayne mentioned something about fights, though?'

The bloody blabbermouth!

'Let's just say it wasn't a happy time in my life, and one of the reasons why I left Stoke as soon as I could.' I suppose there's only half a lie there.

'Are you going to tell Tom?'

'Not yet.' Shelley's frown makes me continue. 'I'm worried he'll go off me before things have even begun.'

'I thought you were planning on leaving?' She nudges me playfully. 'If you're as smitten then as you are now, you'll be staying.'

'Oh, behave.' I nudge her back.

'Please stay. I don't think anyone makes me laugh as much as you do.'

'I'll think about it.' I get up. 'Top-up?'

While I refill our glasses, I think more about our conversation. It's lovely that Shelley wants me to stay, so it's a pity I can't tell Tom everything about my background. But there's more to it than even Wayne has found out. Still, it's nice to think about being here longer than planned. Even if I do have a few things to sort out first.

I sit in the shadows outside Wayne's house for two nights before I spot him coming out of his brother's flat. He turns right and goes down the street. At the corner, he turns right again, and I race after him. I cross over and keep my head down. Even in the dark, it's hard to follow someone on foot without being seen, but I stay close enough behind so that Wayne won't hear me or turn around unexpectedly.

A few minutes later, he disappears into the Rose and Crown. Quickly, I retrace my steps back to the flat he came out of and knock on the door. If anyone is home, I'll ask for someone else and then pretend I have the wrong address.

But there's no reply. The flat is in darkness. Annoyingly, the kitchen window is on the latch, but it's an upstairs flat. I'm not able to shimmy up a drainpipe because there isn't one near enough. There is, however, a shed in the corner of the rear garden.

Seeing it padlocked, I peer through a grubby side window. There's a sheet covering something in the corner. I get out my phone and use its torch. At the bottom, I see a couple of white boxes sticking out. It looks like more knockoff gear, but I don't want to break in and alert Wayne, especially as he's done the same to me. It'll be a dead giveaway.

Figuring I've got enough on him for now, the only other alternative I have is to follow him and see what he gets up to on a regular basis. I can't decide if that's going to be worth my time. I like a challenge, but surveillance work is long hours and often inconclusive.

Now I sound like a detective. I laugh inwardly, then sigh in frustration.

Passing Wayne's car, I take out my door key and run it along its side. The car is old, and I don't even know if he'll notice. And yes, it's petty, but satisfying all the same.

CHAPTER THIRTY-NINE

I've taken Isla out to the park while Tom finishes off an urgent job. On the way back, we stop for a chocolate bar and sit on the wall outside the shops. Just then, someone calls my name. I turn to see Kerry Arington. I groan inwardly. She's the last person I want to see. And as I'm with Isla, I'll have to be polite.

'Clara? It is you!'

'Hi. It's Kerry, isn't it?'

'It is. Brody said he'd bumped into you a while ago, and then he recognised you sitting on the wall the other night. But I wasn't free and when I'd finished my client, you'd gone. Mind you, it isn't hard in our city to bump into the same people. No one usually strays far from where they work, rest, and play.' She smiles. 'It's so lovely to see you. You're looking well. How is life treating you?'

'It's having its moments,' I say truthfully.

'Is this your daughter? She's very pretty.'

'Oh, no. Isla is—'

'My mum died, and Clara helps my dad to take care of me,' Isla says. 'She can be my new mummy anytime, though.'

'Now there's an endorsement if ever I heard one!' Kerry laughs. 'Clara, you must come round one evening. Brody would love to show you his man cave, and we can have a giggle with the karaoke machine.'

Not on your life.

'I'd like that very much.'

'Great! I don't work late every night, thank God.' She hands me her phone. 'Pop me your number in there, and we can arrange something soon.'

Unable to get out of it, I tap in my details. Isla has gone to take the empty wrappers to the bin. There's a pause when Kerry hands back my phone, and then she totally surprises me.

'I'm sorry I was such a bitch to you at school,' she says quietly. 'It sounds stupid now, but you were the one who every boy wanted to be with and—'

'Me?' I find that hard to believe.

'Yes! You could have had your pick. Well, when you weren't trying to fight one of them anyway.'

I can't help but smile. 'That sounds like me.' My phone rings. I see it's the estate agent calling. 'I have to take this,' I tell her.

'Okay. Speak soon, then. Lovely to meet you, Isla,' Kerry shouts before leaving.

I take the call, the smile on my face getting wider. Mark has had an offer for the house that he thinks I should consider.

'I don't think you'll get a better one,' he says. 'It's

five thousand more than the last one, and I thought that was pretty generous.'

'Accept it,' I say, annoyed at his rudeness again. 'How long will it take for all to be sorted?'

'Two or three months.'

I finish the call, take Isla home, and almost bounce upstairs. I feel as if a weight has been lifted from my shoulders. Once the house is sold, I'll be free to do whatever I please.

I put on some music and dance around the living room. I have a buyer for the house! At last I'll be able to leave my past behind. This will be a new start. Away from Wedgwood Street, away from the memories, away from the area I grew up in.

Away from Tom and Isla, and Shelley and Roberta?

My shoulders sag at the thought. Could I really put roots down in Stoke again, after so long away and all the tragedy I've suffered here during my earlier years?

It feels time to make some decisions about what to do next with my life. It would be nice to settle somewhere.

After the death of my parents, I didn't seem to fit in anywhere. Being the odd one out at school was as bad as being at home with my grandparents. When I moved up to secondary school, and Amy and Kerry formed a bond that seemed as good as the one I'd had with Amy, I found myself alone for the most part. I kept myself to myself, sitting with no one during classes, hiding wherever I could during breaks. I began to enjoy my own company.

Sports lessons were a nightmare unless I was running. Running I could do alone, if it wasn't a relay race. But I'd always be one of the kids who no one wanted on their side, and I could never understand why. My parents were dead, nothing that had happened to me would rub off on anyone else.

Soon I was resorting to violence if anyone came near me. I made myself into a target, became a challenge for fun and tricks. I was sent to see the headmaster, and my grandparents were called into school. Neither of them turned up.

Of course Nan said she was sorry when I got home from school. She said she'd been all for going to see what she could do, and then Derek had stopped her. He said he was proud of me for sticking up for myself. He said children at school nowadays were mollycoddled and a good slap every now and then would do them the world of good.

I knew that only too well. I kept away from Derek as much as possible, especially when he was drunk. Getting the back of his hand across my legs stung, my skin burning like it was on fire, and it happened too often, not just now and then.

One night when I was watching TV with Nan, sitting on the sofa with her, Derek came home earlier than expected. He'd still had a drink, but he'd got a gash on his face and a black eye. Nan jumped to her feet immediately. I rushed into the kitchen, coming back with a wet tea towel.

'What's happened, love?' Nan asked him, reaching up to dab at his eye.

'It's all your fault.' Derek backhanded her, and she flew across the room.

'Nan!' I rushed to her aid.

Derek grabbed my hair and pulled me up.

'Leave her alone,' he seethed. 'She's been talking.' He pointed to his eye. 'That's what I got this for.'

I screamed, the pain intensifying as his grip increased.

'Derek, please,' Jean said. 'Blame me for whatever it is I've done, but not Clara.'

Derek let go, and I fell back onto the settee. He was an inch from Nan's face now.

'You told Harry about what I'd been doing.'

'I didn't.'

'Are you calling him a liar?' He stood up straight, tall and menacing.

'No, I—'

'I've had that no-good wife of his giving me what for. And when I gave *her* what for, Harry attacked me.' He raised his hand in the air again as a warning. 'If you weren't a good housekeeper, I'd have you out of here like a shot. Keep your trap shut.' Then he turned to me. 'And you, it's about time you earned your keep.'

'Derek, no,' Nan cried.

Derek lashed out at Jean again. This time she remained quiet.

I said nothing, too. I'd learned when it was best to speak and when not.

'You can come to work with me tomorrow night,' Derek said.

He left us then, staggering into the kitchen. I immediately went to see to Nan.

But she pushed me away. 'I'm sorry, Clara. There are things your granddad does. I'm not proud of that, but if he wants you involved, I'm too scared to stop him.'

'What do you mean?' My bottom lip trembled.

'You'll see, tomorrow.'

Now, I remember the stained, threadbare carpet. I recall, right there, learning that no one was going to look out for me. I could only depend on myself. And it changed everything.

I shudder. A few minutes ago, I felt so alive, like there are better things coming my way. So why do memories of my past still taunt me, making me think that things will never change?

CHAPTER FORTY

'Are you ready to talk more about Evan yet?' Emma asks me at my next appointment.

'What do you want to know? That we had an unconventional marriage? That I hustled men when I was with him? And then when it was over, I dabbled with drugs and went through a low patch?'

Emma says nothing, showing no emotion at my outburst. Yet I wonder why I've come out with all that at this session. Maybe I want to shock her, to see how much she's willing to listen. Perhaps I want to get it off my chest now I'm comfortable with these sessions. Or am I thinking that telling Emma might ease my conscience because I'm lying to Tom?

'I was a different person than when I'd first arrived at Manchester when I was seventeen,' I say instead. 'Landing there had been scary, yet I'm nothing but resourceful. I managed to pick a handbag, and money from a wallet before I'd left the train station, which got me a room for a couple of nights at a small guest house.

I found a job as a barmaid at a hotel and learned to stand on my own two feet. I worked in different bars while hustling on the side.'

'Hustling in what way?'

'Sleeping with men and stealing their wallets before I left. Everyone carried cash back then. I wasn't proud of myself, but I kept my nose clean, not attracting attention, and worked on my own.'

One of the less glamorous evenings springs to my mind. Martin, the guy I'd landed, was about fifty, but he was extremely drunk by the end of the night. I was waiting at the taxi rank with him.

'I'm cold,' he'd said, slinging an arm over my shoulder. 'You can warm me up when you get to my place.'

'And you're sure there'll be no one home?' I'd asked him several times but wanted to hear it again.

'We have the house to ourselves.' He leaned forward to kiss my mouth, and I turned my head to the right so he caught me on the cheek.

The next taxi to arrive was ours, and we got into the back. Martin gave out his address, and I made a mental note of it. It was in a nice part of town at least.

No sooner had the taxi pulled away, his lips and hands were all over me. I didn't mind too much because he was so drunk I doubted he'd be awake when we got to our destination. Which suited me fine.

I thought what I'd do when I got in later that evening. Maybe I'd order some food, put my feet up, open a bottle of wine. Since I'd moved to my flat, the place and area were a tip, but I'd enjoyed having my own space. Still, that was dependent on me paying my rent as I was already two weeks behind. And I'd only met my landlord twice, and that had been enough. I wasn't sleeping with him if he offered it in lieu of rent.

Martin's eyes were closing, so I sat back in the seat, giving him time to drop off. His hand rested on my thigh, but I resisted slapping it away.

'Do we have far to go?' I asked the driver.

'A couple of minutes. Want me to drop you off somewhere afterwards?'

I turned to see Martin, mouth wide open, dribble hanging from his bottom lip. 'Yes, please. Can you wait for me?'

'Will do.'

We drew up in front of his property. Nice gaff. Shame I wasn't going to stay for a while, but I knew when my bets were hedged.

I nudged Martin awake. 'We're here.'

I staggered down the path with him, struggling to get out his keys. Once inside, I laid him out on the settee. He was asleep before I'd counted to three. Maybe helped a little by the sedative I'd slipped into his drink earlier.

I checked his pockets, found his wallet, and his phone. It wasn't hard to slide down the zip to his jeans, fiddle around inside, and get his old fella out on show. The poor thing seemed like it was cold.

Click, click, click.

Perfect.

Then I quickly had a look around the house. His laptop was there for the taking, but I wasn't tempted. I wanted things Martin wouldn't miss straightaway. I hoped he'd wake with a guilty conscience and then crap himself when he saw the photo on his phone.

I *hoped* he'd take his time in reporting his cards stolen, too, but there was no harm in getting as much cash as I could before I went home. Silly fool had kept his PIN in his wallet.

I closed the front door with a sigh. It had been a fruitful evening, and I hadn't had to sleep with him, always a bonus.

'Where to?' the cab driver asked.

'Back into town, please.'

'Ready to go again?' He chuckled.

'Always.'

I wasn't stupid enough to let him have my address or anywhere near it. Still, I'd got through another week. It might not be my idea of paradise, but I was surviving. And it was better than prison, which might be the other option if I went back to Stoke.

'It was supposed to be a way to survive until I got on my feet,' I tell Emma now, not wanting to share everything with her. 'But the money I could make was addictive. At times, a man would get rough with me, but I knew how to handle myself. Mostly they came off worse if they tried anything stupid.'

'Did that happen often?' Emma asks.

'It was an occupational hazard, I suppose. But I was always able to get myself out of any funny business. It's hard to think about it now.'

Even as I say it, I know I'll do it again if I have to, to survive.

CHAPTER FORTY-ONE

Tom and I have brought Isla to the park. Even though I'm sitting on an extremely hard wrought-iron bench, I could get used to this. The noise is deafening as kids race around the playground in front of us. We both have an eye on Isla, who's diving from the swings to the roundabout and back again. Now, though, she's at the top of the slide, waving frantically at us.

I want to pinch myself, and not in a self-harm way. It's Saturday afternoon, and I am spending it with Tom and Isla. It seems right. I turn to see his legs out, one foot crossed over the other.

Maybe I could have a baby with Tom.

I gasp.

'Are you okay?' Tom asks.

'Yes.' I try not to seem flustered. The thought had taken me by surprise.

'Did you do this often with Sasha?' I ask, pushing it back to where it had come from.

'Usually it was one or the other of us who brought

Isla here. You know what it's like when you're busy. I wish I'd taken time now.' Tom smiles. 'Obviously that's changed because I'm here with you, but we did take things for granted when Isla was younger.'

'It's nice to see, though. I can barely remember any happy times with my dad. He was never around. My mum was at work trying to make ends meet, and my dad would piss it all up the wall.'

'You don't recall anything as a child?'

I think for a moment. 'I remember him taking me to a sweet shop and giving me the change from his pocket. I bought a Sherbet Dip Dab, a mixture with Fruit Salads, and a gobstopper. Weird how I can recall that detail. Perhaps it's because I was more interested in the sweets.'

'I preferred Black Jacks myself.'

I nudge him playfully.

'Dad, look at me!' Isla shouts from the top of the climbing frame.

Tom waves to her. 'I want to yell at her, tell her to come down from there in case she falls.'

'It isn't very high,' I soothe.

'You should see what I got up to when I was her age. We were lighting fires in the woods and all sorts.'

'And here I am thinking that there isn't a bad boy in you.' I chuckle.

'To be honest, I didn't dare misbehave as my father was strict. He used to tan my hide if I was late.'

'Tan your hide? You sound like you're from the Victorian ages!'

'You know what I mean.'

'Actually, I don't. I remember waking up one night

alone and standing in the front window crying. Turned out my mum had gone to find my dad at the pub. He was furious, and I went to sleep with them arguing, wishing I hadn't woken up at all.' I sigh. 'My parents really screwed me up. I wish it didn't hang over me all the time.'

'Were you in Manchester during the Covid lockdowns?'

I nod. 'What a hideous time in anyone's life that was. But I guess, for me, some good did come out of it. I volunteered at our local food bank, and I loved it.'

I'm lying again. I did nothing of the sort. But this time, I'm embarrassed at the need to fib.

Like most people, I try not to think about 2020. The first lockdown had been particularly bad. I'd been living with Damien then, more off than on. He'd been trying to find somewhere else to live when everything came to a halt.

Being cooped up for so long with one person is a nightmare, especially if that person doesn't want to be with you. Covid shone a light on our relationship, how damaging it was, how abusive we were to each other. When things were going okay, everything was fine. But when they weren't, we would fight, hurting each other with slaps and fists, rather than words.

After my marriage to Evan ended, I swore I wouldn't get myself in a mess again. But it happened over and over, and it was always me who threw the first punch. My life seemed to be a circle of violence. No matter how I tried not to choose the wrong partner, or be happy alone, something would send me off the rails.

By the time of the second lockdown, I'd ended that

relationship and enjoyed the peace of being alone. It felt better, somehow, being isolated purposely. That was when I started walking during the evenings and at night-time.

I glance at Tom surreptitiously. Will I hurt *him* if I stick around? The fact he isn't a loser, or a liar, or a thief is a good plus to think I might not. But I can't be sure. I hate that about myself.

'I'm going to a friend's house tomorrow evening. Well, two friends really.' I explain who Brody and Kerry are, but not why I've decided to go. I don't want to tell Tom that I'm envious and yet curious to see inside their home.

'A mini school reunion,' he says. 'Are you looking forward to it?'

'Yes, I think I am, but we didn't get on all that well at school. I had a fling with Brody behind Kerry's back when I was younger. I think I'll be keeping that to myself.'

Tom laughs. 'I imagine he will, too.'

Isla comes running over to them. 'I'm thirsty. Can we go to the pavilion café now, please?'

As Isla races ahead, I walk alongside Tom, all the while wanting to feel his hand in mine. But I do have great fun imagining where those hands will be later if all goes well.

I go to work on Monday morning with a smile on my face. I hadn't expected things to be so good between us. We'd ended up having tea out, and it had been wonderful. It gave me a taste of what life could be like, being part of a family.

There doesn't seem to be anything better.

CHAPTER FORTY-TWO

I go by foot to the Arington home. I don't want to risk them seeing my nan's car, firstly because it's a wreck, and secondly because I'd lied to Brody when I first bumped into him. Luckily, it isn't raining.

With my stomach in knots, I walk up the drive. I've daydreamed about the interior of the house for weeks and, now I'm about to step inside, it feels strange.

Before I can ring the bell, the front door is thrown open, and Kerry envelopes me in a big hug.

It takes me by surprise and puts my hackles up. Is there some ulterior motive behind her invite? Is she going to gloat, making out she is superior? Because, if so, she'll probably find a glass of wine thrown in her face.

'Brody's just rang to say he's on his way.' Kerry points through to the kitchen. 'He won't be long. I've managed to get two of the three kids into bed. The baby is still snuffling, but I think she's settling.'

I remind myself to stay calm as I go inside. The

hallway is painted white with colourful family portraits lined along one wall. I remove my coat and hang it on a coat rack, glancing at the rows of tiny shoes underneath its bench.

I step into the kitchen, and it's almost a surprise to see it's nothing like I'd imagined. Kerry has gone for the traditional cottage design, with cream shaker units and wooden work tops. A large vase of orange lilies stands on an island. The walls are painted a pale tangerine above cream tiles, and there's a bank of windows on the back wall where I can see a landscaped garden. I know I'll be daydreaming about this even more now. At least it'll be accurate.

'I won't be a minute.' Kerry disappears and comes back within seconds. She waves me over, a finger on her lips to ensure I'll be quiet.

'Look at her.' Kerry sighs. 'She's so adorable... when she's asleep.'

I peep into the Moses basket to see a little girl lying on her back. Her arms are in the air, a teddy pushed down the side, and she has a smile of content on her face. I'm not sure who she's more like, her mum or her dad. But I do know one thing.

'She's gorgeous,' I whisper, trying not to cry at the thought of never having that for myself.

'She's far too big for this basket, but I brought it down so I can keep an eye on her. She hasn't been sleeping well lately.' Kerry stifles a yawn. 'I'm knackered, to be honest.'

'You look good for it,' I compliment. 'Motherhood suits you.'

'Thanks. Anyway, less about me.' Kerry grabs my

hand. 'Let's have a drink while we wait for Brody. We have a lot to catch up on.'

I almost walk out right there and then. I don't want to lie a lot this evening, but it's going to be tough not to, and, as well, not trip myself up.

In the kitchen, Kerry checks the food in the oven, pours wine for us both, and we go to sit in the attached orangery.

'What do you do for work?' Kerry asks.

I'm a serial liar.

'I'm an author.'

'Wow.' Kerry seems impressed. 'I'm an avid reader. What have you written?'

'*Lessons in Love. Everyone Loves Melissa. I Love You, Love Me.*' I rattle off a few books I've read recently.

'You wrote those? I've read *Lessons in Love.* It's amazing! So you write in a pen name?'

Oops. It's best I get out of that lie rather than dig myself a bigger hole.

'Just kidding! I am a freelance writer, though. I have my own flat in Salford, so I do lots for the local paper, and then I pitch to the national magazines.' Oh, how the lies roll off my tongue.

'Do you specialise in a topic?'

How to be a weirdo?

'No, I'll make a story out of anything I see fit.' I stop. 'Not for gratuitous means. I like my words to be truthful. No sleaze from me.'

'Are you online? Where can I read something you've done?'

The front door opens, and Brody shouts out that he's home. Kerry scuttles over to the oven, and I relax a little. I didn't expect to get such a grilling, and my lies are already winding me up in knots, but I seem to have got away with a few for now.

Surprisingly, with Brody arriving the conversation has become more about what he's doing. For a while, I chat along with them as we eat. When I laugh at something Kerry says, I gasp inwardly. Wait. Am I enjoying myself, being here with these two?

We reminisce about our younger years, I catch up with the local gossip and know it's inevitable that one of them will ask why I went to live in Manchester. It's Kerry.

'When I was seventeen, I went to stay with a cousin and got a job in a bar,' I tell her.

'I didn't know you had cousins.'

'Did I say that? Sorry, I meant a friend. From there, I went to uni and did a media degree. While I was doing that, I got myself a few gigs writing on magazines, networked like crazy, and then freelanced.'

'That's so commendable. We love being our own bosses, don't we, Brody?'

'Yeah, when we don't have too much stress. It's bloody hard work.' He pulls a face.

'I started my business after having our first child, Joshua,' Kerry explains. 'I'd been working in a beauty salon since leaving school, and the next step was always to have my own place. So when I was pregnant and then on maternity leave, we set up KA Nails and Beauty. You should call in. I'll give you a manicure on the house.'

I find myself hiding my hands in my lap, so Kerry won't see how terrible my nails are. I haven't painted them in a good while, let alone had a manicure in a salon.

Why is that? Why don't I take more care of myself? Is the answer that I don't want to make myself too attractive to men, bring any attention to myself nowadays? Men have always brought trouble to me.

Then I think of Tom and how he's changed my life over the past few weeks. He would have enjoyed it here with me.

'That's really kind of you,' I say. 'I'll book in when I'm free.'

Finally the evening ends, and to my mind it's been a success. Kerry's middle child, Nancy, came downstairs for a glass of water. The baby slept straight through, and I didn't see the eldest child at all.

I sit in the living room, finishing off a coffee, and realise that I've enjoyed the evening a lot, despite cringing at my lies earlier. Both Kerry and Brody have made me feel so welcome. I wish I was in a position where I could return the favour, especially with Tom. I can see him getting on well with them both.

When Brody offers me a lift home, I think about declining and walking to clear my head, but then I say yes. It will give me the chance to say something to him in private about what happened between us before I left Stoke.

'We were kids, Clara,' he says, turning briefly to me with a grin. 'I remember it being very nice, and I was unfaithful to Kerry at the time, but I told her about it ages ago.'

'You did?' I can't hide my shock.

'Yeah, we were playing some kind of truth and lies

game. I was going for the shock factor when I had to tell the truth.'

'And she didn't mind?'

'We were married by then. She punched me on the arm, though, and it hurt like hell.'

I laugh, wondering again what it would be like to have that kind of relationship with someone. It must be amazing to last from childhood sweethearts. Now I've seen them from the other side, it's admirable. More importantly, I can tell they really love each other.

I bet their arguments don't end up with fights before they make up.

And when I think about things regarding nature versus nurture, and my upbringing making me the way I am, well, it can't be just that. Kerry's family were as rough as mine, and look how she's turned out.

So maybe there's hope for me yet.

CHAPTER FORTY-THREE

Later that week, I'm sitting at the table in the kitchen when there's an almighty crash from downstairs. I freeze, listening intently. Then I hear crying, yelling, and the scrape of what sounds like a table being pushed across the floor.

'Shelley.' I race to the kitchen drawer where I put the key to flat two, and then out into the hallway. Even before I've got to the bottom of the stairs, Tom is opening his door.

'What the hell's going on in there?' he asks, a look of panic on his face.

'Tom, is everything all right?'

I glance up to see Roberta on the landing.

'It's Shelley. Wayne's hurting her.' I bang on the door. 'Shelley!'

Roberta is level with me soon and stands next to Tom. There's no answer, screaming coming from inside.

'I have a key. I'm going in.'

'Wait,' Tom cries. 'I think we should call the police and let them sort it out.'

'She could be dead by then.' I shake my head. 'I can't let that happen.' I bang on the door once more, put the key in the lock, and open it.

'Shelley, it's Clara, are you—'

I don't get any further because I'm bowled out of the way by Wayne. He pushes past Tom and is away from the building before anyone can react. But I saw the anger in his eyes, the blood on his fists. I run into the flat.

'Shelley?' I shout.

There's no reply, but by this time I'm in the living room. She's in the kitchen, and I drop to the floor next to her. Her eyes are closed, there's blood all over her face and droplets on the front of her blouse.

Images of a kitchen floor eighteen years ago come rushing to my mind, but I banish them immediately. I need to concentrate on the job in hand.

Behind, Tom is on his phone, talking to the emergency services. I try to rouse Shelley again. Her eyes flicker open, and I smile with relief.

'Hey. Don't worry. You're going to be okay. Help is on its way.'

'Wayne.' Shelley tries to sit up, moaning as she holds on to her stomach.

I push her down gently. 'He's gone. Tom's called for an ambulance. You lie still for now.'

'They're on their way.' Tom rights an overturned chair. 'Is she all right?'

There is blood trickling from a cut on Shelley's cheekbone. Her eyes are already blackening, and there are some horrid red marks coming out around her neck. But she's alive.

'I think so.' I glance up at Tom, Roberta standing behind him. 'That bastard did this to her. He has to pay.'

'The police will press charges,' Tom says. 'He'll go back inside for this.'

'He deserves that after what he's done.' Roberta shakes her head. 'I'll help tidy up once Shelley has been seen to.'

'I think the police will want to take photos, get prints et cetera,' Tom surmises. 'I hope he goes down for a very long time.'

He leaves to wait for the ambulance and to check on Isla. Roberta, needing something to do, decides to make tea for everyone upstairs.

I'm itching to clean up. There's blood everywhere, on the table, across the floor and kitchen units. Why has Wayne attacked Shelley so brutally? To cause that much damage, he must have been in one hell of a rage. It's all I can do to shut out what I'm imagining.

The ambulance is there within ten minutes. I explain briefly what I think has happened.

'What's her name?' a female paramedic asks.

'Shelley.'

'Hello, Shelley, love. I'm Tina, and this great big hunk with me is Will. We're just going to examine you.' Tina kneels on the floor next to her, while Will gets out the necessary equipment from his backpack.

I feel a hand on my shoulder. It's Tom. He's reaching out for me then, and I grasp it as I stand.

'The police are here,' he says.

There are two male officers in uniform standing behind him.

'What's her surname?' the younger of the two asks.

'Lovett,' I tell him. 'He's Wayne Stallington. I haven't known her for long. I live upstairs. The house has been converted into four flats. It belongs to Roberta Fisher, flat three.'

'She's upstairs,' Tom replies, stepping into the hall. 'She'll be back soon.'

'And the person who did this,' the officer continues. 'Does he live here, too?'

'He used to,' I say. 'He lives in Doulton Street, number twenty-two, but spends a lot of time here, unfortunately. He's been to prison for GBH, came out about a year ago and hasn't left her alone since.'

'And he's named Stallington, you say? Wayne?'

I turn to see the older officer getting a notepad out. I nod.

'I know the family. Did you witness anything?'

'No. We might have stopped him going further, but we didn't get in quick enough. She gave me a key in case this ever happened again.'

The officer finishes writing his notes. 'We'll get an arrest warrant out for him.'

I point to the spare room. 'You might want to search in there before you go. The wardrobe is full of stolen goods, and they don't belong to Shelley. I bet he made her store them here.'

Tom gives her hand a squeeze as the officer goes into the room. His eyes widen when he sees the number of boxes once the wardrobe door is opened.

'Is that all knockoff?' he asks, perplexed.

'Roberta's going to be worried sick,' I say quietly.

'Don't worry,' the officer tells them. 'We'll bag it up and get it all removed over the next few hours.'

I leave the police to do their work and pop back into the living room to see how Shelley is.

'She's doing fine.' Tina steps away for a moment to talk to me. 'I don't think there's anything life-threatening, but we're taking her to A and E. She'll need x-rays, scans, and stitches at the very least.'

'Can I go to the hospital with her? She has family I can contact to meet her there.'

'Yes, of course. We'll be ready to go in a few minutes.' Tina touches my arm. 'She's lucky you stopped him before he did even more damage.'

Although I'm grateful for her comment, the images of what's happened will take a lot longer to fade than Shelley's bruises.

CHAPTER FORTY-FOUR

The incident with Shelley and Wayne has left me desperately in need of a chat with Emma.

'Can I talk to you about anything?' I ask her, immediately after we're seated in the bay window.

Emma sits forward a little. 'Yes, of course. What's bothering you?'

'There's so much I need to get off my chest. My neighbour got attacked by her partner the other night, and I... it brought back memories I'd rather it not have.' I glance out of the window for a moment. 'But there's much more than that. My life has been such a mess.'

'Whatever you tell me is confidential, Clara. I'm here to help.'

'I went to prison for six months, and when I came out, Louise had moved in and she was pregnant by Evan,' I blurt out.

'Well, there is a lot to unpack there,' Emma replies. 'Shall we start at the beginning?'

A silence descends on the room. I can't speak.

Then I find I can't stop.

'Even though I wasn't happy with Evan, I stayed with him because I had nowhere to go. He was still shoplifting, but robbing places left, right, and centre too. He worked alone, so I went along with him sometimes. I would wait for him in the car.

'But for the last job I did with him, he brought in a mate of his. Stuart had given him details of a lock-up with a ton of electrical goods that could be shifted quickly on the markets. They were going halves with the money they'd earn when the gear was sold on.

'I didn't like Stuart when I met him. I don't know why, sixth sense or something, but I didn't trust him. When we took the stuff Evan had stolen over to him, he got cocky about giving us our fair share. They had a bit of a scuffle, and eventually we left with half of the loot.

'We were on our way home when the police caught up with us. Turns out his mate had grassed on us. I pulled over, and as I did, Evan legged it. He was gone before they had a chance to speak to him. So I was caught with a car full of knockoff gear.

'They linked me to the robbery through finding my car appearing on CCTV nearby. I could clearly be seen as the driver. I was arrested, charged, and then sent to prison.'

'Was that your first offence?'

I nod. 'It was humiliating and degrading, and I never want to go there again.'

'What about Evan? How long did he go to prison for?'

'He didn't do any time.'

Emma seems confused.

'I refused to give his name. I thought he'd be grateful to me, but it was then I realised that he only cared about himself. He never came to visit me when I was inside. Not one time.' I clench my hand into a fist and resist the urge to punch the palm of the other. 'I did three months, and when I was let out, I went home, and I couldn't get my key to fit. The locks had been changed. I banged on the door, and guess who answered? Louise. She just smirked at me, said I wasn't welcome there anymore, and then told me about the baby they were expecting.

'We started mouthing off at each other, and Evan finally came to the door. He wouldn't let me in either. He said our marriage was over and then he handed me two black bin liners full of my belongings and shut the door in my face. I had nowhere to live, again.'

'Did you come back to Stoke?'

'No, I had an appointment arranged with a probation officer, so she sorted out a hostel for me to stay in. I'd opened myself a bank account when I first got to Manchester and put six hundred pounds in it. I never touched it so, once I'd ordered a new debit card, I had a bit of cash to get me by. The hostel was horrible. I had to share a room with two other women, but I needed a roof over my head. Then I found myself a live-in job at a hotel. I'm good at cleaning up other people's mess.'

'That must have been tough to go through.'

I nod. 'I filed for divorce, which, surprise, surprise, Evan didn't contest, and I've never really trusted anyone else since. I've had a few relationships, but they've always ended up out of control or miserable.' I picture Tom. What will he think of me if he ever finds out?

While Emma makes coffee, I take a moment to reflect. I have mostly carried the secrecy of my prison sentence around with me since my release. It won't solve any of my problems, but it's such a relief to get it all off my chest.

'You're such a survivor, Clara,' Emma tells me. 'Most people would have crumbled if that had happened to them. The betrayal, the prison sentence, the rejection from Evan. You took everything in your stride.'

'I didn't really have a choice.'

Once the session has finished, I go home. Before going up to my flat, I knock to see if Shelley is back. They've released her from hospital now everything has been checked over. Her last message says that Wayne hasn't been arrested yet and she's going to stay with her parents for a few days. She's waiting for her brother to pick her up.

When she opens the door, Shelley grimaces as she tries to smile. Her eyes are less swollen, there are butterfly stitches on her cut, and the bruising around her neck has come out immensely. A bandage covers her right wrist, two fingers taped together on her hand.

My face drops. 'Oh, Shelley, what has he done to you?'

'A right proper job, that's what.'

We hug each other before going through to the living room. I sit next to Shelley on the settee.

'Still nothing from the police?' I ask.

'No. They visited the flat, but his brother says he hasn't seen him. The shift officers are patrolling the area, searching for his car. They say it's just a matter of time.'

'When is your brother coming to collect you?'

'After he's finished work, an hour or so now. I doubt Wayne will turn up here again, but you never know with him.'

'Well, I'm pleased I won't have to worry about you in here on your own. I was going to suggest I sleep on your sofa.'

Shelley smiles, and then winces. 'Thanks. It means a lot to have a friend like you.'

My heart sinks. I'd been hoping to sort Wayne out so that he didn't attack Shelley ever again. But I didn't feel like following him the other night as planned. I told myself I'd do it the next day instead. That day never came.

Yet, how could I have known Wayne would react so violently when he next saw Shelley?

'This is why I didn't give you a spare key to my flat,' I tell her. 'I couldn't be sure he wouldn't use it to let himself in when I wasn't here.' I lower my eyes momentarily. 'I'm so sorry if any of this is my fault.'

'What do you mean?'

'Wayne didn't like me interfering. I might have made him worse.'

'This isn't anything to do with you. Wayne has always blown hot and cold. The slightest thing sets him off. He accused me of going through the stuff in the spare room. As if I'd touch any of that.'

I balk inwardly. Was this my doing after all? Has he found out the watch is missing? I can't ask her outright even though I want to.

'I do feel responsible,' I say. 'Maybe I wound him up.'

'Clara! I won't have you feeling that way. You *rescued* me. You have nothing to be sorry for. I just hope it wasn't too bad for you. I bet it brought back a lot of memories.'

Far too many. I shake my head, though. 'It's okay, especially because I was able to stop him.'

'I don't know what would have happened if you hadn't let yourself in when you did.' Shelley's hand goes to her neck, and her eyes mist over at the thought.

Her phone rings. It's the police. I listen intently while I wait for her to finish.

Shelley disconnects the call and sighs. 'They haven't found him yet.'

'There can't be many places he can hide.'

'He won't tell anyone what he's done so he'll have a few friends he can call on, I suppose.'

'Do you know any of them?'

'No, more's the pity.'

'Perhaps the police might know some of his associates' addresses from their records.'

'I hope so. At least they keep me informed.'

I give her a hug. 'You'll let me know the minute you hear?'

'I will.'

Later that evening, I decide to have a wander round. I pull my hood up as it's raining, but I don't really care about getting wet. If Shelley's right and Wayne is acting as if nothing has happened, he might be in the pub I followed him to the other night. If so, I can ring the police and let them know.

Seeing Shelley beaten and bruised reminds me so much of my mum after one of my dad's attacks. My parents are never far from my mind when incidences like this happen. It doesn't take much to bring it all hurtling towards me. And Shelley has become like a sister to me. I care about what happens to her.

But Emma was right that morning. I have survived so much that I should be able to get through this, too.

I have no interest in watching my usual families. I just want to find Wayne. There are no lights on in his brother's flat, so I have a quick scan through the windows in the pub to see if I can spot him. But he doesn't seem to be there either.

He can't lie low for ever. He'll be arrested soon, and then hopefully with the stolen goods the police have, he'll be sent down again. Before he can do any further damage. Or I can do some to him.

CHAPTER FORTY-FIVE

I'm exhausted when I go into work the next morning. I've kept in touch with Shelley via messages, but Wayne hasn't been caught yet.

I sit down at my desk, glancing over at Sam's office to see his door is closed. There are two women in with him who I don't recognise.

'Where's Tess today?' I ask when I see her chair is empty.

'She's not coming here again,' Lisa says. 'Before she left yesterday, she said she was making a complaint about Sam. For inappropriate conduct. Did she mention that to you?'

'Yes. I was the one who told her to complain. The guy is a leech.'

'Didn't he try it on with you?' Fran joins in, excitement all over her face at the thought of something going on. 'You seemed pretty close a few weeks back.'

'You never said.' Lisa's tone is accusatory.

I ignore her remark but speak to them both. 'He

was all talk in the end. Especially after I'd given him a kick in the balls.'

Fran and Lisa both gasp.

'I'm joking!' I laugh, hoping to throw them off the scent. 'Although I wish it was true. I don't like Sam, never have, so he deserves what he gets. Is that who's in his office with him?' I feign casual interest at the two women who are sitting with him.

'Yes. They're from HR,' Fran remarks. 'Maybe she's already put in a complaint.'

It isn't long before we find out. The door to Sam's office opens, and all heads go down as if we're all busy.

'Clara, could I have a word, please?' Sam says.

I get up slowly, my skin reddening as I feel every eye on me. But at least it'll be good to get my side of things out in the open.

Sam holds the door for me, and I go inside. He points to a seat, and I sit opposite the three of them. What's going on? *Is* this something to do with Tess making a complaint? Or has Sam told them about my behaviour?

'Clara, this is Manda Thompson and Sharon Bignall from our head office HR department,' Sam tells me.

There isn't a faint smile between them. The older one is hunched forward, with grey-blonde hair tied back in a ponytail and squinty blue eyes behind glasses. The younger woman wears a suit that's far too tight, overemphasised makeup, and a look of disinterest at my arrival. I notice her surreptitiously glancing at Sam. Surely not another one of his groupies.

'They're here today,' Sam goes on, 'because it's come to our attention that you've been doing some work outside the office, claiming it was on behalf of Stoke Helps Out.'

'I don't know what you mean.' My voice comes out croaky, so I clear my throat.

'Mrs Nellie Wootton. Mr Graham Handy.' Sam waves his hand in a circle. 'Need I go on?'

Apprehension rushes through me, making me light-headed. They've found out. I'm not able to refute it.

'I was helping, that's all,' I reply. 'I did it in my own time and I was well behaved in clients' homes.'

'That doesn't make it right,' Sharon speaks up.

I turn to her. 'Have you had any complaints?'

'No,' she admits. 'But you can't swan around impersonating one of our officers.'

'I can't get DRB clearance, but I wanted to offer support. If anything, I made light of the work that Fran wasn't doing and took it upon myself to help *her*.'

'Blaming someone else for your misdemeanours is appalling, Clara,' Sharon says.

'I didn't steal anything, if that's what you're inferring.'

Sharon holds out her hand. 'I need your ID pass.'

I glare at her, then remove my lanyard and slap it into her open palm.

'I'll need your password so we can delete anything you've been working on,' Manda speaks for the first time. 'I must say, I'm extremely disappointed in you, and distraught that you would even do such a thing. We at Stoke Helps Out pride ourselves on integrity and trust.'

'I was *trying* to help,' I protest.

'You have brought the organisation into disrepute

through your actions. Luckily, the matter might not go any further, so I don't think we'll be pressing charges.'

'Charges?' I balk.

'You were trespassing. Your role was office-based purposely, and you were not to work in the community alone, as well you knew. Who else have you been... visiting?'

I say nothing. Let them find out for themselves. I've done no harm.

'We're still checking our records and will be contacting anyone you've been dealing with. In the meantime, your contract will be terminated immediately.' Sharon shakes her head now as if she can't believe what's happened. 'Sam, can you go with Clara to make sure she empties her desk of her belongings and then stay with her until she leaves the premises?'

Sam nods, standing up.

I sit still for a moment, stunned and unable to work out what to do for the best. I can stay and plead my case, but they won't listen. They've come to the assumption that once a criminal, always a criminal.

I think of telling them about Sam's behaviour but realise it won't be wise. Shouted out in the heat of the moment, and after what they've found out, it would look bad, even though I do have photographic evidence. But not here, not now. There's nothing for it but to leave with my head held high before the rumour mill gathers momentum. I stand, pulling up my shoulders, and return to my desk.

A deathly silence falls across the room as, again, everyone stops to watch what's going on. I decide not to make a fuss. They'll be expecting it, so I won't give them the satisfaction. Instead, I collect what items are mine – a used mug I'm not leaving behind, the Snoopy diary I treated myself to at Christmas, a cardigan off the back of my chair. Is this all I have to take?

Sam shows me out, not saying a word until we're at the exit downstairs. Then, of course he has to get in a parting shot.

'I must admit, I didn't have you down as a con artist.' His lip curls up in derision. 'I'm shocked at your level of deceit.'

'Pot, kettle, and black come to mind,' I throw back at him.

He sniggers. 'Boy, am I glad to see the back of you.'

'Don't be too sure about that. Your time will come.'

I let the door swing shut in his face and throw him the finger before leaving. At least I've got in the last word.

I drive away from the office and park outside a nearby supermarket to gather my thoughts.

'Fuck, fuck, fuck!' I bang my fist on the steering wheel. How can this happen now, just when everything is going well? It's the first time I've kept out of trouble for so long.

I'm not sure whether to go back to Cedric House. I can't be sure who they will have been in contact with. Roberta may have been part of the initial investigation. If not, I have a bit of leeway and could, perhaps, bag up my things and leave quickly without having to face anyone. But then again, no one at Stoke Helps Out knows I'm living in Cedric House, so I could stay there until I figure out what to do next.

No, I'll have to go to Wedgwood Street. At least there I can pretend nothing has happened. I can think that neither Tom, nor Shelley, possibly not even Roberta, will find out what I've been up to.

If only I could keep it that way.

It's too late. I've ruined everything. I'll have to leave as soon as I can. There isn't any point staying now. No one will want to know me once they find out what I've done. Despite wanting to help, I've royally fucked up again.

Because it's only now, when it will all be taken away from me, that I register how much I want the chance to be with Tom, and Isla.

How much I enjoy living in Cedric House, despite the problems with Wayne.

How my chance at happiness has been taken away again.

CHAPTER FORTY-SIX

Tom was surprised to see Roberta in the hall as he got home with Isla that afternoon.

'Hi, Roberta,' Isla said. 'We've been studying World War Two today. Were you alive then? Can you tell me about it?'

Tom groaned. 'You can't ask questions like that, Isles. It's quite rude to assume someone's age.' He winked at Roberta, who was usually quite forgiving about Isla's slip-ups. But when she didn't smile, he stopped. 'Are you okay?'

'No, I...' Roberta stalled. 'Could you spare me a minute to change a lightbulb, please? It's in the bedroom, and I can't get to it easily.'

'Yes, of course.' Tom opened his front door to let Isla in. 'I won't be long, duck.'

Tom jogged upstairs and followed Roberta into her flat. It still surprised him how much better it was looking since Clara had helped with the clearance, how homely.

Roberta sat down and patted the settee next to her. 'I have something I think you ought to know.'

'What is it?'

'I've seen how fond of Clara you've grown, so this is going to come as a shock. I had a call from the charity this morning, the one who employed her to come out and visit.'

'Stoke Helps Out?'

Roberta nodded. 'Clara isn't a support worker there. She's been hired as an administration assistant. She isn't supposed to be meeting clients outside of the office.'

'Why not?'

Roberta wrung her hands. 'Because she's been to prison.'

Tom's blood ran cold. That couldn't be right. Clara would have told him, and there was no way he'd let her near Isla if she could be a danger to her.

'Did they say what she'd done?'

'No, because of the Data Protection Act. I'm not sure they should have told me in the first instance as they backtracked quickly afterwards.'

'That's ridiculous. She's been in your house – in my flat – and we don't know what she's done before that?' He got out his phone and fired a quick message to Clara, asking where she was. 'Have you spoken to her about it?'

'No. I... I'm not sure how I should feel because she's been lying to us, and yet, I quite like her. I can see she's had a troubled past, but she's obviously been trying to get over that.'

'But we don't know anything about her!'

'It can't be much. She comes across as loyal and friendly.'

'It's a side she's showing us.' Tom felt duped. Why hadn't she said anything to him? They'd spoken about their pasts. Was any of what she'd told him true? He ran a hand through his hair.

'Tell me what you know about her,' he said.

'She was sharing a flat with a girl who had moved in her boyfriend, and she felt like a gooseberry so asked if she could rent number four.'

'Did she know it was empty before she came?'

Roberta paused, then shook her head. 'No, she couldn't have. Only people in here knew that.'

'Did she tell you what she did before she came back to Stoke? Where she worked before?'

'No.'

'Did she mention family, friends? Her husband?'

'Husband?' Roberta frowned. 'She told me she'd never married.'

'She's divorced.'

'Perhaps she doesn't like to talk about it, then.'

'It makes me wonder if anything we know about her is true.' Tom glanced at his phone. No new messages. 'I must see her. I need to find out what's going on.'

They sat in silence while he called her. But there was no reply.

'Is she here, do you know?' Tom asked. 'In her flat?'

'I haven't been across. I wanted to wait for you, to see if we should visit together.'

'Do you have a key if she isn't there?'

'Yes, but I'm not using it yet. It wouldn't be right.'

'She might be inside.'

'Then she'll answer the door and tell us what happened.'

Tom slapped his hand down on the cushion. 'You think what she's done is okay?'

'Of course not, but I believe everyone has the right to explain their actions. When I've heard Clara's side of things, then I'll decide what to do next. Because if she has been untrustworthy, then she can't stay here regardless. And even then, there are tenancy laws I must abide by.'

Together they went to flat four. Tom knocked on the door, but there was no answer and no noise from inside. He knocked again.

'Clara, it's Tom, and Roberta. We need to talk to you.'

Still no answer. Exasperated, Tom sent another message.

'You'll let me know if you reach her?' Roberta asked.

Tom nodded. He watched as Roberta went back to her flat and then he went down to Isla.

All through the evening, Tom rang Clara, but the calls remained unanswered. After putting Isla to bed, he paced the living room, glancing out of the window as if by magic Clara would appear. He wasn't sure if she was in and not answering the door, or if the flat was empty. But he needed to see her.

He had to find out why she'd befriended people and lied about her background. Worse, why had she been to prison? He struggled to imagine the woman he cared deeply about locked up in a cell.

And how awful would it have to be before he refused to let her near his daughter? If it was a minor offence, perhaps something she did when she was younger, then it would depend on what it was. But until then his mind was imagining all sorts. Hell, she could be a killer for all he knew.

He flopped down on the settee, adrenaline pumping. It was stupid to think that. Clara wasn't capable of anything so violent. Was she?

Sure, she threw a mean punch, but even that was down to the need to protect herself, or him in the one instance. After what had happened to her parents, he couldn't blame her for that. There were some people who would always take advantage of others. It was better to be prepared.

At half past nine, he checked on Isla, to see she was asleep. Then, leaving the front door on the latch, he went upstairs to try one last time. Outside Clara's door, he raised his hand to knock and hesitated.

Was he sure he wanted to know?

What if it was so bad that there was no coming back from it? Tom didn't want to think about that because Clara had brought something fun to his life again. After Sasha died, he wasn't sure there would be anyone else for him. What would life be without Clara?

He went back downstairs. If it was going to be distressing, he couldn't deal with it now.

CHAPTER FORTY-SEVEN

Feeling out of sorts, the next day I book an extra session with Emma. But now, skittish before I've sat down, I'm not sure it's a good idea. Yet somehow the chats with Emma seem to be the only way I can let out my feelings.

I'm torn. Should I own up and tell Emma what has happened, or is it better to keep quiet about it and talk about things in general? I've grown used to being with her and don't want her to think ill of me. Maybe what I've done is too much to share.

But, even though I have no wages coming in, so perhaps it isn't wise to spend Nan's money on therapy, I have to speak to someone about it, and Emma hasn't been put off when I mentioned my prison stay during my last session.

So I tell her.

We chat in general about my reasons, and then Emma suggests something totally weird.

'Why don't you write a letter to yourself, Clara?'

I frown. 'What do you mean?'

'I think it might be a good exercise for forgiveness. You're so hard on yourself.'

'I deserve to be. I've made a mess of everything.'

'Not all of it. You think you've done wrong by young Clara and yet, from where I'm sitting, it's quite the opposite. You've kept your inner child as safe as possible.'

'I got her into some difficult situations.'

'And you got her out of them.'

'But I've deceived people I care about!'

'Why do you think that is?'

I take a moment to think what to say next. Growing up as I have, lying and thieving was part of my life. It was Derek who turned me into a pickpocket, but it isn't all down to him.

'I lied, I robbed, and I fought as a way to look after myself,' I tell Emma. 'Before I left home, I stole three thousand pounds to keep me going. Of course I denied it when my nan asked about it. I used to tell myself it was my compensation, for what Derek put me through, but really, I didn't want to be there anyway. I wanted a life away from the crap and everything else I hated.'

'May I ask where you got the money from?'

'There was always cash in the house, and when I found out where it was kept, I'd steal a bit here and there, not enough for him to notice. Derek used to run illegal fights, lots of bets going on. I found the old ledger when I was clearing out the sideboard.'

'What kind of illegal fights?'

'Fist fighting. It could get quite bloody at times, nasty stuff. The harder the men fought, the more money the winner got. Derek taught me how to pick pockets while I was there, one of the only decent things he showed me because it came in handy when I was older.'

I shudder as I recall what I'd had to do.

'The worst was cleaning up afterwards. I had to sweep away the sawdust. There would be blood mixed in with it. It was disgusting. I was thirteen the first time I had to do it, and it made me throw up.'

We take a short break, giving me time to recover from the anguish the session is causing. My resentment is building up again. Talking about it doesn't seem to be helping me this week. It's making me even angrier.

Emma starts again when I'm ready. 'Why did you feel the need to lie to everyone in Cedric House?'

'I didn't want anyone knowing my background and what I'd done before I moved in,' I reply. 'It would have meant me not getting the flat if I'd told Roberta I'd been to prison. Can you imagine how she'll feel now, when she learns the truth about me? I've been in her home, through her belongings when we cleared out the rubbish. I bet she'll think I stole things to sell on.' I think about the watch I hid from Wayne. I make a fist and punch the arm of the chair.

'It's good to be angry, Clara.' Emma sits forward, resting her elbows on her knees. 'What's really eating at you?'

A tear falls from my eye, and I wipe at it furiously as more follow. 'Everyone will immediately think I'm a thief when they hear what I went to prison for.'

'Has anyone accused you of stealing?'

'No, and I haven't taken anything, but they'll assume I did it for that reason. To see what I could pilfer, and not to help people out.'

'You can't be sure that everyone is thinking that about you.'

'Mud sticks.'

'But your new friends don't know that about your past, so why would you assume they would think that?'

'They'll find out. I... maybe I know I might be tempted to steal.'

'Have you?'

I think back to Nellie, always trying to give me money as I was leaving. That shows progress, I suppose.

'No, I haven't. But if I want to change completely, I have to be the one to instigate it.' I sit forward abruptly. 'I don't think these sessions are helping me anymore. I don't need you telling me how it is. I *know* how it is. I've lived it, remember, and I live it every day inside my head.'

'Which is why you're here right now. Trying to make sense of things.'

I pause. 'I'm sorry. That was rude.' I stand up quickly, knowing my anger is yet again getting the better of me. 'I have to go.'

Emma doesn't try to stop me, but she does speak as I get to the door.

'Try writing that letter, Clara, or at least get your thoughts down on paper. That might help you more than you think. See you next week.'

I leave the room without another word. I storm out into the rainy day that matches my mood, annoyed with

Emma now. What good will writing things down do? Because I can never tell anyone everything that's happened.

Nor about the night that someone nearly lost their life because of me.

CHAPTER FORTY-EIGHT

After my session with Emma, I go straight to Wedgwood Street. I can't stop the memories flying at me, and it's difficult to shut them out. In my old bedroom, I get into bed and cover my head with the duvet.

Maybe I'll take Emma's advice later and write things down, but I'm not calm enough right now. Because something else is going round and round my head. It's a memory I haven't thought about in a long time because I've blocked it out with shame. It was my fault someone got badly hurt.

It all started with Derek. Everything started with him.

After the night he struck my nan, and then told me I'd have to go to work with him, I'd been curious to find out what he wanted me to do. So when he knocked on my bedroom door and then came in after tea, I was ready. But he surprised me by sitting on my bed.

'Come here a minute, I want to talk to you,' he'd said.

I did as I was told.

'You remember what I said last night, about you coming to work with me?'

'At the factory?'

Derek was a labourer on an industrial site a few streets away.

'Not quite.' He reached his hand over to me, and I froze when he wiped his hand across my forehead. 'You're growing up into a pretty thing. I know men who'd like to be, how shall I say, friendly with you, so you need to be careful. But I think you're old enough now to earn your keep.'

'What will I have to do?' I whisper.

'I'll show you tonight, and then I expect you'll be helping a couple of times a month. Get your coat. We're going in five minutes.'

I left with Derek shortly afterwards.

'Where are we going?' I asked, running along the path after him.

'You'll see when you get there.'

It was dark and freezing cold, so I was glad we could go in the car. But Derek walked past it.

'Come on, keep up,' he muttered.

'How long will it take?'

'A few minutes.'

'How far is it?'

He stopped and I almost bumped into him. 'Look, less of the questions. Just be quiet.'

I folded my arms, against the cold rather than being insubordinate. It took ten minutes of me running to keep up with his long strides before Derek turned off a street and went along a dirt track. Almost immediately, I lost my footing on the uneven surface.

'Watch where you're going,' he snapped, stopping me from falling by putting out a hand. 'They're bloody big potholes along here. Don't turn your ankle.'

I glanced at the ground but couldn't see much. Then I stepped into a puddle and gave out a yelp.

'Stop being a baby. We don't have far to go now.'

Lights came from behind them, and they moved to one side to let a van go past. The area opened up then, to rows of garages. We went through the middle of them and down another dark path. For a moment, I was petrified and then a building I recognised came into view.

'Are we going to Holdcroft's Farm?' I queried.

'Yes, the barn on the bottom field.'

'It would have been quicker to go the front way.'

'Too many people about.'

'Why?'

Derek sighed. 'Just shut up, will you!'

I muttered quietly. I didn't like Derek when he was mean. I was only asking because I didn't know.

A minute later, and we were at the barn. There were lots of men hanging around outside it. Derek unlocked a padlock and pulled the doors open, and they all followed him inside.

I stayed where I was, unsure whether to make a run for it now and risk a good hiding. But Derek noticed and came back for me. He grabbed me roughly by the arm and took me inside.

'Marian!' Derek shouted and waved to a woman as old as my nan in the back of the barn.

She came over to him, all of a dither.

'Hello, Derek love, and who is this sweet one? Is this your granddaughter? She's a bit young, isn't she?'

'You said you wanted out, and Jean will be helping her when you're not around. Besides, it's about time she earned her keep.'

'Yes, but—'

He cut her off with a stern glare. Then he turned to me.

'I'll sit you with Marian, and she'll show you what to do. The next time you'll be doing it on your own, so make sure you listen carefully to everything she says. And if you see any police, you come straight to me.'

I nodded, almost feeling otherworldly. Derek shouted to another man in the distance. I saw a gap open in the middle of the floor and a young boy throwing sawdust on it. What were these men here to do?

Fear coursed through me. I was thirteen and knew all about young girls and boys being messed with by adults. Derek wouldn't do that to me, would he? I burst into tears.

'Oh, do stop your blithering.' Marian pulled me by the arm. 'You're not going to be in any danger. As long as you do as you're told, you'll be fine.'

Marian led me back to the front entrance, where there was a small table and two chairs, a silver cash box, and a book of raffle tickets. A queue of men waited by the side of it.

Marian took a seat and patted the other one. 'Sit

down next to me and watch what I do. It's simple really. It's five pounds to get in, and you give them a ticket. Any who say they want to bet, you send to your grand-dad. Is that clear?'

'Yes,' I said, even though I didn't really understand.

'And if you see the police, I want you to run like hell. Do you hear?'

'Derek told me to find him.'

'Your *granddad* will have enough on his plate.'

'Come on, Marian,' a man in the queue cried. 'The first fight will be over before we've got in at this rate.'

'Keep your hair on, Mickey Sullivan,' Marian quipped. 'Oh, silly me. You don't have any, do you?'

When laughter and light-hearted banter started up, I relaxed a little. If all I had to do was sit here, then it was better than what I'd anticipated. It wouldn't take me long to learn what to do, and I could see the advantages to it already. A ticket going amiss might earn me a fiver for myself.

I'd been left to man the door alone after two sessions with Marian. I hadn't minded that so much. The men were respectful, and no one bothered me. But as I grew older, once the fighting began, Derek made me find opportunities to steal money from elsewhere, which was a challenge each time but risky, too. Of course it was only a matter of time before I was caught.

I'd stood behind the man while the first fight got going. There was a young lad in the ring, Phil Dwyer. He was sixteen, a few months older than me. I hated watching the fights but saw that Phil was giving as good as he got and seemed to be on a winning streak.

The man egged him on, and when he raised a fist and cheered, I slipped my hand into his pocket. I had his wallet when he suddenly grabbed me.

'What the fuck are you up to?'

'Get off me,' I shrieked, hoping someone might hear and come to help.

But the man dragged me out of the barn and around to the side. Everyone was too busy watching the end of the fight to notice.

'Give it back to me,' he said.

'Don't know what you're talking about.'

'My wallet. You pilfered it.'

'No, I didn't.' I held up my hand so he could see it was empty. Of course, I'd had the sense to drop it when he'd caught me.

'You little bitch,' he seethed. He came close to me.

I could smell his stale breath and pulled a face, turning my head to the side.

'There was two hundred quid in that wallet, and I know some other thief will have found it by now, so you'll have to pay it back.'

'Where am I going to get that kind of money from?' I moaned. 'I'm fifteen.'

'You can steal it from your granddad.'

'I don't think so.'

'Then you'll have to pay in another way.'

He tried to kiss me, but I squirmed, slapping at him. He grabbed for my wrists, so I bunched my hands in fists ready to strike out.

'Hey, leave her alone,' a voice said from behind me.

It was Phil Dwyer. Sweat was oozing out of him, his chest still bare after the fight, and he had a black eye and a cut on his nose.

'Thought *you* were in the ring,' the man said.

'I've won my match. Thought *I'd* see what you were up to with Clara.'

I beamed. He knew my name.

'Mind your own business.'

The man threw a punch. Phil blocked it, hitting him in the mouth. But it wasn't long before the older man got the advantage of the younger. While they grappled with each other, I took the opportunity to run.

When I got up the next morning, I heard Phil had been beaten so badly Derek had to drive him home. His parents called for an ambulance. The police had been kept out of it so far.

Derek blamed me. 'You nearly ruined everything, you silly cow.'

'He attacked me when I was working for you,' I told him. 'But don't worry, I won't be doing it anymore.'

'You'll do as you're told.'

'You can't make me.'

Derek sliced his hand across my face. I dropped to my knees with the force, my ears ringing.

'You'll do as I say or else you can pack your bags and leave right now.'

Despite the wrath of Derek, I refused to take part in anything else. He'd threatened to chuck me out on the streets several times, but I stood up for myself when he hit me. I said I'd tell all if he made me leave.

It was a good showdown at the time. But it's all my life has been about. Fighting for survival.

And I am so tired of it.

CHAPTER FORTY-NINE

I choose a time when I think Cedric House is likely to be empty of its residents. I know Tom goes into his office most mornings. It's him I want to avoid really. Shelley will probably still be staying with her brother. I hope Roberta doesn't come to her door, but if she does, I'll have to apologise and take her wrath if she's found out the truth.

I take a deep breath and let myself into the hallway, tiptoeing as quietly as I can up the stairs. Inside the flat, I gather my things. Most of it will have to stay behind, but I need my clothes and shoes, my notebook, letters from my nan, and the photo of my mum. There's a little food left over in the fridge, so I bag it up to take down to the bin.

Before I leave, I stand in the middle of the room, trying not to cry. I've been my happiest here, something I hadn't anticipated. But it's too late to dwell on what could have been now. I need to hurry.

A noise downstairs makes me stop. I go over to the spyhole in the door and see Roberta climbing the stairs. She pauses on the landing and looks at my door. For a second, I think she's going to head my way, but with a sorry shake of her head she lets herself into flat three.

There's no time to take all my belongings now, so I grab the bag with my personal stuff inside it and sneak out. I don't have the energy to talk to Roberta, nor do I want to see the disappointment on her face as I've lied to her.

After being unable to sleep, I finally doze in the early hours. I wake at half past eight to the sound of my phone ringing. I reach for it on the floor beside me, hoping it isn't Tom again. I'm not ready to speak to him yet, knowing that things will be over between us. I don't think I'll ever be ready for that.

The call is from Andy.

'Hey, Clara. Just checking in as I missed you last night. Is everything okay?'

I pinch the bridge of my nose. I'd forgotten about the anger management meeting. Would I have gone, though? I very much doubted I could have coped with it, even if it might have been to my benefit.

'Clara, are you there?' Andy goes on.

'Yes.' My voice is hoarse after crying myself to sleep.

'What's wrong?'

'I'm fine.'

'No, you're not. What's happened?'

Whether it's the concern in his voice or the fact

that I have someone to talk to, or someone who cares about me, I don't know. I break down.

'I'm in such a mess.'

'What kind of a mess?'

'One I can't get out of.'

There's silence down the line, then he speaks again.

'You're not hurt, are you?'

'No.'

'Have you hurt someone, then?'

I say nothing.

'Where are you?'

'Home.' My laughter sounds insane even to me. 'Totally the wrong word for it.'

'Clara, I'm worried about you. Give me your address.'

'I can't.'

'Why not?'

'It's too... too...'

'Too what? You're not making sense.'

Too hideous for anyone to see. And too raw for me to see anyone after what I've done. But I need to talk to someone, and right now, Andy is offering to help. A few months earlier, I would never have asked anyone for it. Now I know I have to.

'Andy... will you come?'

'I'll be right there. Text me your address.'

'You promise not to judge?'

'As if I'd do that.'

I disconnect the call and send Andy my details before I can change my mind. I'm not sure how long he'll be so, still in yesterday's clothes, I brush my teeth and wash my face.

I stare at myself in the mirror, barely recognising the person in front of me. I'm pale, eyes dark but puffy from crying. Eyes that have seen too much. Lips that can't raise a smile.

I will have to do.

I go downstairs to wait for Andy. He arrives within ten minutes and parks outside. I open the front door and see him walking towards me, his eyes widening.

'Christ, Clara, what's happened?' He takes me in his arms and closes the door behind us.

'I... I... fucked up again,' I say between gulps of air.

Andy guides me into the living room and sits me down on the settee.

I notice his eyes scanning the room as if seeing me for the first time. 'It's why I'm selling it,' I say.

'What do you mean?'

'I can see your disgust.'

'You're mistaken.' He shakes his head. 'It takes me back to my childhood. I had a shit home like this, too, remember.'

I gaze down at the carpet. Of all people, I shouldn't be so quick to judge. Andy is my friend, and he's offering to help. I should accept it for once without sniping.

He makes hot drinks for us, and slowly, painfully, I tell him what's happened.

'Shit, that is a mess,' Andy concurs when I've finished.

I glare at him pointedly. But I see he's teasing, a faint smile on his lips.

'Why did you lie about it, though?' He shakes his head. 'At work, I mean? I don't understand.'

'With my record, I couldn't get cleared to do anything outside the office. I was only working there part-time, twenty hours a week. So I went to visit clients in my own time.'

'Wait, you didn't get paid?' Andy looks on in amazement.

'No. I had so much time on my hands when my nan died and I had to wait to sell the house, so I thought if I helped other people while I was here, I... I might fix myself, too.' I shrug slightly. 'I can't believe how pathetic that sounds now.'

'It doesn't. I know I wouldn't work for nothing. How did you get by, then?'

'My nan left me some money, so I'm using that.' I don't say how Jean came about it. That would have been a step too far, to let him know everything.

'So what are you going to do about it?' Andy asks next.

'There's nothing I can do. They'll all hate me when they find out, if they don't know already. Tom has been ringing me, but I haven't had the courage to speak to him. I suppose I'll go back to Manchester once this house is sold.'

'Do they know you were seeing clients in your own time?'

'No, but they'll know I've been to prison, and they won't want me around.'

'You went to prison years ago.'

'The record is forever, you know that.'

'No, that's not what this is all about. What's really wrong, underneath all this? Because something is hurting you, and I don't think you'll be able to let go until you share it with someone.'

'That's the thing, Andy,' I cry. 'I don't *know* what's hurting me. I've been a bitch for most of my life, but nothing bad has happened to me physically. I wasn't raped, or sexually abused as a child. I wasn't locked in a room or left alone to starve. I wasn't made to service men when I was too young to know better. I wasn't—'

'You *were* abused, Clara. You were starved of love. People will never realise what an affect it has on a child if it hasn't happened to them. I do, so listen to me. Your parents and your grandparents had a duty of care to you, and they failed. It's them who messed up, not you.'

I haven't told Andy much about my past, the reason why I left my grandparents when I was seventeen. But I have confided lots of things about my childhood to him.

Maybe he's right. I hadn't been looked after well, despite my nan's best intentions. Before that, as a small child I grew up in a house where there was a little love, but feeling like I wasn't wanted. It must have played on my mind, influencing my choices all those years ago.

And yet I could have changed when I got to Manchester. If my nan hadn't lied to me, I would have stayed in Stoke, or moved on in my own time.

Should I get in touch with Tom and tell him the reasons behind me being the way I am? About what I thought I'd done, and then found out I hadn't? Will it explain things enough for him to forgive me?

I'm not sure I'll be able to find the words.

'Will you do me a favour?' I ask Andy, when he's getting ready to leave. 'Will you fetch the few things I have at Cedric House, please? They're all bagged up. I don't think I can face anyone yet, especially Roberta, the woman I helped. She'll be so shocked at what I did.'

'Sure. Would you like me to do it today?'

I nod, tears spilling from my eyes again. It isn't that I can't face seeing anyone. It's because I've been so happy in flat four. It's become home to me already. Something I haven't realised until it is too late.

CHAPTER FIFTY

At Cedric House, Tom was sitting facing the front window. He hadn't been able to concentrate on work at all, constantly checking his phone to see if Clara had responded to any of his messages.

He spotted a man coming down the path towards the front door. No one buzzed him in, but Tom didn't see him leave either. Doing his neighbourly duties, he went out for a nosy.

There was no one in the hallway, so he hung around. Eventually the man reappeared, from the direction of Clara's flat. He was carrying several black bin bags. Tom was about to say something when the man addressed him.

'It's Tom, isn't it?'

Tom nodded, startled to hear the man knew his name. He still didn't recognise him.

'I'm Andy, a friend of Clara's. She's asked me to fetch her belongings as she doesn't think she'll be welcome here anymore.'

'Ah, she's told you what happened.' Tom was annoyed Clara had spoken to him first. 'I haven't seen her for two nights. I've been calling, but she hasn't picked up. Is she okay?'

'No, mate, she's not. She's in bits, the worst I've ever seen her.'

'Can I ask where you know her from?'

Andy stepped down, coming level with him. 'I'm not sure that's my place to say, but I've known her about four months, and I think she's sound. She's had a rough time of things lately. Maybe you should talk to her, face to face. You'd be surprised to find out what she's really been doing, and why. It would all make sense to you then.'

'I don't know where she's staying.'

'At her grandparents' house. It's been sold, so she'll be off when everything is sorted. That's if you don't talk her out of it first.'

'What?' Tom balked. 'I didn't even know she had a house to sell.'

'She's been hiding things from you, I admit. It's because of her upbringing. She's ashamed and wants to be happy. But she can't because she says she's let *you* down.'

'She has.'

'That's not fair.' Andy walked a few steps away but stopped. 'She's been judged as a nobody for most of her life, and it will break her if she knows you're thinking that, too.'

Tom bowed his head for a moment, ashamed he'd jumped to conclusions. Clara wasn't a nobody to him. But she had lied.

'Do you know what she went through as a child?' Andy asked.

'About her parents? Yes.'

'Anything else?'

'No.'

'That's half her story, but you haven't lived through it like she did regardless. Like *I* did.' He prodded himself in the chest. 'Have you ever been punched so hard by your dad that you've ended up with broken ribs? Had cigarettes put out on you, just for the fun of it? Thought when you're older that the only way to show someone you love them is to hurt them? To get attention by a punch or a slap?' He huffed. 'I bet you were brought up with two loving parents who stayed together, and you had a great upbringing.'

Tom said nothing because Andy was right.

'The way me and Clara are?' Andy continued. 'It's what people can grow into without love as a child. All I'm asking is that you go and talk to her. She's hurting and she needs to explain what's been going on. And you need to listen. She's been happy since meeting you. I'd go so far as to say that she loves you.'

Tom couldn't think about that right now. He shook his head.

'I can't.'

'Why not?'

'I... I don't know.'

'Then she doesn't need you.' Andy turned to go.

Tom couldn't let him do that. 'Where can I find her?'

'Glad to see you've manned up.' Andy paused. 'She lives at twenty-five Wedgwood Street, in the middle of the Bennett Estate. And don't pull your face when you step inside it. According to Clara it was a house, not a home anyway.'

After Andy left, Tom sat on the stairs and reflected on their conversation. He had wanted Clara to come here so he could see her, talk to her. He'd go so far as to say he'd been waiting for her to show up.

He took out his phone, idly scrolling through his recent photos. Him with Clara. Clara and Isla. The three of them together. Lots with Clara on her own.

He paused at one of her, enlarged it, and stared at her face. Already it seemed so familiar to him. The shape of her button nose, the curve of her lips. Those deep-set blue eyes, and that wonderful smile that lit up her face.

He swapped it for one of Sasha, and his shoulders dropped. He missed her every day, and what could have been. The future he'd been robbed of. The mother Isla should have had for many more years. Maybe they'd have had another child. He would have liked at least one more.

Recently he'd enjoyed sharing things he would have told Sasha about with Clara. Telling her about Isla's antics at school, of how well she was doing in maths and English. Asking her opinion on an outfit to buy her. He'd thought about redecorating her bedroom, but Clara had said it was beautiful as it was.

He feared getting things wrong as Isla grew from a girl to a teen, even though they'd been a team before Clara had come on the scene. And yet, he knew Isla loved spending time with Clara.

He couldn't get her off his mind. Maybe it was time to go to her.

He'd think what to say and go that afternoon. He was too emotional right now.

CHAPTER FIFTY-ONE

Since Andy left, I spend all my time lying on the settee. I try to eat a slice of toast, but after the first bite reminds me of cardboard, I throw it away.

Mostly I stare at photos of Tom on my phone, with me, and with Isla. Flicking through them over and over, torturing myself of what could have been.

Now it's nearing lunchtime, and still my mind won't switch off. There have been no new messages from Tom since the last one at quarter to nine this morning. I imagine him getting back home after dropping Isla to school and hoping I'm the first thing he thinks about. But now there's been no further contact, it can't be true.

Last night, I was all set to write a letter to myself. I'm not sure Emma's idea will work, but I'm willing to try anything to take the emptiness away. Rid me of my fear of being alone again. And perhaps writing out how I feel might give me some kind of closure. So I root out a notepad and pen. So far, the words haven't come.

I decide to try again now.

Inside everyone is a child wanting to feel loved, protected, and safe. I'm sorry I let you down, but my head has been in a mess for the most part. It isn't much fun being me at any age, really. My dark thoughts get me down. I don't want to be like this, and yet coming back here has started it all again.

Life isn't just about love, but it helps everyone to get by, doesn't it? When you've been starved of it as a child, I think you become obsessed with it when you're older. I wanted Evan to love me, and I was prepared to put up with anything to stay with him. The relationship was over long before it ended, but I belonged to someone, and I didn't want that to be over.

And of course, there wasn't just Evan. There had been Damien, and Carl, and a brief encounter with Pablo. Each time became worse than the last.

I'm sorry I never loved you enough to find someone special and chose men who made things much worse. You deserved to be loved, to meet someone who would keep you safe.

Your parents weren't capable of that.

Your grandparents weren't capable of that.

The way Evan treated you was wrong.

But all that happened, and I'm sorry. If I was brave enough, I could have walked away earlier. Yet I liked the fighting, too. How could that be right?

What kind of sick person does that? Hits someone for a reaction? Harms themselves to feel something, let the pain take away the deep hole inside of them that they can never fill?

The baby you lost — that wasn't your fault. It might even be something to do with Evan. I should have found out for certain that I couldn't carry a child full-term. I'm going to do that now. It's the least I can do for you.

I haven't shown you how to have a good life, have I? And although I can blame others because I didn't know how to love someone unconditionally, I am to blame for being so hostile. So angry, so obsessed with everything being perfect.

I'm not sure what's going to happen next. But I will apologise now if I get it wrong. I only want what's best for you. I love you, Clara. I will protect you until the day I die.

Like I haven't protected you at all until now.

Somewhere in the middle of the words, the writing changes from a letter into a rant, and everything pours out of me.

Violence is always going to be inside me. I need to learn how to control it because I don't want to live like this. I'm not sure I'm even strong enough to continue.

Why am I such a loser?

Why does Kerry have so much, after how she was at school?

Why does Sam have what I want, and yet he dicks around trying to destroy it?

Why do I sabotage what I have, and could continue to have with Tom, because I don't feel worthy?

I deserve to be happy, too.

But I've done some nasty things.

I wanted to damage Sam's marriage because he hurt me.

I wanted to get even with Wayne because he reminds me of my dad, and Derek, and I know he's no good for Shelley.

I even ruined Shelley's friendship because I don't deserve to have her as a friend after what happened with Wayne.

I never want to be nasty to Tom.

Sometimes I know I try too hard. I daren't love someone, but I'm desperately lonely. Scared of hurting someone I love or making a fool of myself. Look at what happened with Sam. He's a prick, but stupid Clara, overreacting.

I need to do something about me. I can't live like this anymore. No matter who I try to help so that it fixes me inside, I know I can't mend myself.

Why can't I be happy? Why can't—

A knock on the front door startles me. I freeze, pen in hand, hoping that whoever it is might go away.

When there's another knock, I go to the front window. Careful not to be seen, I peep around the curtain, praying it isn't the police.

It isn't anyone in uniform. It's Tom.

I'm not sure I want to see him either, but eventually, I move through to the hall and open the door. He has his back to me at first but turns when he sees me. His hands are shoved into his pockets.

My heart skips a few beats at the sight of him. I want things to be right between us so badly.

'How did you find me?' I ask.

'I bumped into Andy when he was collecting your things. Well, actually I was watching out for you and saw him instead. I was hoping you'd visit and then we could have had a chat.'

'I'm not sure I want to hear what you have to say.'

'*You're* judging me?' He shakes his head.

I don't speak, scared to say anything in case he leaves.

'Can I come in or not?' he says finally.

I don't want him to see the inside of the house, but how can I say that without embarrassing myself further? Between these walls, in every room, if he looks hard enough, he will find tainted dreams, cracks filled with lies, cries of pain, drunken rages, tears of anger. Do I really want to lower myself any further in his eyes?

But I step aside to let him in, nevertheless.

There *are* things we need to say to each other.

CHAPTER FIFTY-TWO

It's strange to see Tom in my grandparents' house. I try not to see it through his eyes. The peeling wallpaper, the nicotine-stained ceilings and woodwork. Fist-sized holes punched in several doors. Everything grey, dismal, dreary. A dying spider plant that I've failed to resuscitate. A relic of a TV, and furniture not fit to give away.

'You can sit down,' I tell him, lying on the settee and throwing the blanket over my legs. 'It might be tatty, but everything is clean, because I've made sure of that myself.'

He chooses the armchair across from me. 'Roberta told me what had been going on. She's been contacted by Stoke Helps Out.'

My body deflates. They know everything, of course they do. Well, most of it.

'How can I trust you after all the lies?' he adds.

'I agree. Why would you want to?'

'So why did you do it?'

'I had a chance to better myself when I went to

Manchester, leaving my past behind. But I failed. So when I came back to Stoke, I decided I would be someone else instead of angry Clara. I can't change my name without a whole load of hassle, so I invented a new backstory, appearing to be bubbly behind my fear of being alone.' I reach for a cushion and hold it in front of my chest. 'But then my lies tripped me up. And I realised I was as weak as the old Clara. I guess bad people can't help being bad.'

'That's nonsense. You have so many good points, and you don't realise how strong you are.'

'That's what Emma told me, she's my therapist.'

'Therapist?'

'I started seeing her a few weeks ago, trying to understand why I lash out when someone hurts me or angers me. She said I still see myself as that little girl who was always told to clean up her mum's blood after she'd been beaten by her dad. I've tried not to be like him all my life, yet I keep finding trouble.'

'It's good that you're talking to someone about it all. Andy said I was wrong about you and that I should ask you more about your work.'

The mention of Andy makes me smile, even if it's faint. 'I met a good friend in him.'

'What did he mean?'

'I like helping people. It makes me feel good about myself.' I explain about why I'd worked for no payment. 'I cleaned up for their clients in my own time. I enjoy the sense of putting things back together again, making things perfect so that everything will be okay when I'm finished.'

'Were you ever going to tell me the truth?' Tom

pinches the bridge of his nose, closing his eyes momentarily. 'I feel as if I only know half of you.'

The tears I've been holding back fall. I hadn't wanted to cry, I don't want any sympathy. Yet the man sitting across from me means so much that I can't help it. I want him to move across and sit by my side, put his hand in mine and say everything is going to be fine.

But it isn't, is it? Unless... can I be totally honest with him, now that I haven't got anything to lose? I'm not sure I even know the truth between my lies anymore.

'I thought I was lucky when I found Cedric House, but meeting you was even better,' I say. 'You showed me how a relationship could be. For the first time in my life, you made me feel safe. Loved. Hopeful for the future. But that's all gone. Who's there to take care of me now? I react to things I don't like with violence, and I really don't want to do that. But I struggle to be normal because I inherited my father's genes.'

'You tell yourself that, but that's not true. It's an excuse.'

'How would you know? All my life I've had to fight and steal.' I point at the room. 'Would you have liked to grow up here? Be dragged up, actually?'

'No, but that doesn't mean you have to be a victim all your life.'

'Says the man who grew up with two parents living in the same home and feeling safe and secure because of it!'

'That's what Andy said, and it's still not fair.'

'Neither is labelling me. When I wake up, every morning I try my best to be and feel fine. To stop the past from ruining my future. Do you know how hard that is? So don't lecture me on trying to just get on with things.' I point to my temple next. 'Everything my dad did to my mum, everything he did to me, I remember. All the time. I bet you don't have such dark memories with your perfect family as you grew up.'

An awkward silence descends on the room. Tom is the first to break it.

'Tell me the truth, from the beginning.'

'It will take me forever.' And it won't be the truth. It can't be, can it? Because I don't think he'd like the real Clara.

'I have as long as it takes,' he urges.

So I tell him what I can, what he doesn't know already. About the times I've cleaned up the blood after my father attacked my mother. About the times he'd hit me, too. Growing up with my grandparents. Surviving at school.

I tell him about the thieving, the shoplifting, the crimes me and Evan got away with. His marriage proposal and how we worked as a team. The miscarriage, the child I mourned, the despair at not being a mother. The fear I will never hold my own baby.

I tell him about my violent relationship with Damien, and the other men, and then choosing to be alone for two years. Not wanting to mix with people, or meet anyone else, for fear of hurting them or damaging myself. How I'd enjoyed lockdowns, knowing I wasn't the only one who couldn't mix with others. How it made me less lonely.

I tell him what it felt like to come back to Stoke

knowing my nan was dying. All the demons in the house that were still waiting for me.

I tell him of my hopes and dreams, and how I'd thought from a little girl that my life would be so much better when I was older.

Finally, I mention the fallout with Wayne, the anger management classes, and my therapy visits with Emma. How I've been trying to understand in what way my past affects me, trying to cope and deal with it, to make a better future for myself.

And as I speak, I see myself as a ten-year-old girl standing in the corner of the room. I watch as I change from a child to a teenager to the woman I am today.

I see myself through Tom's eyes.

Damaged.

Untrustworthy.

Unlovable.

It's then I know that, because of my actions, I have lost something special. Someone who would have changed my life for the better.

No, someone who has done that already.

Spending time with Tom, and Roberta and Shelley, and talking to Emma and Andy, makes me realise that even if the argument does start off as nature versus nurture, essentially it's down to me which path to walk. I've taken the wrong one for so long.

I've hit roadblocks.

I've negotiated detours.

I've crashed and burned.

I've veered off the road.

I've gone off-road completely for a couple of years.

I've taken umpteen wrong turnings, and then I've

landed where I belonged. Right here. Where it all began.

I've come full circle.

I wrap my arms around my knees as I clutch them to my chest, trying to comfort myself. My face wet with tears, eyes swollen. Still wanting to be loved, needing someone to care for me.

I know I've lost him.

And yet...

All the time he's sat and listened, Tom hasn't once judged. In fact, he hasn't said a word, except when he needed something clarifying. His hands have formed fists, thumped the arms of the chair on occasion, and stretched out in anger.

I made him feel like that. And I hate myself all over again.

Finally, I tell him what happened when I was seventeen, and about the day my nan told me to leave.

'She lied to me, Tom. She lied to me about Derek.'

CHAPTER FIFTY-THREE

Eleven Years Ago

Clara walked down the road towards home. It was nearly midnight, and she'd had the most amazing evening. She stepped on and off the pavement, giggling to herself. She'd been to a party, expecting nothing more than a laugh and a catch-up with a couple of lads, when she'd felt someone's eyes on her. She'd turned her head to see Brody Arington. She'd given him a dazzling smile, and he'd soon come over to talk to her.

Clara had always liked Brody, even though she was warned off by his cow of a girlfriend a couple of years ago. At the time, she hadn't seen his attraction, but since then the boy had gone from a scraggly teenager to the makings of a man.

Which was why she thought it a perfect opportunity to get her own back when he offered her a lift home. Brody wasn't drinking, and the fact that he wasn't intoxicated, so couldn't blame his slip-up on being under the influence, made it more special. He wanted to be with her.

He'd dropped her off, after a lot of heavy petting beforehand. It had taken all her willpower to stop, the thrill of getting one over on Kerry outweighing the issues if they got caught. But at the last minute, she'd stopped and given him a blow job instead. Maybe next time she'd sleep with him.

Despite dating Kerry, Brody had said he wanted to see Clara again, and they'd arranged to go for lunch tomorrow, but seeing was believing. She had her doubts he'd turn up at all but, if so, she would keep him keen. Make sure he treated her like a lady.

Her house came into view and she frowned. There were lights blaring from most of the windows, one upstairs open. Noises drifted towards her. A yell followed by an angry voice, the slap of a palm across a face.

'Nan.' Clara ran quickly, struggling with her key in the lock with her haste to get inside.

In the hallway, she gasped. Was that blood she could see on the carpet?

A muffled scream came from above, and she took the stairs two at a time. Across the landing, her grandparents' bedroom door was open, and she could see directly inside. Derek was straddling Jean, his hands around her neck. Jean was struggling for air, pawing at his hands, trying to pull them away.

If Clara didn't stop him, Derek would kill the one person she cared about.

Looking around, the first thing she spotted was a

hardback book on the bedside table. She picked it up and swiped it at his head.

Derek fell to the side, and she went at him again.

'Leave her alone,' she screamed.

Derek grabbed her wrist, gripping it so hard that she was forced to drop the book. He slapped her across the face, sending her reeling.

'Don't you ever come near me again, you ungrateful bitch,' he roared.

Clara said nothing, knowing it would make matters worse. The best thing she could do now to calm the situation down was wait for him to leave the room. He would go to bed and then she could help her nan.

Jean was sitting up now, back to the headboard as far away from Derek as possible, a hand to her neck where red blotches were already becoming angry bruises. She inhaled deeply to fill her lungs.

Memories of her dad attacking her mum sprang to Clara's mind. Fists flying, screaming, blood, a knife.

The night...

She kept her back to the wall, so she could see what Derek would do next. She needed him out of the room. Then she could clean up her nan. But equally she didn't want to antagonise him.

'You'd better pack your bags, Clara,' he muttered. 'Your time here is over. I want you out by the morning, and don't ever come back.'

Clara glanced at her nan whose eyes brimmed with tears, her face racked with fear. She waited until Derek left the room and staggered across the landing and, when she saw he was going downstairs, something snapped. She ran at him, arms outstretched, and pushed him down the stairs.

Clara didn't think of the consequences. She just wanted Derek to feel the same pain as he'd inflicted on Jean.

Later that evening, she would recall every knock, every thump, every thud as he fell headfirst.

He landed at the bottom of the stairs, hitting the wall ahead before the steps turned into the hallway. His body lay in an awkward position. Clara could tell he'd broken a leg, hopefully his neck, too.

'Clara! What have you done?' Jean stepped past her, on her way down to see to Derek.

Clara grabbed her arm. 'He deserved that after what he did to you.'

'You shouldn't have pushed him.'

'He was hurting you.'

'You might have killed him!'

'Would you be glad if I had?'

'Oh, child. I don't care about that. I care about you getting into trouble. I'll have to call for an ambulance, and the police might come.'

Clara caught her breath. 'We could tell them he missed his step and he fell backwards.'

'What about me, the bruising?' Jean sounded unsure. 'They will see what he did.'

'You were downstairs.' Her words rushed out. 'I came in and stopped him, told him to go to bed but he didn't make it.'

'I'd better go and see to him.'

Clara watched Jean race downstairs to check on Derek. She didn't want to get her story straight. She wanted everyone to know what she'd done. He was an evil bastard and deserved all he got.

After what she'd witnessed happening to her mum when she was younger, Clara fought hard not to be like her father. But there were times she relished how alike they were... and that had been one of them.

CHAPTER FIFTY-FOUR

Eleven Years Ago

It was a long night before Nan came home from the hospital after Derek was taken away by ambulance. Clara was frantic, unable to sleep much. She'd sat on the settee so that she could hear when she got in. All the time she kept thinking about what would happen if Derek was dead.

She could go to prison for pushing him down the stairs. At the moment she had no need to worry. When Nan had left in the ambulance with Derek, he'd been unconscious but breathing. Nan had backed her up by saying he'd fallen, but if it looked suspicious in any way, if he died, the police might investigate things further.

Clara had cleaned up the blood that had come from his head wound, scrubbing at the wall and carpet with the strongest thing she could find. Then she'd sat in the dark waiting.

She was in the window when she saw a taxi drop

Nan off. Clara raced to the front door, opening it before she got there.

'Is everything okay?' she asked, frantic to see signs of reassurance. 'How is he?'

'Let me come inside and I'll tell you.'

Goosebumps erupted over Clara's arms as she followed her. Jean took off her coat while Clara put on the kettle. She wanted to scream at her, to know how Derek was, but she knew she'd have to wait.

Jean sat down at the table and, once she had a mug of tea in front of her, she wrapped her hands around it and stared at Clara.

'It's bad news, I'm afraid,' she said. 'Your granddad's spinal cord is severed, and it's unable to be fixed. He's paralysed from the waist down.'

Clara gasped. 'I didn't mean to hurt him that much.'

'I know you didn't, love. He's still unconscious at the moment, so they're not sure if he has any damage to his brain.'

'You mean he might die?' Clara hadn't expected her thoughts to be true.

'I'm not sure.'

'Oh, Nan, what will I do if he does?'

'I've been thinking about that.' Jean pulled her handbag across the table and took out an envelope. Tears pricked her eyes, one falling that she wiped away. 'Clara, it pains me to say this, but just in case he doesn't make it, I want you to leave.'

'I can't.'

'Think of the alternative. You might be sent to prison.'

Clara sat back in her chair, as if to put distance

between the two of them. 'We told the paramedics that he fell. You haven't said anything else, have you?'

'No, but what happens if he wakes up fine and then decides to tell the police that you pushed him?'

'You'll back me up that I didn't.' Clara paused. 'Won't you?'

'If he's okay when he wakes up, he'll know that I saw what happened. Your granddad will use that against me. I'll have to look after him for the rest of his life if he can come home. How we're going to manage in this house, I don't know. We may have to move into an adapted property.'

'Stop!' Clara covered her ears with her hands. 'I can't leave you alone with him. Life was unbearable enough before.'

'I can't take the risk, Clara. I love you so much, and I know this will come as a shock, but you have to leave.' She slid across the envelope. 'There's six hundred pounds in there. It's all I can get.'

'But where will I go?'

'Manchester, or Birmingham. Liverpool, or further up north. You'll be able to get a job doing something. Perhaps with live-in accommodation.'

'It's not as easy as that. I won't go.'

'Then I'll have no choice but to tell the truth if things take a turn for the worse.'

'You can't.'

'I'd have to, and if you're not here, the police won't be able to find you.' She reached for Clara's hands and gripped them tightly. 'Child, I want you to have a better life. You've spent far too much time here with us, and your granddad will just get worse.'

'But you're my only family. What if he dies? You'll be on your own.'

'Then I'll be safe in the knowledge that you're away from here, and you won't be going to prison. When things have quietened down, then maybe you can come back.'

Clara sat quietly for a moment. It wasn't an easy thing to up sticks and leave the place you'd grown up in. That had provided a roof over your head, even if there was no love and laughter. Where would she stay, where would she work? She had her job at the pub waiting on tables. Maybe she could hunker down there until everything had blown over.

'No.' Jean shook her head.

'What?'

'I know what you're thinking, and you're not going to stay at the pub. You need to leave the area completely.'

'But they'd let me stay until I found somewhere new!'

'No! You must leave, and I suggest you go this morning. The sooner the better.'

'What aren't you telling me, Nan?'

'I just want you to be safe. You can ring me when you're settled and—'

'You're really going to throw me out?'

'It's for your own good.'

'You're just as bad as my parents.' Clara pouted. 'All I've ever wanted is a home and a family to love me.'

'I do love you!'

'You love him more.'

'That's not true.'

'Then let me stay.'

'Just go, Clara! I can't protect you now.'

Clara stood up, the chair screeching across the floor. 'Don't worry, I won't be under your feet for much longer.' She snatched up the envelope of money. 'I'll be gone within the hour.'

CHAPTER FIFTY-FIVE

'What do you mean she lied to you?' Tom asks me.

'When my nan phoned me out of the blue and told me she had cancer and no longer than six months left to live, she asked if I'd be able to take care of her until she died,' I tell him.

'That seems a bit much, after how you were treated.'

'I know, but I was on a zero-hour contract, cleaning in a hotel, and lodging in a grotty flat, so I said yes. But I was dreading seeing Derek. I'd never seen him since I'd pushed him down the stairs and I didn't know what to expect. That's when she told me he'd died a few months earlier.'

I see the colour drain from Tom's face, his features sag. 'She never contacted you to let you know?'

I shake my head.

'And then she let you think he was still alive until you got back?'

'Yes.'

'Jesus, do all your family lie?'

'That's not fair! And that *is* my family. Nan was all I had in the end.'

'Sorry, I just feel so angry on your behalf.' He waves his hand, urging me to carry on.

'It was strange walking up the path and knocking on the door. I burst into tears when I saw her.' I sniff and wipe my nose with a tissue. 'She was so thin, most of her hair had gone, and she seemed old and frail. She'd recently finished a round of chemotherapy, and it had knocked her about.

'We chatted for about half an hour, and then she dropped the bombshell.' I take a moment to catch a breath, my heart beating out of my chest. 'Derek hadn't been paralysed at all.'

I close my eyes for a moment, recalling how angry I'd felt. I still remember every detail of that night eleven years ago, and the morning after, as if it happened yesterday. It's been horrendous knowing I hurt Derek, even after everything he put me through over the years since my parents died. The guilt of what I did has been hard to live with.

Yet I was duped, played, conned. Whatever you wish to call it. And it hurt. So to see Tom looking so aghast makes me feel slightly better. Because it had been wrong. And yet, I have come to understand why.

Tom sits back in the chair, almost as deflated as I am. 'Fuck, that was cruel.'

I nod. 'She wanted to get me away from Derek so that he didn't damage me any further. I love her for that, and I hate her for it, too. Because I knew she suffered at his hands when I wasn't around. It was the same with my mum. Often when my dad or Derek saw me, or heard me telling them to stop, the red mist would disappear. But that was as a child.

'When I was seventeen, Nan knew that Derek and I would eventually start fighting between ourselves. She didn't want anything to happen to me on his account. She didn't want the circle of violence to continue. Derek was a vicious man, and he'd raised my dad to be the same. She didn't want me to be like either of them.'

'But you're not.'

'She thought if she lied to me and got me to leave, that I'd have a better life. I never told her it was probably worse for me that way. I felt so alone at times. I didn't have much, but I had to give up everything I knew and start again from scratch.'

'That's a lot to go through on your own.'

'Don't get me wrong. I was angry with her at first, but then I realised it was done. I couldn't change anything, and my nan was dying. So I shut it away and got on with what needed doing. I quite enjoyed it until I couldn't do it anymore. She went into a hospice for her final week. I was so grateful that she'd get the right care. I thought I'd have more time with her, but three days later, she was gone.'

'I'm sorry.'

I shrug. 'I was a bit numb at the time. I went off the rails drinking to block out the pain for a couple of weeks, feeling sorry for myself all alone again. But Nan had provided for me in a way, leaving the house to me. And a few thousand pounds in cash. You remember me telling you about the fights? Well, Nan wasn't as stupid as she led me to believe. Turned out she'd been siphoning money, too, right up until they stopped. She was the one who updated the ledger.

'She gave the money to me before she died. So, once I felt able to cope, I pulled myself together and made a plan. Being back on the estate in this house made me feel like a loser. I thought selling it would be the best thing to do, so I could move to somewhere else. Start afresh.

'But I worry I'm always going to be violent. There only has to be one thing that goes wrong, and I go up like a bottle of champagne.' I'm crying openly now. 'I know my nan meant well, but she made me believe I was evil inside. I'll never understand why she stayed with Derek. I told her all I'd ever wanted was to feel safe and loved, to have a family and a home to call my own.'

Tom wipes at tears that are trickling down his face.

'You need to fight to get on in this world,' I go on. 'With wit, with deviousness, with your fists. Derek told me that. He said people like us amount to nothing otherwise.'

'You know that's not true.'

'I know I wanted to hit out at Wayne because he found out everything about me. It was stupid, and it was my fault Shelley was hurt. It was hard seeing her so badly injured. Men shouldn't be allowed to do what they want to women, and vice versa. There should be consequences.'

'There are, prison. I'm sure Wayne will be back inside by now. He broke the conditions of his parole.'

'He'll come bothering Shelley as soon as he gets out.'

'I know it sounds harsh, but if that happens, then

she'll deal with it. But actions have to have conse-quences.'

I lower my eyes momentarily. My actions have them, too.

'I'm scared I'll be like this forever. Reacting to violence even if I'm not searching it out. There will always be the Waynes of this world who want to spoil things.'

'Then look past them!'

'That's easy for you to say. As a child, I was made to feel like I was an inconvenience, having to fight, liter-ally, for everything. I became obsessed with love, finding the right man to accept me as a damaged soul. Is it too much to ask to belong to someone who will love me back unconditionally?'

I stare at Tom, pleading with him to say something, anything, to put me at ease.

But he doesn't.

Eventually, Tom stands up. 'I have to collect Isla from school.'

'There's something else before you go.' I tell him what happened with Bill Fisher's watch and where he can find it.

'Why didn't you tell me any of that at the time?' he asks.

'I wanted to sort it out on my own. I ended up getting Shelley into a lot of trouble, though. I think Wayne took it out on her.'

'I doubt he's clever enough for that.' He gives me a

faint smile. 'I'll tell Roberta where it is.' He turns to go again.

'Tom.' My voice comes out as a whisper this time. 'I would never hurt you, nor Isla.'

'How do I know? How do *you* know?' he cries. 'How do you convince *me*?'

My stomach flips and then drops, seeing the pain etched on his face. The anguish I've caused. How can I ever make up for that?

Tom shakes his head. 'I can't be with you right now.'

And then he's gone.

I sit on the settee for a long time afterwards, feeling lost. I'm back where I started, having made such a mess of my life. I've been given all the chances. I'm the only one who can help myself now.

But I'm not sure I can do that here. I'll stay until the house sale goes through and be gone as soon as the papers are signed. Because coming back has been too much. It hasn't mended me as I'd hoped.

Coming back has finished me off completely.

CHAPTER FIFTY-SIX

When Tom got home with Isla, he settled her in and then nipped upstairs to see Roberta. He wanted to put her mind at rest as well as let her know about the watch.

Roberta beckoned him in. 'Have you seen Clara?'

'Yes.'

'How is she?'

'She's... in her words, she's broken, and I'm not sure if she can be fixed.'

As quick as he could, he explained what he'd learned. Roberta's mouth dropped open on several occasions.

'That poor woman,' she said once he'd finished. 'I don't know how she's coped with all that from a young age. No wonder she's been struggling.'

'It doesn't make what she did right.'

'I know, but she was trying to make amends. She was working voluntarily, you said.'

'Yes.'

'Funny how the charity missed out that detail. That's very commendable.' Roberta threw a hand around the room. 'Look what she did for me. I would have paid her if I'd known.'

Tom wasn't sold. 'What happens if she hits out whenever she's angry? You saw what she did to Wayne.'

'When we had lunch? I thought that was rather good, if I'm honest.'

'But—'

'You saw what *he* did to Shelley. It pained me so much to see her hurt like that, and I'm glad he'll go to prison for it. Now, imagine you'd been brought up with that kind of violence, how would it have affected you?'

Tom drops his gaze momentarily.

'Clara is broken, Tom, but I think she needs the chance to be mended.'

'I... I can't have her near Isla.'

'Do you really think she would hurt her?'

'I don't know, that's the problem.'

'So you'll live without her just in case?' Roberta folded her arms. 'That's poppycock. I've seen you two together. You make a great couple, and after losing Sasha, you and Isla need someone like Clara to make you complete. You deserve to have what Bill and I had. As well, you get to share it with Isla.'

Tom's eyes brimmed with tears at the thought of the women in his life. Sasha who he'd lost, Isla, his darling daughter, and Clara, who had stolen his heart over the past few months.

'I know what Sasha would tell you to do.' Roberta chuckled. 'I used to love her forthrightness. She'd tell you to sort this mess out and get on with it.'

'It's not that easy.'

'Do you love Clara?'

Tom didn't like being put on the spot, but eventually he shrugged. 'I was falling in love with her, I guess.'

'Why?'

'She makes me laugh. She makes me feel alive, whole again after so much pain and sorrow. I look forward to seeing her whenever she isn't with me. There's an air of fun about her, maybe once in a while too manic. And she loves having Isla around, which is a must for me.'

'Can you see yourself having children with her?'

Tom raised his eyebrows. 'That's a bit presumptuous.'

Roberta stared at him, waiting for a response.

'What is this?' He smirked. 'The "How To Make Tom Cringe Show"? You know men aren't good at sharing their feelings.'

'Then you should try harder.'

Tom went downstairs to Isla then and spent a pleasant but quiet evening with her. It was the tonic required for him to switch off for a while. But Isla asked about Clara when he tucked her into bed.

'Have you seen her today?'

'I haven't, sweetheart,' Tom lied. He cursed inwardly. Even he was at it. But there were times when little white ones were necessary.

'Where is she?' Isla went on, her bottom lip quivering. 'Did you scare her away?'

'Of course not.' He wiped a hand across her forehead. 'But grown-ups often fall out and go their separate ways. Sometimes things don't work out as planned.'

'I like Clara, Dad. Please try and find her. I want to see her, too. I miss her.'

What a day to punch a man when he's down, he mused.

'I promise to sort things out soon.' Tom paused. 'Isla, do you think it's time we moved out of Cedric House and found a place all to ourselves?'

'Noooo.' Isla shook her head vehemently. 'I like it here. And what happens if Clara visits, and she doesn't know where we are?'

'Okay, that's fine if you want to stay.'

'I do. I like it that Mummy is here, too.'

Tom bit down hard on his bottom lip to stop a sob escaping, wondering if Isla sensed Sasha or was recalling memories.

'Goodnight, poppet.' He kissed her on the cheek, noticing her eyes already closing.

'Night, Dad.'

In the living room, Tom poured a glass of wine and collapsed on the settee. It had been a draining day, and he had a lot of thinking to do.

CHAPTER FIFTY-SEVEN

It's been two hours since Tom left, and I find myself needing to ease my pain in the only way I think might help. I have to get out of the house.

Traffic is busy as I walk to the cemetery, thinking about what I've messed up over the past few months. I've been instrumental in getting Sam to sleep with me, and then got angry with him when he didn't want me anymore. I've prompted Wayne to react in the guise of sorting him out for Shelley. I've pushed my way into Roberta's home under false pretences. I've immersed myself into Tom's and Isla's lives without thinking things through.

My strides are quick and long, but the world is on my shoulders. I'm finally at the cemetery, passing by Sasha Simson's grave and continuing to where my parents have been laid to rest. But when I get near, it's Derek's grave I want to see. I need to make sure he's dead. How mad is that? I need to know he'll never bother me again. Can never harm me again.

And I can move on when I know that.

I stand in front of my grandparents' grave. I stare at Derek's name, engraved on the headstone.

'You bastard!' I cry. 'You never loved me. You never knew how to show love to my dad, so he became a monster, too. And I trusted you. As a child, you should have sheltered me, not had me doing jobs for you and putting me in danger.

'I'm glad I pushed you down the stairs. I'm glad I never came back to see you alive. I am angry at Nan for lying to me, but I know deep down that she was right to do what she did. To save me from spending the rest of my life with you. Becoming like you.

'But I did that anyway!' I sob. 'I hate you for instilling in me the horrors from my childhood that made me a bitter and hard woman. You started my life off on the wrong footing. Well, it stops right here. I won't let what you did, and what I thought I'd done, define me for the rest of my life. I deserve better, and I am going to find my happiness. I thought I had it, but that chance has been taken from me. So now it's up to me to go out into the world and find my place. Without anyone to blame but myself.'

I pause to catch my breath, noticing then an elderly man in the distance. He's tending to a gravestone. The surroundings are so peaceful. I hope I haven't disturbed him.

I take out the newspaper clipping I've placed in my pocket, giving it one last read.

Double Death Ruled as Murder/Suicide

Stoke News, 19 October 2006

A coroner has returned a victim of murder/suicide after the death of Jennifer and Duncan Cooper. Jennifer Cooper, 34, was found with severe head and facial injuries, a stab wound to the stomach, and multiple defence wounds. Duncan Cooper, 36, then took a knife to himself.

They are survived by their daughter, now eleven. She witnessed the attack, only then telling anyone that it was a regular occurrence.

'This is, yet again, a tragic case of a woman in her prime losing her life at the hands of a violent man,' Detective Super-intend Shaw said. 'What that little girl must have seen will haunt her forever. No child should have to live in danger, in fear of their lives. My heart goes out to her and her remaining family.'

I rip the paper into tiny pieces. I move to sit at a bench and shove it all in the bin beside me. Sitting there on my own, I let my worries fade away for a moment. It's a beautiful place to be.

Deep in thought a few minutes later, I don't notice the man I saw earlier coming towards me until he's almost standing in front of me. He looks to be in his eighties, a checked cap on his head with a few tufts of grey hair showing at the sides. He's wearing a navy suit, with a woollen waistcoat, a white shirt, and a purple tie. His black shoes are shiny, as if he's polished them that morning. Maybe he has.

He smiles at me.

I wipe at my eyes and smile back.

'Are you all right, duck? I don't mean to pry, and tell me to mind my own business, but you seemed a bit upset earlier. Have you lost someone recently?'

'My nan,' I tell him. 'She was the only member of family I had left.'

'Oh, that is terribly sad. You're so young.' He points to the bench. 'May I?'

I nod and scoot along a bit to make room for him.

'I'm George.' He tips his cap.

I smile at the gesture and tell him my name. He gets out a small bag from his pocket and offers me a mint. I take it, unwrap the paper, and pop it in my mouth.

'I love these things,' he says. 'But they play havoc with my dentures, especially if the middle is sticky!'

I find myself smiling again, then laughing.

'That's better,' he says. 'I'm glad in Stoke we can chat to strangers and not feel silly. I'd hate to live somewhere so busy that people rush on by.'

'I've lived in Manchester for eleven years, and that's mostly the same. I still chat to anyone, though. You'd be surprised how many people reply or smile even.'

'Smiles are free.' He chuckles. 'Will you be staying in Stoke or going back?'

'Going back.' I let out my breath dramatically at the thought.

'That's a big sigh. Have you got decisions to make?'

'Not really. I don't feel like I belong here anymore. I've lived away for so long.'

'Home is where the heart is.' He looks ahead. 'I feel more at home here than I do in my little bungalow since Maureen died. We were married for forty-seven years.'

'Wow.' I can't help myself.

'I'm lost without her, which is why I come here every day, rain or shine.' He pats his knee. 'It gives the old body a workout. I do miss talking to her, though.'

'Do you have children?'

'Three boys, eight grandchildren, and five great-grandchildren so far.'

I smile. 'I'm going to have children, grandchildren and great-grandchildren one day.'

'Good for you. They all keep me young.'

It's nearing six p.m. I turn to George and offer my hand. 'It was very nice to meet you, George, I hope you have a wonderful evening.'

'Likewise, Clara.' He shakes it. 'And please go easy on yourself. I can see you're troubled by something. It's never as bad as it seems.'

I want to say so much more but instead I stand and walk away.

I trudge along my usual roads, past the families I love to watch. The Mini owners, the TV couple, and the gamers are at home as I walk on. Still my mind won't stop going over and over the past few days.

I can't wait until the house is sold now. I don't want to stay there with memories haunting me, my own mistakes included. And it's wise to get out of Stoke. I have enough money to tide me over.

First thing in the morning, I'll drive back in my nan's car. It'll come in handy until the house is sold, and then I'll get a better one. Nothing fancy or new. Just a nice set of wheels to get me from A to B.

Wherever that might be next.

CHAPTER FIFTY-EIGHT

That evening, I pack my belongings into the back of the car and head off to bed for the last time. I'm glad I won't ever have to sleep here again. It's been so bad for me, creating all kinds of feelings and obsessions.

I think about Cedric House as I go from room to room. I never meant to trick Roberta. I really did just want to help her, and I loved staying in flat four. It was a home for me, even in the little time I was there.

More to the point, what I hadn't intended to find was a family. Roberta, Tom and Isla, and Shelley. By being with them all, it opened my eyes to what I might be able to have if I left my past behind. And to do that, I had to lie to everyone there.

I bet Shelly wished I'd never set foot in Cedric House. But when I met her, she reminded me so much of my mum, and I wanted to help her out of her dire situation. I wonder if she knew I called him Wanky Wayne all the time? I still think it's apt, especially after what he tried to do to her.

Shelley was always so kind to me. I enjoyed our few nights in together, our chats when we put the world to rights. I'm not sure she'll ever know how good it felt to have a friend, someone who didn't know my past. But I was the friend who turned into a nightmare.

It's half past eleven before I finally go to bed and curl up under the covers. Surprisingly after the day I've had, I drop off to sleep quite quickly. But not before thinking of Tom, what he might be making of everything. Of me. I go to sleep dreaming of what could have been.

It's an hour later when I awake. Something has startled me. I lie in the dark, waiting to hear if it's my imagination, that a dream I had hasn't crept into reality. A few seconds pass, and I let out my breath. But then, I hear another noise.

Someone is in the house.

I pull back the covers and creep to the door. It's ajar as I never like sleeping with it closed. A flash of light at the bottom of the stairs looks like a torch. How the hell did someone get in?

I glance around, searching for something to use as a weapon, but I'm hindered as there is nothing. My fists will have to do if necessary.

I go to investigate, tiptoeing down the stairs until a creak on the bottom step alerts the intruder and I see a shadow of a person in the doorway. In a flash, I switch the hall light on, hoping to startle whoever it is.

Wayne is coming out of the living room.

'What the hell are you doing here?' I cry.

'I thought you'd be at Cedric House.'

'And?'

'I've come for what's mine.'

I ignore his comment. 'The police are searching for you.'

'What for?'

'You hurt Shelley really bad this time.' I rush to unlock the front door, to tell him to get out.

Wayne grabs my arm. 'I want a word with you.'

'If you've come to gloat, you're too late because I'm leaving. Now, take your hand off me.'

'Good riddance, I say. Especially seeing as you wanted me gone.'

'What are you doing here anyway?'

'I told you, I want what's mine.'

'I don't have anything of yours.'

'The watch you stole from me. I know it was you and that Shelley must have told you about it. It's worth a tidy bit, and I've been waiting for the right buyer. I found out it was gone just before—'

'You punched two barrels of shit out of Shelley. She never said anything, by the way. But you thieved that watch from Roberta, so I put it back.'

'You expect me to believe that?' He sneers. 'Once a thief, always a thief. I know it's in here somewhere.'

'Get away from me.' I yank my arm away.

He pushes me so hard, I fall to the floor. In seconds, he's lying on top of me.

'I've always wanted to be in this position with you. How about it, Clara? Now that Tom won't want you after all your lies.'

I turn my head to the side as he moves his face towards mine. He ends up kissing my cheek. He holds my hands either side of my head while I buck underneath him. Overpowering me, he tries to kiss me again, but this time I bite his lip.

'Grheihgmmm.'

He can't get away from me because my teeth have clamped down. I stare into his beady eyes. Then I let go.

His hand covers his mouth, and I scramble to my feet. The only place I can run is upstairs. I take them two at a time.

But he's right behind me, grabbing my ankle and pulling me down again. I reach the landing but hit the floor with a bang. He flicks me over, straddling me. His eyes are full of hate, a demonic darkness I know isn't there just to intimidate me. He means to harm me, and he has the advantage again.

He smashes his fist in my face.

For a moment, I see stars but then I free a hand and punch him back. I push him off me and he falls to the side. Both of us scramble to our feet. We stand facing each other, catching our breath.

'I warned you to stay away, but you didn't listen,' Wayne seethes. 'Now, where's the watch?'

'I told you, I gave it back to Roberta. She'd have got it eventually, though. The spare room where you hid your treasure? When the police were called to see what you'd done to Shelley, I asked them what she should do with all your stuff in the wardrobe. Shelley thought she'd be in trouble for keeping it there, but they said it was all down to you. They have it all now, so that's something else they'll charge you with.'

'You fucking bitch.'

He comes at me again, but I dodge him, my fist

connecting with his back. We're at the top of the stairs, and he grabs for me again. With all my might, I shove him.

Wayne tumbles backwards, barrelling down at speed. He cracks his head on the wall, knocking himself out, and drops to the floor like a rag doll.

It's as if history is repeating itself, just like what happened to Derek all those years ago.

Like that last time, I don't care if he's dead.

For a few seconds.

Then reality crashes into me. I grab my hair and bunch it in my fists. There's no movement from downstairs. I wish I could go back in time to erase everything.

I stand at the top of the stairs, scared to go down to face what I've done. I need to see if Wayne is alive. If he's dead, I'll be sent back to prison, and I vowed I wouldn't go there again. No one will believe it was self-defence.

I drop my head and sob. I'm never going to get straightened out, am I? I'll always be a true Cooper. Whenever things are going well, I screw up. I can't help myself. This isn't self-sabotage. This is just plain stupid Clara.

I sit on the top step, reminding me of how I'd done the same as a child. Afraid. Lonely. Worried.

No, he can't be dead. I couldn't have killed him. I wasn't strong enough the first time it had happened with Derek, so what makes me think I am now?

I finally go down to him. His eyes are closed. I kneel by his side, but as I check for a pulse on his neck he stirs. I see red.

'It's. All. Your. Fault,' I say, picking up his head and ramming it into the wall on each word.

But then I stop. I want to kill him, but I can't. For starters, it will halt the sale of the house. Who would want to buy a property where a murder had taken place? As well, I'd have to go on the run, and I'd need the money to do that.

And where the hell would I put his body if I tried to cover up what I'd done? The only place I might be able to drag it to is my car. I could perhaps shove him in the boot, but where would I dispose of him?

Besides, I can't kill him. Because that's what everyone thinks I will do. And I'm better than that.

Be brave, Clara.

I realise then how I can get him out of the picture. He deserves to suffer because of what he did to Shelley.

Upstairs again, I get my phone and practise what I'm going to say a few times in the bathroom mirror. I rip at the corner of my T-shirt. My eye is blackening where he punched me, so I look a state anyway. I mess my hair up, so it seems as if he's been rougher with me.

At the top of the stairs, I sit and stare down at Wayne. He's still out for the count, so I dial 999.

'I need the police,' I sob hysterically to the operator. 'Someone broke into my house and tried to rape me. He's still here. Help me, please!'

CHAPTER FIFTY-NINE

It's early next morning when I leave the police station. I've been treated well, given breakfast after having to wait a while for someone to come and see me. I was offered a lift home, but I declined.

I'm restless and find myself walking into the city centre. I see there are messages on my phone from Shelley, numerous missed calls, too. I know the police will have been in touch to tell her Wayne is in custody. Maybe they told her what had happened in Wedgwood Street, I can't know for certain, because I won't be getting in touch with her.

Last night when the police arrived, Wayne was conscious again but unable to get up from the floor. He'd obviously concussed himself when he fell in his haste to get away. That's what I told the officer when I gave a statement, anyway.

I was interviewed in a soft room, treated like a witness, and I played my part so well. They knew Wayne was wanted for the attack on Shelley, so I filled them in about him stealing the watch and me putting it back, and how he'd broken into my house with the sole intention of raping me.

My injuries were logged and photographed. I left the station knowing he'll be recalled back to prison for breach of his license in connection with Shelley and the stolen goods. What he's done to me is extra, and he'll go to court for that in time.

The forensic team has been through my grandparents' house overnight, getting samples of everything they need, and I can return there now. If only I want to. I think about Cedric House where I'd much prefer to go. I long to visit once more before I leave Stoke for the last time, yet I know I can't.

Before I catch the bus to Wedgwood Street, I have a last wander through the town. There isn't much left in Hanley now the high street has been decimated. So many boarded-up shops and others filled with donations from charity shops, vape stores, or mobile phone companies.

I walk through the Potteries Shopping Centre before my feet take me to the multi-storey car park. I go up to the top floor so I can see over the city I assumed I'd grow old and grey in. It isn't a bad place as cities go. Its people are friendly, the best. I wish I'd been able to settle on my return.

I hate to leave Tom behind. He won't trust me around Isla anymore, and I can't say I blame him, although I would never hurt her. It's why I can't bear to be around now it's over. Because those lies I told him? How will he ever believe anything I say now I've cried wolf so many times?

He's right when he said what happened to my parents shouldn't define me. What happened when I went to live with my grandparents caused the most damage. You see, even now I don't know how a relationship works. I never had what Tom had with Sasha, what Roberta had with Bill, what Kerry has with Brody. I've only ever known destructive love. Tom will be better off without me.

A car parks up, and its occupants jump out and are soon on their way. The floor is empty of people. Without a second thought, I hitch myself onto the barrier wall and sit on it, hanging my legs over the other side. There's a pitched roof for the floor below that would stop me from falling directly down, but it would be so freeing to jump. No one will miss me. Because no matter where I go, innocent people get hurt. I can't have that on my conscience anymore.

I recall the night my parents died, the catalyst, the trigger as Emma would say.

CHAPTER SIXTY

Eighteen Years Ago

Clara was sitting on the edge of the bed, her hands covering her ears. She rocked back and forth. The banging had woken her first. Then the screams. It was getting more regular, and she hated it. Because she knew what would happen soon.

No, please. I didn't—

I don't believe a word that comes out of your mouth. You made me look a fool. And now you're going to pay for it.

As fist hit skin, Clara crept to the top of the stairs. Sometimes if he saw her, Dad would stop. Often, he'd make such a mess of Mum and never remember anything in the morning. Clara had patched her up ever since she'd been able.

But now she was ten, Clara wasn't sure Mum could cope with much more. Dad had been brutal, these past few months especially. And he'd started hitting Mum where it showed, not even bothering that other people might see.

The noise quietened. Clara stood up to go back to her room, but then the kitchen door opened before she had time to scurry across the landing. Dad spotted her and she held her breath. He came up the stairs, a scowl crossing his face.

'Shift yourself,' he said when he was two steps down from her.

She squeezed as far into the wall as she could, eyes tightly shut, too, waiting for him to have a go at her next.

This time, he continued up the stairs.

'Get down there and clean up,' he muttered.

Clara didn't breathe until she heard the bedroom door close behind him. Then she rushed downstairs. But when she stepped into the kitchen, she could see drops of blood splattered on the tiles, all over the floor, and across the table. She had never seen so much of it.

Mum was sitting on the floor with her back against the sink unit. Her head leaned to one side, her eyes staring ahead.

Clara's hand covered her mouth.

She couldn't be dead... could she? She'd be left with her dad, and he might hit her even more. There was nowhere else she could go, and no one to talk to about how nasty he was. She couldn't tell Nan and Granddad. They might not believe her.

No, Mum wouldn't be dead. Clara had seen her passed out due to pain before.

Yet this time seemed different.

'Mum?' Clara inched towards her, trying not to step in the blood that was puddling by her mum's side, dripping down her jeans and onto the floor.

'Mum,' she whispered, her lower lip trembling when there was no response. Clara inched her foot forward and prodded her with a toe.

Still no response, not a flicker of an eyelid. Not a hint of a groan.

'Mum!' Clara kneeled and took hold of her hand. It was all floppy.

She screamed, so loud and so long that she wasn't certain she would stop.

'What the hell's wrong with—' Duncan tore into the kitchen and stopped.

'She's dead!' Clara sobbed. 'You've killed her!'

'No, she can't be.' Duncan ran his hands through his hair and pulled. He paced the room, unable to take in what had happened. 'She just needs a drink of water and then she'll be fine. Get one for her.'

Clara did as she was told and reached into the cupboard for a glass. She filled it with water from the tap, all the while her dad speaking to her mum. He had kneeled next to her now.

'Jen, love. Come on, wake up. Jen? I'm sorry. I overreacted and I... I promise it won't happen again, Jen. Jen!'

Clara handed the glass to him. Gently, Dad lifted it to her mum's lips. But she didn't respond. Her mouth remained closed, the water dripping down her chin, her neck, and onto her chest.

'You've killed her!' Clara sobbed. 'My mum... you've killed her.'

'I'm sorry.' Duncan brought Jen up into his arms and held her to his chest while he cried, too. 'I'm so sorry.'

Clara sat on her knees, not caring that there was blood on her pyjamas and all over her hands. Then she spied the knife Dad had used. There was blood on that, too, on the blade. Her mum's.

Dad saw her looking at it. He turned to his wife, wiping a hand over her face. 'Goodbye, Jen. I love you, and I'm so sorry. It shouldn't have ended like this.'

Clara stayed quiet beside him, wondering what to do. They sat in shocked silence for a few minutes.

'Clara, love,' Duncan spoke at last. 'Will you fetch the phone, please? I need to call for an ambulance.'

Clara rushed through into the living room. The handset wasn't in its cradle. Her eyes searched around until she found it down the side of the armchair. Quickly, she ran back into the kitchen.

The sight that greeted her made her come to a stop.

Dad was now sitting with his back to the units. The knife he'd used was held out in front of his stomach, shaky hands clutching on to its handle.

'Daddy, don't.' Clara dropped to her knees. 'Please, don't.'

'I can't be without her.'

The fear and sorrow in his eyes were reflected in her own. Clara reached out to him, hoping her touch would let him remember that she was still here. She hadn't gone away. She needed protecting, loving, keeping safe.

'What about me?' she whispered.

'I'm sorry, Clara. I can't live with what I've done.' Duncan took her hand and placed it around the handle of the knife. He covered it with his own and, with a groan, inched the blade towards his chest.

Clara tried to pull away, but he held on tight.

'I'm a monster, Clara. I deserve to die. I killed your mum.'

'You're a bad man.'

'I am and I'm sorry, but she made me so angry and—'

Clara tried to shut out the things he was saying. It wasn't her mum's fault. It was his, and he was never going to take the blame, was he? He'd lie about what happened. He'd say her mum was violent back, and she wasn't. Clara glanced over at her, but it was too painful to see her now.

What would happen if he was dead? She would have no parents. She'd be an orphan. But she'd be safe, wouldn't she?

'Do it, Clara,' Duncan urged. 'What are you waiting for? I can't do it on my own. Do it!'

Clara gave an angry roar and, with one almighty push, plunged the knife into his chest. She watched as blood poured from his wound, covering her fingers. It flowed down onto the floor, mixing with her mum's. She had never seen so much.

Duncan reached for her then. 'I'm sorry,' he whispered, his face contorting with pain.

Clara couldn't bear to see anymore. She ran into the living room, keeping her eyes shut tight for fear of seeing something else that would stay in her memory forever. She didn't want to see the same look in his eyes as she'd seen in her mum's. Staring at nothing. Dead.

The phone was still in her hand. She knew what she

had to do and yet she couldn't. Not yet. She sat there, shivering, shaking her head. It can't have happened. It can't.

But she knew it had, and her palm and fingerprints were on the knife handle. She had to tell someone. And she had to lie.

999, what's your emergency?

My dad has hurt my mum, and then he hurt himself.

―――――

My phone goes off in my pocket. I pull it out to see it's Tom calling. I reject his call and look down at the ground. The people below are like ants milling around, the cars and lorries passing past on Potteries Way like toys.

I put my hands either side of myself. I could push off this wall in a second. It would be so easy to end the pain, hear nothing but silence. Shut out the thoughts in my head.

I can almost feel myself sailing through the air, thankful it will be over.

Because I'm not sure I can face the world alone again.

CHAPTER SIXTY-ONE

Three Months Later

'Come on, Isles,' Tom shouted, throwing on his jacket. 'I'm going to be late if you don't hurry up.'

'Do I have to go upstairs to Roberta?' Isla walked towards him, dragging her feet. 'Can't I stay down here on my own? I am ten years old, not a baby.'

'Of course you can't stay here.' Tom opened the front door and ushered her out. 'It's parents' evening. What would your teachers think of me if I left you home alone?'

Roberta was at the top of the stairs. Isla danced up to her.

'I won't be too long,' Tom spoke to Roberta. 'If she's been good at school, I might even bring back a pizza for us to share.'

Isla turned, wide-eyed, and smiled. 'Yay!'

'Come on, love.' Roberta held out her hand to Isla. 'I have chocolate ice cream and cookies to demolish before that.'

Tom shook his head, laughing as he got into his car. Isla was so like her mother that it was almost as if Sasha was still with them. Then again, with Isla a part of them both, that was true.

At school, he spoke to Mrs Lewis, Isla's form teacher.

'She's a wonderful child to teach,' she told him. 'A true chatterbox, though. I often have to tell her to be quiet and concentrate, or at the very least let someone else get a word in edgeways.'

'Yes, that sounds like Isla.' Tom beamed with pride.

'She's particularly come on with her English. She's written some wonderful short stories lately. I find it hard to see they were written by someone so young.'

Tom's face ached from smiling, but it wavered a little then. The stories had been down to Clara, he was sure.

'All in all, Isla seems to have settled down well after losing her mum,' Mrs Lewis finished. 'Her classmates were great, rallying round to look after her, and I've seen her schoolwork improve in general again. How are things going for you?'

Tom wasn't used to anyone asking after him. 'Oh, fine, thanks. I'm getting by. It's good to hear about Isla. It has been hard for her, for both of us. We seem to have a team of two now.' He wished he could have said it consisted of three, that Clara was sitting here with him.

In the living room later that evening, Isla tucked up

in bed, Tom's thoughts returned to Clara. He was still wondering if he'd made the right decision to break contact completely, not to keep in touch. Having said that, when he had sorted out what to do, he'd raced round to her grandparents' house and banged on the door. But the neighbour next door said she'd gone.

Clara had moved on. It had been painful to know. And she hadn't replied to any of his messages or emails, nor answered his calls after that. The silence spoke volumes. Tom had let her down. He hadn't given her a chance, and he very much regretted that now.

Perhaps with all her baggage it was the best thing for them. Sometimes, he couldn't help thinking he'd had a lucky escape.

But mostly, he was waiting for his broken heart to mend.

CHAPTER SIXTY-TWO

I walk around the harbour, bobbing between people as they pass by on the pavement. I'm going to a bar I found a week ago. Usually, it's a delight to sit and just be, with no one around to bother me. But tonight I'm meeting someone.

The sun is still treating us to its evening's rays. I look up, smiling when it warms my face. I find it pleasant here in Bournemouth. It's the first place I thought of because there's a direct train from Manchester. And it's by the sea, what more could I ask for?

My nan's old relic has gone to the scrapyard, and I'm now the owner of a snazzy new-to-me red vehicle. The sale of the house went through. The money is in the bank, and I'm not going to spend it rashly. I'll let it sit there until I decide where I want to lay my hat.

It's funny, though, having money. I feel secure because of that, knowing I can come and go anywhere I please. That's good for me. You never know when I might need to make another swift exit.

I'm not going to waste my inheritance. I'm going to make it work for me, get what I want with it. And that's security. I'm in a small flat near to the seafront, which I love. I'm staying for the summer at least, but it's great having the resources to be wherever I choose.

When I went back to Manchester after leaving Stoke, I kept my head down, determined to stay on the straight and narrow. I steered clear of the crazy gang of people I knew could lead me astray with their partying and drugs. Now, I'm feeling much better, more like my old self.

The thing with Wayne still hangs over my head. The police told me he's up in court in four months, but even if he gets a longer sentence, there'll be a time when he's out. Maybe he'll come after Shelley again. Or maybe he'll come after me now, turn his anger towards me. Life is so uncertain for us all, but I'm not going to dwell on it.

A couple walking past catch my eye. They're about my age. The man is pushing a pram with a young baby in it, the woman talking animatedly by his side, and a young boy of about four is keeping close on a bike. I smile, still yearning to be a mum myself. One day at a time, Clara. The future's mine for the taking.

At the bar, I order myself a glass of wine, find a booth, and slip inside it. While I wait for Lewis to arrive, I scan the photos I took. I'll never stop thinking about Tom and Isla and wondering how Roberta and Shelley are doing. Even now, I feel as if I've lost a family as well as a home. But I'm in a much better place now. No demons of the past to come and get me.

And let's face it, it hasn't all been bad. I resisted the urge to send a letter to Sam's wife, including the damning photos of me and her husband. Misha is better off without him, but they have kids, and I don't want to be the one to split up a family. Sam will probably do that of his own accord if he keeps messing around with women. I'll let him be his own downfall.

I've kept in touch with Emma over Zoom and found that to be truly worthwhile. Who knew how much therapy actually worked? If you'd asked me that a year ago, I would have laughed in your face.

And at least she'll never know the truth between the lies I've told her, too, about my time in prison. I was never Evan's driver. I was put away because I lost my temper one night when I caught him and Louise having sex. In our bed of all places. So blatant, rubbing my nose in it.

In a rage, I threw Evan from her and into the wall. While he was catching his breath, I laid into Louise. All the fury of the past few years escaped in one big flurry, poor Louise. I got eighteen months for that. Evan divorced me while I was locked away.

I'm not mad about it now. Honestly, I've never felt safer than when I was inside. At least I had a roof over my head, was fed and watered, and didn't want for a thing. Freedom is overrated when you have a warped mind like mine.

I thought I could change when I had to go back to Stoke. I was the only person who could look after my nan. I had a need. It was wonderful. But she spoiled it all by wanting to clear her conscience, knowing she hadn't got long to live.

When she told me about Derek, I was horrified. Yet as she went on to tell me how she'd lived her life in fear, I found a new respect for her. She shouldn't have lied to me for all those years, though. I was proud of myself then, too, as I could have taken what life she had left by putting a pillow over her face.

But that was supposed to have been the end of it all. A new beginning for me. If Wayne hadn't pushed my buttons, and Sam hadn't been such a bastard, I would have been fine. I could have lived a good life with Tom and Isla, in Cedric House.

A man I recognise from his online profile steps through the door. He glances around and then waves when he spots me. Even as he's getting nearer, I'm wondering how I approach things with a potential new partner. Do I tell the truth this time? Or lies within the truth—even a whole new bundle of lies?

Or is he one for hustling only? I'm definitely not telling him my name for now.

'Hi, Sarah?' Lewis leans closer and plants a kiss on my cheek. 'This is a great place to meet. Can I get you a top-up?'

'Yes, please, that would be lovely.'

I watch him move to the bar to place an order. He seems relaxed in his manner, friendly, too, just what I need.

This is another chance for me.

To lie again—I mean, to *try* again.

The End

First of all, I'd like to say a huge thank you for choosing to read Safe at Home. I hope you enjoyed getting to know the characters, Clara in particular. I had so much fun writing her.

If you did enjoy Safe at Home, I would be grateful if you would leave a small review or a star rating on your Kindle. I'd love to know what you thought. It's always good to hear from you.

Why not join my reader group? I love to keep in touch with my readers, and send a newsletter every few weeks. I also reveal covers, titles and blurbs exclusively to you first.

Join Team Sherratt

ALL BOOKS BY MEL SHERRATT

These books are continually added to so please
Click here for details about all my books on one page

DS Allie Shenton Series

Taunting the Dead

Follow the Leader

Only the Brave

Broken Promises

Hidden Secrets

Twisted Lives

Family Matters

The Estate Series (4 book series)

Somewhere to Hide

Behind a Closed Door

Fighting for Survival

Written in the Scars

Eden Berrisford Crime Dramas (2 book series)

The Girls Next Door

Don't Look Behind You

DS Grace Allendale Series (4 book series)

Hush Hush

Tick Tock

Liar Liar

Good Girl

Standalone Psychological Thrillers

Watching over You

The Lies You Tell

Ten Days

The Life She Wants

Missing Girls

Safe at Home

ACKNOWLEDGMENTS

Thanks to my amazing fella, Chris, who looks out for me so that I can do the writing. I wish I could take credit for all the twists in my books but he's actually more devious than I am when it comes down to it – in the nicest possible way. We're a great team – a perfect combination.

Thanks to Alison Niebieszczanski, Caroline Mitchell, Louise Ross, Imogen Clark, Talli Roland and Sharon Sant, who give me far more friendship, support and encouragement than I deserve.

Thanks to my amazing early reader team - you know who you are! I'm so blessed to have you on board.

A special thanks to my agent, David Headley, for having faith in me.

Finally, thanks to all my readers who keep in touch with me via Twitter and Facebook. Your kind words always make me smile – and get out my laptop. Long may it continue.

ABOUT THE AUTHOR

Ever since I can remember, I've been a meddler of words. Born and raised in Stoke-on-Trent, Staffordshire, I used the city as a backdrop for my first novel, TAUNTING THE DEAD, and it went on to be a Kindle #1 bestseller. I couldn't believe my eyes when it became the number 8 UK Kindle KDP bestselling books of 2012.

Since then, I've sold over two million books. My writing comes under a few different headings - grit-lit, thriller, psychological suspense, police procedural, emotional dramas to name a few. I like writing about fear and emotion – the cause and effect of crime – what makes a character do something. I also like to add a mixture of topics to each book.

When I'm not using my hometown as a setting, working as a housing officer for eight years gave me the background to create a fictional estate with good and bad characters, and they are all perfect for murder and mayhem.

But I'm a romantic at heart and have always wanted to write about characters that are not necessarily involved in the darker side of life. Coffee, cakes and friends are three of my favourite things, hence I write women's fiction under the pen name of Marcie Steele.

Printed in Dunstable, United Kingdom